Isha,

Unscripted

Isha, Unscripted

SAJNI PATEL

BERKLEY

New York

BERKLEY
An imprint of Penguin Random House LLC
penguinrandomhouse.com

Copyright © 2023 by Sajni Patel
Readers Guide copyright © 2023 by Sajni Patel
Excerpt copyright © 2023 by Sajni Patel

Library of Congress Cataloging-in-Publication Data

Names: Patel, Sajni, 1981- author.
Title: Isha, unscripted / Sajni Patel.
Description: First edition. | New York: Berkley, 2023.
Identifiers: LCCN 2022025630 (print) | LCCN 2022025631 (ebook) |
ISBN 9780593547830 (trade paperback) | ISBN 9780593547847 (ebook)
Subjects: LCGFT: Novels.
Classification: LCC PS3616.A86649 I84 2023 (print) |
LCC PS3616.A86649 (ebook) | DDC 813/.6—dc23/eng/20220531
LC record available at https://lccn.loc.gov/2022025630
LC ebook record available at https://lccn.loc.gov/2022025631

First Edition: February 2023

Printed in the United States of America
1st Printing

Book design by George Towne

To the Brohan.
I know you didn't want a book inspired by
your awesomeness, yet here we are.
You're too amazing not to share with the world.

Chapter 1

When Mummie sent me off to college ten years ago with a prayer over my head and a sweet to my lips, she'd said, "Excel in school, beta. Don't bring shame to your family."

Shame came.

Everyone and their uncle had my dad's ear on how he could've possibly allowed this embarrassment to continue. That was right. The Asian equivalent to American kids going to raves and experimenting was being a lit major. Every auntie locked up her sons when I came around toting my voluptuous love of the arts and sultry grasp of grammar. Forbid that my mastery over the written word seduce good Indian boys.

Worse yet? I left college.

Hello, two-time college dropout, was that you?

Third time was a charm. But it wasn't exactly what my parents had hoped for.

"A degree in *film and theater*!" Papa had bellowed. "Was *that* what I've been paying for this *entire* time?"

Um. Yep. Surprise . . .

"Oh, ma . . ." Mummie had muttered, rubbing her temples in complete dismay and invoking the gods to ask what she'd done in her past lives to deserve this punishment.

I swore their yells haunted the house to this day like wraiths reminding me that I wasn't meeting my potential.

In the past six months, to make matters worse for a struggling creative soul, rent had skyrocketed (thanks, Apple, Tesla, SpaceX, and other Californians mass migrating to Austin and tipping over the market), and without a full-time job, I ended up moving back home.

Whomp-whomp. Adulting fail.

So here I was: twenty-eight, somewhat jobless, practically friendless, and living back with my parents. What a prize, right?

And, yes, yes, I know twenty-eight sounded too damn old to be living with one's parents. But not-so-fun life fact: things don't always turn out to our best expectations, no matter how hard we try.

To add insult to injury, I was destined to spend yet another Friday night home alone.

Papa grabbed his keys from the kitchen counter and tilted an invisible hat to me. "I'm off!" he said. I wished I had his big weekend-project energy. It practically sizzled through the air.

"Are you sure you trust YouTube enough to fix Uncle's broken sink?" I asked warily.

"Ah. We're civil engineers." He shrugged as if that explained anything, or in some way gave him handyman superpowers.

"Right. Because Indians can suddenly do anything when they don't want to pay a professional."

"Between us and YouTube, we can fix anything."

"Can you, though?" I asked from the kitchen, the heat from the stove warming my side.

He flashed a grin. Wow. I was jealous of his sense of confidence as he went in headfirst with a wrench in hand to tackle a plumbing issue he'd never seen before at someone else's house. And he didn't even bother wearing jeans and a T-shirt like someone who was about to tackle a sink. He was, as always, decked out in a button-down shirt and khakis. I mean, talk about dad swagger.

He jerked his chin toward the simmering pot at my side. "Making Maggi?" he asked, referring to the desi version of Top Ramen and quintessential food for singles.

"No noodles tonight," I replied. Then I remembered. "Oh, here!" I said, whipping toward the cabinet beside the pantry and then back to Papa to hand him his blood pressure medicine. "You usually have this with dinner, but since you're eating over there, take it now. You don't need food with it."

"Thank you, beta," he said, taking the medicine with a swig from the cup of water I offered. "Always looking out for me."

"Of course, I'll always look out for you."

"What's on the agenda for you tonight?" he asked as I walked him to the foyer.

My younger brother, Mohit, rushed down the stairs like a thunderclap. Rogue, my ferocious miniature Yorkie, barked with annoyance from the living room around the hallway.

"Motiben's going to binge on chocolate in her sweats," Mohit jested. "Like every Friday night."

He shoulder-shoved me and I shoved him back. "That is *not* what I do."

"Sure, sure." He hopped into one shoe, then another, and flew out the door before Papa even slipped into his loafers.

Papa shook his head and called after him, "Be safe!"

Then he smiled warmly at me and patted my head. "Make use of a lovely night, huh?"

"Hah," I said as I closed the door after him, my back hitting the wall as I stared into the near-deserted house.

I returned to the kitchen and checked the timer. Another minute should do.

Mummie walked into the space between the open-concept kitchen and living room, all dolled up to hit the town with her auntie squad.

"My spinster daughter," she teased dramatically with a cluck of her tongue as she twisted on the backs of her earrings. "Did you even change out of your pajamas today?"

"Yes," I muttered, glancing down at my faded green sweatpants and gray T-shirt, the delicious scent from my coffee-and-sugar-scrub soap still lingering on my skin.

"If you made an effort to meet people, you'd dress better and look nicer."

"Hmm . . ." I mumbled. How could my own mother, after all this time, equate my introverted nature to laziness?

"What are you doing? Cooking?" she asked from the hallway.

I placed a hand on my hip and leaned against the counter, watching boiling water roll the little pink plastic item over as it floated at the top of the saucepan.

"Can I sterilize my menstrual cup in peace?"

The color drained from her face. "In my cha pot!"

"It's the small one. Mummie, you never use this."

"That's unsanitary, *Isha*," she chastised.

"Umm, no. The entire point of boiling is to make it sanitary. It's clean before it goes into the pot."

"Why can't you just use pads?" she heaved out, exasperated.

"Don't be disgusting," I teased.

"Unmarried girls use pads."

I rolled my eyes. "Mummie. You're a nurse. You know mighty well that tampons and menstrual cups didn't take my virginity. I mean . . . that sort of monumental moment would be quite disappointing, huh?" I couldn't help but grin.

Then it came. The inevitable. With a deep sigh, as if bringing this up caused my mother a great deal of stress, she said, "Your papa and I have been discussing your life."

I knew this conversation was bound to roar back to life, and yet I wasn't entirely prepared for it.

"You can't keep living like this. You are an adult. You're almost thirty. You *must* find a job, a real career. It took you eight years to finish college. You've been out of school for two years chasing this dream, beta. It's time to get serious and get to work," she said firmly as she braided her hair.

"I do have a job," I protested. But also, why did it matter if it had taken me so long to finish college as long as I finished with the degree meant for me?

"What? This writing business? I don't see income from it."

If words could cut, then my mom had just slayed me. "I mean the freelance communications job."

She waved her hand, dismissing my attempt to pass that off as enough. "That's not a steady job. You need continuous income, forty hours a week if not more, good benefits, 401(k), grow your savings, think of building up for a house and marriage, retirement, for so many things you have left to do in life. You're working part time so you can focus on writing, and that has been a dead end."

I scrolled through my email. C'mon, agent extraordinaire. Where were you with a lifeline by declaring you'd sold my script? But alas, there was no such miraculous, long-awaited email to support my stance.

Mummie sighed as she took a good look at me, her eyes crinkling in the corners, before touching my cheek. "So much potential."

Ouch. Having an Asian parent say that to their eldest child was a verbal stab straight to the gut, an absolute disembowelment. I felt the pain down to my emotional bones.

She went on. "Don't let it go to waste. You're not going to be young much longer. You should be working as much as possible while you can, while you're strong and healthy, and making as much money as possible. A full-time, regular job with consistent income and benefits plus a side hustle. Make this writing thing a hobby if you must keep pursuing it."

Her tone was soft. Her words were meant to gently push me out into the world, usher me into reality. My mother was, in essence, disappointed in me. Even at my age, her words sent my heart fluttering deep into despair, possibly never to be seen again. I wondered if her disappointment would hurt this much at forty. Worse yet, I wondered if she would still be disappointed in me at forty.

Probably. I would probably be sitting right here on this couch in my sweats on a Friday night while she went out to party with the aunties and Mohit was married with kids. In fact, my future sister-in-law would probably be cooking dinner and quietly wondering what the hell was wrong with me and how she hadn't signed up to take care of me when she married my brother.

Mummie checked her phone when it pinged. "Heena Auntie says there are lots of openings at the IRS."

I rolled my eyes and opened my mouth to defend my degree and explain how working at a desk for fifteen dollars an hour was a bit embarrassing and time spent there was time taken away from writing. But I didn't have much of a leg to stand on.

Mummie sashayed across the room to get her purse and said sternly, "The career websites are always available. In fact, your papa and I have to put our foot down. Apply now. No more arguing about this. We've been too lenient."

I needed to get back onto my own two feet. I needed to sell a script. Or get a full-time job, but a job that helped me advance toward my goals. Not just anything. And this wasn't a new thought for me. It wasn't as if I hadn't tried, and horribly failed, at getting through the door. Because the truth was, little known to my parents, that I'd tried very hard to get into a steady role, but at production companies and outlets that could help me get my foot into the industry. If they knew that I had a spreadsheet of over two hundred failed applications, they would never understand why it had been this difficult for me when it seemed so easy for others to get work.

She added, "And go back to mandir and make some friends at least. Get one aspect of your life together before it's too late and you're set in these bad ways."

"Do you mean if the entire Indian community thinks I'm a failure better suited to be brushed under the rug like Mohit's slew of subpar grades?" I asked, my eyebrow cocked. Wow, that didn't sound bitter at all.

She waved off my comment. "Eh? It's okay if your brother

has senioritis and doesn't put in as much effort in the last months of his classes. He'll still get his degree. He already has a nice job, you know. They're not going to retract his offer because he has a few Cs. He is set. But you need to get set. I only want what's best for you. In a couple of years, you're going to be thirty and look back at all this wasted time and regret it. What will you have to show for yourself, huh?"

What she meant to say was that they didn't have to worry about Mohit the way they had to worry about me.

I was genuinely proud of my baby brother. But by now, "wasted potential" had become synonymous with Isha Patel.

I was screwed if she wasn't going to back down, and the disturbing tentacles of an anxiety attack slowly reared at the edge of my thoughts.

"Maybe you'll make friends and find a nice Indian boy, no?"

I almost cackled. What nice Indian boy? None of the guys at mandir came around me. It was as if they might combust if they laid eyes on this wild child of wasted potential.

"What say you, Rogue-alicious?" I asked my Yorkie.

She played viciously with her pink stuffed pig no bigger than a tennis ball. She sat on the edge of the couch with her toy between her paws, chirping and nipping wildly like she had an entire monologue to execute. Then she looked me dead in the eye and gave her toy a swat, pushing it over the edge to join the other toys. It was like she was sending a message to her other toys that snitches get stitches.

I petted her soft, shiny, dark brown coat and sucked my teeth. "Rogue says no."

Mummie grabbed her keys on her way to the foyer, where she rummaged through the shoe rack for her best sandals. "Remember, you have twenty-four hours in a day and the majority of that time should now be spent on job applications," she said. "In fact, I want to see proof. Otherwise . . ."

I arched a brow. Lord, what was worse than my parents treating me like a child and me feeling like said child trapped in this unmoving nightmare?

"We'll have to get the family elders involved," she said matter-of-factly, and then just left.

I swallowed hard.

Well . . . damn. I might as well be on trial for career crimes against my kin.

My heart tried to catapult out of my chest as I panted for air. Going to the family elders was a desperate move that could only end with me leaving my family in shame or being manipulated into a future they wholly controlled.

With my menstrual cup in its pouch, I picked up Rogue and walked through the hall. She had her claw at my throat and side-eyed me as if saying *I'll cut you, bitch* if I made one false move.

I went upstairs in a sort of dizzy haze. I could barely breathe as I walked into my room, put away the pouch, and paced. My skin itched and my neck was on fire. Until I finally slumped into my desk chair and checked my shared drive.

"Let's see, let's see," I mumbled, scratching a nonexistent itch on my chin, as Rogue chomped down on kibble near my feet.

As soon as the video presentation of my script was ready, I could go full blast on any and every pitch session coming up. On websites, social media, in person . . . anywhere. I dropped my head back. *C'mon. Please, universe, let me have this before my family descends upon me.*

I tapped the dark wood desk and waited. And waited. But

Rohan, my cousin and video editor, hadn't finished with the file. I swiveled in my chair and immediately faced a tower of screenplays and screenwriting books quivering in the corner, ready to topple over with a single breath. My entire room was covered in colorful palls of four-by-four Post-its, the love of my life, and smelled of scented Sharpies, the mistress of my life. The window seat was littered with Starburst wrappers and coffee cups, the ambrosia of the gods, around a sprawling of notebooks filled with pages of scribbled notes and finalized storyboards.

Directly in front of me was a large, double-sided, portable whiteboard covered with storyboards and panels of my latest script.

Almost like a prayer, I whispered to the black-and-blue sketched panels, "This script has to be *the one*."

I felt it in my bones. Just the sight of my story coming to life in visuals as the main character, Priyanka, tried to make a name for herself in the entertainment industry as an actress held back by the murder she'd witnessed sent shivers down my spine. A perfect mix of mystery, thriller, and comedy—it was magic bleeding from my fingertips. A vision of story and conflict erupting across my thoughts, transferred onto pages, and visualized in storyboards.

"Priyanka, girl, you can make it. I know you can."

I sighed. If I could love concepts the way people loved significant others, then this would be the one. Right down to the gut clenching and wobbly knees and hitched breaths.

Every dream hinged on this script. It was my "lucky eight," because it turned out that "lucky seven" wasn't a thing after all and we were way past "third time's a charm."

Seven scripts had come and gone, set on fire by the cruel

words of Hollywood and currently used as kindling in some overpriced L.A. house where agents toasted to the fire kept burning by my dreams. But this one? The script that I had just finished and polished and run through every critique partner and writing group was the one. I called it *The Avenged*. It would avenge the death of all the scripts before it, but also, it was the actual title. A chilling but sometimes funny tale of a woman trying to achieve her goals in a harsh reality. They said write what you know, so this was pretty much my life. Well, ya know, aside from the murder part.

Above the whiteboard were framed articles—the most prized being a write-up in which I was featured as one of Matthew McConaughey's screenwriting students when he taught the course at UT.

I smiled at the articles and closed my eyes, taking a few breaths to combat the spark of naysaying my mother had incubated in my creative soul. These articles reminded me that I had potential and had accomplishments. They reminded me that I could do this and never give up.

An antsy sensation skittered up my back and lodged into the base of my skull as Mummie's words ricocheted through my thoughts. My entire family-controlled future flashed across my vision: sitting in a cubicle at a pointless job or returning to college for a degree in a field I loathed.

I needed to get out of here and out of my head.

Scrolling through social media to scope out who might be in town and available didn't help. Veronica was the first person to come to mind, and the first post to pop up on my feed. She knew how to cheer me up. Aside from being bubbly and optimistic, she was in a similar familial situation. Who knew Indian and Filipino parents could be so alike?

Oh. She was already out and about at a cute little eatery in south Austin sharing appetizers and toasting drinks.

#LoveMyGirls.

A few more seconds of quick scrolling showed that any friend who would understand my dilemma was already out with others, busy with husbands or kids, or not in town.

At least social media saved me from having to hear rejections.

Just then, because the boy somehow always knew, Rohan texted.

Rohan: Eh. What you doing?

Isha: Wasting my life, apparently. What's up?

Rohan: You hungry?

Isha: Sure. I can always go for some tacos.

Rohan: I know a place downtown you might like.

I rolled my eyes. I was too old for downtown traffic and crowds. As if Rohan knew what I was thinking, he added.

Rohan: Dude. I'm driving. And paying. So let's go.

I smiled. He knew me so well. My younger cousin was such a sweet kid and always there when I needed him.

Chapter 2

"Thanks for driving!" I told Rohan over his beloved Hindi music blasting through the car. I might've thought of my baby cousin as a kid, but the boy was a man. Complete with stubble, an iron stomach, and the most laid-back style in existence.

"Yeah," he said, pulling out onto the street and taking a turn to get onto the main road, bobbing his head to a Bollywood beat and tapping the steering wheel.

"Look at you. Getting out of sweatpants." He snickered, giving me a look over.

"Har har." Yet I did a little shimmy because darn him, getting out of sweatpants made me feel fancy, even if my slim jeans and blouse were far from it.

He noticed a cute redhead in an SUV to the left when she glanced at us. Rohan gripped the steering wheel with one hand, trying to look like most guys who thought they were cool or hard-core driving this way. I almost wanted to mom it up and tell him to adjust both hands properly on the wheel and keep his eyes on the road.

When we stopped at the next red light, he turned from me, no doubt giving the woman a wink or . . . whatever he did to flirt.

I couldn't help it. I reached over and pinched his full cheeks and said in a baby voice, "Look who's growing up. Who's a grown boy? You are. Yes, you are!"

The woman laughed while Rohan shrugged me off and flared his nostrils. "Stop, dude. What are you doing?"

"You're so cute trying to flirt," I said, grinning and trying not to giggle.

"Exactly. I'm trying to flirt. Why you gotta do that?"

The light turned green. The cute redhead turned left and we went straight.

Rohan groaned. "Woman. Do that again and I will leave you on the side of the road."

I laughed. "No, you won't."

"I'll do it right now," he warned, his eyebrows high. "I will pull this car over and leave you."

"Can you do so by Sonic so I can at least get a slush?"

"You think you're funny."

"Thanks again for taking me out. I really need this." I hit my head against the back of the seat and stared at the visor, letting out a haggard sigh.

"Need a drink that bad? It's been, what? A whole week. Does someone have a problem?"

I guffawed. "I don't *need* a drink. I just need to get out of my head and relax, stop thinking about selling this script. It's stressing me out. My entire life is between writing, pitching, taking care of the family, and fighting off the pangs of failure. Ya know?"

"Um. I'm extremely happy and successful, so no, I don't know," he replied in that half-solemn, half-jesting tone of his. Pair that with his constant smirk and one could literally never tell if he was serious or joking or being sarcastic or a mixture of anything in between.

Even though Rohan hadn't followed the conventional path in our family, he truly seemed happy now that he was out of his depressed episode. Maybe he didn't have the skyrocketing career our parents wished for him, but that didn't determine his worth and I was sick with anger for anyone who might've made him feel less than.

But then he laughed and said, "Nah. I totally understand. We're from the same family, remember? My parents bug me about going back to college every *single* day. And my brother hounds me about at least trying to find a better job, every *single* day. Between the three of them, they drive me nuts. Not to mention, whenever I see your parents. I love them, but they bring it up every time we see each other. And so does every uncle, which is one of the reasons I don't go to mandir. I don't need to feel bad about myself. Neither do you. We're good people. And you're trying really hard. It'll happen. And then you can throw it in everyone's faces."

My heart swelled. Even in his monotone, honest way, he was the sweetest and always made me feel better. "Aw. I'd hug you, but you'd probably pull the car over and abandon me."

"I see a Sonic up the street," he warned.

"They mean well, you know? Our parents," I reminded him solemnly, even as my gut twisted in remembrance of the conversation with my mom earlier.

"Yeah. Well, it doesn't feel that way sometimes."

"I agree." Which was why I wholeheartedly defended Rohan every time someone came at him. The boy had a full-time job that required overtime half the month, and he never complained. He cooked like a chef every other day for his entire family of four (his parents and brother). He cleaned and did house chores. He dropped whatever he was doing if someone asked him for a ride or for help. He never said no. He took care of his mom's growing medical needs. He was the one who did the grocery shopping and anything else that needed to get done around the house or for his parents. He never seemed to get angry or annoyed. He was selfless.

There was a term in Gujarati called *dayo*, meaning smart, but also, in the context of Rohan, it meant he was a good boy. Everyone, no matter what they thought of his education or job, said he was bo dayo. Basically, I would die for this kid.

He was Rohan. The ultimate son/brother/cousin/friend. He was also the ultimate bro, which was why he was *the Brohan*. Down for anything, anytime, and always had my back.

"Thanks for not telling my parents about me drinking," he said.

"Thanks for not telling my parents that I drink *and* still eat meat."

"I got your back, bro."

I grinned. "Are you almost done with the video edits?"

"Yeah. Just a little bit more. Will probably be ready tomorrow."

"You're so fast. Thanks for doing that."

"Anything to help you, Motiben."

I smiled warmly. We weren't technically siblings, but he

never hesitated to refer to me as his elder sister. "Where exactly are we going?"

"At a food festival some months back, I met a guy named Seth, whose brother owns this pub on Sixth Street. By the way, he told me he knows your old professor. What's his name? Oh yeah. *Matthew McConaughey*," he said as if that name ever slipped any Austinite's mind.

"Pssh! Everyone thinks they know him."

"He showed me pictures of them hanging out with his grandma. Anyway. I think you'll like the place. It's not super rowdy or freezing cold."

"But does it have food?"

He gave me a lingering flash of side-eye. "Of course," he replied dryly. "I would *never* take you somewhere that doesn't have food. It's more of a bar and grill. Plus, there's karaoke."

I groaned. "No. I'm not doing karaoke."

He drove around the block twice before parallel parking with impressive ease into a tight spot. The way this guy weaved in and out of traffic and perfectly parked made him the prime candidate for any *Fast & Furious* movie. "I bet you'll be smashed and singing within the hour."

"Ha! I will *not* sing."

"My phone is ready to video all of it."

"Don't you dare post any of that!"

"See? Even you know that you'll be up there on stage making a fool of yourself," he added as we climbed out of the car and walked up a block, pushing against the flow of pedestrians.

The humid air cooled on the fringes of a light breeze. Sixth Street came with its Russian roulette game of pleasant scents battling the nauseating stench of back-alley trash and side-street vomiting.

"Remember the first rule of our adventures? No proof that it ever happened. You're breaking rules and that breaks us," I reminded. I swung my cross-body purse over my chest and adjusted it at my hip, wishing that fanny packs could make a comeback to spare the growing ache on my shoulder and neck from bearing the weight of a purse.

"Not even for myself? For those days when I need a good laugh?" He cackled.

"No!"

Ahead, about another pub's length away, a random and creepy AF guy appeared. Complete with red hair, a white-painted face, and a downturned mouth covered in red. I was instantly thrown back to ninth grade leaving softball practice and walking past the adjacent soccer field when a trio of kids in clown costumes came out of nowhere to prank us. I'd never run so fast in my life.

A different kind of anxiety spiked my blood pressure. I leaned toward Rohan as the clown eyed us. "Am I hallucinating or is there a creepy-as-crap clown watching us?"

"Huh?" He followed my gaze. "Oh yeah. That guy. I don't know what his deal is, but he hangs around here sometimes. Maybe he's trying to get people to a specific bar?"

But what sort of marketing was that?

Rohan stopped near a set of unassuming wide, wooden double doors outlined in neon green lights. "This is the spot."

He opened the door for me and we walked right into a wall of noise, music, conversations, laughter, and clanking dishes and mugs. The smell of fried food bombarded my senses, making my mouth water and my stomach growl in heavenly anticipation of eating something very, very tasty.

I shivered from the blast of icy air and rubbed my exposed

arms, my eyes instantly attracted to the fancy bar in the back. A large floor-to-ceiling mirror made up the far wall, reflecting rows and columns of neatly arranged bottles of liquor in all colors and types and prices. Above the bar hung dozens of drinking vessels. It was quite the sparkling collection hanging like a delicate chandelier casting flashes of light.

The bar itself was wide and long, surrounded by barstools occupied by some rowdy patrons laughing and gesturing wildly. Ducking in between them were two bartenders, quite the tasty treats to my sore eyes. One happened to glance up as he passed a drink to a patron.

Our eyes met across the expanse of the large, crowded space. The room stilled for the briefest of seconds, and the noise hushed before roaring back to life.

This . . . felt like a moment. Or was I heady from the cigarette smoke wafting in through the opening doors?

Moment or not, it passed. His second of pause dwindled as he carried on with what seemed like very busy and fast-paced work.

Eh. I'd learned to accept that I wasn't exceptionally gorgeous, not the type who stopped a room dead in its tracks or who typically caught a handsome guy's attention in some swoony, romantic way. If a guy was checking me out, odds were that my underwear was showing or bird poop was dribbling down my hair.

"Want to sit at the bar, a booth, or a table?" Rohan asked over the noise.

I scanned the area. There was a row of tables directly in front of us with chairs on one side and bench seating on the other. Behind the bench seating were a few round tables and a small stage. Crowded pool tables lined the wall to our right, and ahead, several booths. I cocked my chin at a still-cluttered booth as a trio paid for their meal and left. We immediately made a beeline for the only available seats.

We slid into the booth right as a waitress came over to claim her payment and tip from the previous customers while a busser popped up beside her to deftly clean the table. The waitress smiled a big Southern smile and placed two menus in front of us. Within the hardback menu, there was a half page of food, mainly appetizers and shareables, and three pages of drinks.

"What's your poison?" Rohan asked, closing his menu when he'd apparently settled on something.

"Already know what you want?"

"Yep. I decided the first time I ordered here that I wanted to try the entire menu. So, Moscow mules three ways coming up."

"I don't even know what a Moscow mule is. Hmm . . . let's see . . ." I perused the menu.

About five minutes later, the waitress returned and took Rohan's order after checking his ID. For his three drinks, I knew we'd be here for a while. He liked to savor and relax and was never looking to get drunk.

"What do the bartenders recommend for something sweet? Or any off-menu drinks?" I asked the waitress.

"Let me ask, darlin'," she said in a notable Texan drawl. She took our order for queso and stuffed peppers and moved on to another table.

"You sure you want to eat those peppers?" Rohan asked.

"Is that a serious question? You know I love anything stuffed with cream cheese and fried."

He blinked at me and said, "You know you're barely Indian, right?"

"Hey! Jalapeño poppers aren't spicy," I retorted, never mind that he was right in implying my spice tolerance was at toddler level these days.

"They have habaneros mixed into the cream cheese filling."

"I'll take my chances. They come with raspberry sauce, right?" I cocked an eyebrow.

He rolled his eyes before tapping the table. He leaned forward and said, "Tell me what's going on."

"What do you mean?" I asked.

"I know you, Motiben. Something happened and you're about to get stress-smashed."

I relayed the ultimatum my mother had given me. All Rohan had to say about it was, "Damn. That's messed up. But yeah, expected. Why hasn't your agent done anything for you?"

There was a tinge of anger in his question, and I found myself defending Amy for the hundredth time. "She's trying."

"She's not trying hard enough," he shot back.

"She's doing her best. She can't control the producer side of things. They have to be willing to buy, too."

He let out a breath, returning to his calm self. "Well, your parents are pushing you into a corner. I know all y'all. You want to keep the peace and they only see logic. So you have to make a move or they'll put you in a corner and keep you there."

"Like what? I go to networking events, pitchfests, my agent is submitting everywhere. I mean . . . I don't know. Are . . . they right?" I bit my lip and blinked away tears. Was I a mess and needed to get my act together?

"No," he said simply.

Rohan looked off into the void for so long that I thought he might've forgotten I was there. "Matthew McConaughey," he said finally, dragging his gaze back to me. Suddenly he was excited, grinning and his eyes lighting up.

"What . . . about him?"

"He can help."

I laughed so hard that I almost pulled a muscle. Clutching my lower abs, I shook my head. "You almost had me."

"I'm serious!" he replied with a smirk. But see, that half smile of his relayed that he was jesting. Did he even know he was doing that? Saying one thing and sending contradicting signals?

I calmed down and planted my face into my hands. I didn't want to think about my problems and the obvious career decisions that had to be made rather quickly, yet Rohan had a way of easing words out of me. All right, it was more like an undamming, followed by a verbal flood of thoughts and emotions. All he had to do was sit quietly and wait. Darn him and his open, welcoming aura!

Several minutes later, as Rohan and I were getting animated with gesticulations about why I couldn't tell my parents to leave me alone and how irreparable the consequences would be if the family elders were to get involved, I ended with, "And unless I follow the path they set for me, I'm irredeemable in their eyes! Why is our family like this? Or am I in the wrong? Huh? Tell me, and I'll accept it."

"You're not," he promised, his tone getting louder to meet mine.

"Push is coming to shove, Rohan! What choice do I have except to sell a script now or throw away my creative dreams!" I swung my hands out on those last words, hitting someone. So hard that my knuckles felt it.

I gasped, taking a second to register exactly how hard I'd hit someone.

"Oh! I'm so sorry!" I jumped, and then immediately felt a hundred times worse realizing that I'd backhanded/knuckle-slapped a guy's crotch. Eh. Wasn't the first time that had happened, to be honest, and by far the fastest way I'd ever handled a guy's package.

He pinched his lips into a thin line and refrained from pushing a hand down to his groin while bowing over.

Rohan clucked his tongue and shook his head, what he always did when I embarrassed him. I was more surprised that he hadn't covertly pulled out his phone to livestream this entire fiasco of an interaction.

"Oh my god!" I bounced out of the booth and hunched over with him, my hand automatically reaching out to . . . what? Rub his crotch? I mean, that might make him feel better, but . . .

I yelped and pulled my hand back. "Are you all right?"

"Yep," he wheezed. He pressed his lips together as he clutched the back of the booth beside me, in turn blocking me into place. He glanced up at me with intense green eyes. Like, make-a-woman-want-to-commit-to-having-his-baby kind of eyes. They were remarkably stunning against his light brown skin.

I went to touch his arm but pulled back until I finally, gently, placed my hand on his shoulder. "Can I get you something?"

"I'll get some ice. It's fine," he pushed out.

"You don't look fine. What can I do?"

"Agh . . . you can tell me what you'd like to drink?" His left brow hiked up.

"What?" I asked, confused.

"The waitress said you wanted a drink."

"Oh!" I finally understood. The bartender! The one I might've had a moment with from across a crowded room upon my entrance but probably not.

Damn, though, he was kind of fine. Thirst-Trap level of fine. The sort of good-looking guy I'd always heard about but never had the fortune to come across in real life.

"Something off-menu," I finally said, hopeful for a delicious drink but also worried that I'd accidentally assaulted him.

He held up a finger and grunted, "I'll be right back."

Rohan commenced to laughing as soon as Thirst-Trap walked away in what was perhaps his best attempt to seem okay when in actuality, his crotch was probably killing him. A backhanded knuckle slap to the balls was probably not what he was expecting to walk into. Literally.

I plopped back into my seat, mortified. My skin flared hot. Poor guy.

"You need to calm down. So! I'm going to put us on the list for karaoke," Rohan declared.

I groaned, but what a way to get my mind off an attractive guy's crotch. "No. I am *not* singing."

"Even your fave K-pop beats?"

"Even then." No amount of BTS was going to get me up there. And yet I found myself singing a K-pop song in my head at this very moment. Damn Rohan, he knew me so well!

"Eh. You will be once you get to drinking. I think . . ." He leaned back and studied me for a few seconds. "You'll be downing your third drink by the end of the hour and might need another two to get over this setback. Nothing wrong with that."

He eased out of his seat and headed toward the karaoke attendant. There was no stopping him. Worst case, I could just get up and leave when our names were called. The karaoke attendant would only give us a few minutes to claim our spot before he moved on to what was an incomprehensibly packed list of strangers wanting to drunken-tain other strangers.

I was not going to get drunk.

I was not going to have more than two drinks.

I was not going to depend on or lean on alcohol in any way to cope with my lack of success or the anxiety springing up across my thoughts.

I was better than this.

Chapter 3

A shadow fell over my slumped shoulders. I straightened up, fully expecting queso and chips and the infamous spicy jalapeño poppers.

Instead of hot, gooey treats, a delicate martini glass filled to the top with pale yellow liquid and a double cherry on top with a slender twisted lime wedge fitted to the rim appeared. And adjacent to that, what I assumed was Rohan's Moscow mule in the telltale copper mug glistening with beads of condensation.

"Oh," I said, mesmerized by the prettiness of my drink. And then equally enamored by the hand that wiped spilt droplets from the base of the glass. Those were definitely not the hands that belonged to our petite waitress.

My gaze followed the wide hand and the broad forearm beneath a rolled-up blue sleeve. My, what a mighty fine-looking piece of muscular flesh, complete with greenish veins. What was it about forearms, this very non-sensual body part, that suddenly exploded with sexiness? My eyes weren't done wandering, however, no matter the forearm porn urging me to stay put.

My gaze trailed up his tan arm, bulging biceps, and firm-looking shoulders to his face. A . . . sexy half smile with dimples deep enough to fall into. I eventually met those dreamy green eyes again as the bartender retracted his arm, his hand gripping the towel.

Thirst-Trap was making me believe in romance-novel meet-cutes, the way he kept interrupting my night.

"Hello, again," he said, his voice deep, a rumble out of his chest but loud enough to hear over the new roar of the room as a guy took the karaoke mic.

"Oh! Hi," I replied. "How's your, um . . . ya know?" I double-clucked my tongue and jerked my head to the side, somehow meaning this to indicate his groin.

He smirked. "Better. It'll be fine."

"You're going to keep working after being assaulted?"

He chuckled. "I'm taking lots of ice-to-the-crotch breaks."

I clamped down on my laugh while wishing away the flush at my cheeks from sheer embarrassment. "I feel horrible."

He grinned. "You know you're smiling, right?"

"Sorry. It's not funny . . ." I bit my lip. But it kind of was?

"Well, how about this. Try this drink and tell me I'm the best mix-master in the world. But first, can I see your ID?"

"Oh. Yes, sure." I fumbled through my small cross-body purse and handed him my driver's license.

He took the card, looked at it like he was reading more than just my date of birth, and handed it back to me. "A Moscow mule for your . . . friend?"

I clamped down on a smile and said, "My cousin."

"Ah. Good to know," he replied, and smiled. "And for you? You said off-menu. I'm usually pretty good at feeling out someone's choice of drink by a look. I'd say your taste is mild alcohol, fruity rum, tart?" he asked, his eyebrow quirked.

"I usually go for a mix of sweet and tart." I drew the cold glass toward me. "Let's see if you missed the mark."

He raised a hand toward the drink, as if to say *Try me, I rarely miss.*

I took a tentative sip. I wasn't prepared for the complexity exploding on my tongue and carving a name for itself by spelling out T-H-I-R-S-T-T-R-A-P. Vibrant flavors of coconut rum and peach schnapps, subtle hints of tart pineapple and orange juices, and a splash of grenadine sweetness, but there was something else in the mix that left my head whirling just a bit. In the best possible way. I took in a sharp breath.

"Is it too strong?" he asked, as if reading my mind.

I shook my head and smiled up at him, refraining from licking the taste off my lips. "Just what I needed. Okay. This was a hit, not a miss. But that might be pure luck."

He crossed his arms, stretching the fabric of his shirt. "All right. Then let me take another shot and see what else I think you'd enjoy." He eyed me, as if studying me down to my molecular composition to figure out what I'd like.

"But different from this one because I'm a woman of many facets," I said.

"Absolutely. Enjoy."

"Oh! Wait! What's this drink called anyway? In case I want it again?" I took another sip.

He narrowed his eyes, which glistened the slightest bit between the dim of the establishment and the lights hanging over the booth. A slow, wicked smile spread across his lips. "Crotch punisher."

I almost spat out my drink and coughed. "No, it's not!"

"It's called a cowboy quencher," he said with a wink, and walked off.

Oh, *damn*. I might be in love.

"Where did you get that from?" Rohan asked when he returned.

"Thirst-Trap bartender," I replied matter-of-factly, trying so very hard not to look over my shoulder.

"Are you drooling?" he teased, and pointed at my chin.

"Oh!" I wiped the spat-up drink from my face with a napkin.

Our waitress dropped off our order and I took a bite of stuffed pepper, forgetting to let it cool, and kept Rohan's amused stare.

Heat exploded at the back of my throat and sweat trickled down my brow. I wheezed, "Not spicy at all."

He guffawed. "Liar! Your face is red. Drink some water, you weakling."

I gulped down water and my drink, letting the peppers cool for a bit, and dove into sharing queso with him.

I kept the conversation off my parents and on Rohan's vague plans for the future that our parents kept prying him for. "How's work?" I asked per usual.

"Boring," he replied, as always.

I pushed around another popper with a fork. "Going to stick with this job?"

"I think so. Not too much work and people leave me alone. Paperwork is easy, filing away, finding errors." He shrugged. "I'm also thinking of a food truck . . . but my mom doesn't

think I have it in me to do business and work unmanaged
hours."

"I think you do. You love to cook, so it's something you'd
enjoy. And with a food truck, you don't have as much overhead and could work your own hours."

He gave a smile. "Sounds like a lot of work, though, and
expensive."

I nodded. "Well, let me know if you want to brainstorm.
We could list pros and cons of a food truck and figure out
expenses and talk to banks about loans and lean into the market to strategize best locations and vendors."

"I know you love some spreadsheets," he jested.

"Forget spreadsheets! I'll give you the other side of my dry-
erase board."

He held a hand to his chest. "How did I deserve such royal
treatment?"

I stabbed a popper and pointed it at him. "Better be grateful that I love you."

"Well, actually, Seth offered me a position here. To make
up a new menu with some Rohan originals, and teach the
cooks how to make them."

I lit up. "Rohan! That's amazing! Are you going to take it?"

He smiled sheepishly. "Don't get too excited. I'm considering it, but I dunno. Sounds like a lot of work. And I have to
get Seth's approval before he passes me on to his brother, the
owner, and he said his brother is hard to impress."

I clucked my tongue. "Don't overlook an opportunity when
it comes to stepping toward your goals. Besides, this owner is
lucky to even get your time when it comes to your cooking."

He watched me for a moment, his lips pressed together,
and nodded. I really hoped he would take Seth up on this of-

fer, which sounded fantastic. I wanted to know details, but the way Rohan turned quiet, I knew not to push him for more.

He kept checking his phone, laughing and grinning and looking a little impish.

"Who's the girlfriend?" I prodded.

"What? It's my wife," he replied.

The way he answered, smirking with a mischievous glint in his eyes, I didn't quite know if he was joking or telling the truth. Of course, I *knew* he wasn't married. Still. The way he said it . . .

I rolled my eyes and groaned, feeling a little heady after one drink. "So it's Mohinder?"

He clucked his tongue in response.

"Is he back in town?" I bit into the last of the stuffed jalapeño smothered in whatever raspberry jam was left at the bottom of the tiny dipping bowl, bracing for the final high-heat assault.

"Yeah."

"Why aren't you hanging out with your bestie, then?"

He placed his phone down and looked me dead in the eye. "Because I'm here for you."

"That's very sweet. But you should spend time with him. He's not in town often."

Rohan shrugged and dunked a broken chip into a now-tepid puddle of queso. "It's fine. I like hanging with you."

I smiled softly. I knew he meant it. He never lied to me, but he would probably sugarcoat it a bit to spare my feelings. Yet a numbing sadness trickled down my insides and settled into the pit of my gut. Pity. And pity was almost always aimed at the pitiful.

"Stop," he said, reading my face.

"What?"

"You're thinking bad about yourself and that I'm here because you need someone to go out with. Well, shut your face. I'm here because I want to be here. So stop self-deprecating."

"Sheesh. Your tough love is hard to swallow."

"I'm awesome and I know it. And you're awesome, too. So just do everyone a favor and accept it." He glanced behind me as our second round of drinks arrived. Delivered by Thirst-Trap and his hot and heavy forearms.

"Thanks," Rohan told him, exchanging his empty glass for a new one.

"Is this what you came up with?" I said, my gaze lingering with lust on the sultry red drink placed in front of me. *Oh.* Who could deny such a pretty thing? I dragged my gaze away to look up at the bartender.

"Yeah, we have a thing, don't we?" Thirst-Trap said, giving a half smile. "How's this one?"

Rohan eyed us for a second before returning to texting.

I took a tentative sip, expecting and receiving a strong sabotage of liquor and the mellow tang of cranberries and orange. I couldn't help but laugh. "Okay. All right. Two for two."

"Wanna try for three?" he asked.

"Sure," I found myself saying even as the alcohol started hitting my brain cells and my tongue went a little numb with a slur. My alcohol tolerance was laughable, and this drink was about to get me tipsy. At this rate, the next one would get me on the brink of drunk and a fourth would get me karaoke drunk if I wasn't careful.

After Thirst-Trap made sure Rohan was enjoying his drinks, he walked away. Rohan placed his phone down. I knew he was fake texting!

"Dude," he said after a sip.

"It's good?"

"I mean . . ." He cocked his head in Thirst-Trap's direction.

"What? Can't I smile at a guy without being judged? You of all people? Not as if he likes me. Just trying to get us to pay for more drinks." I scoffed. "I'm not ditching you so he can take your innocent motiben home or anything."

"Bros before hos."

I laughed. "Who's a ho?"

"Man-ho," he stated matter-of-factly. "I know one when I see one."

"Oh my lord . . ."

Before we knew it, our glasses were down to the last drops and Rohan waved over the waitress for his final round—with a groan, mind you, because it was a lavender drink—and I was indeed tipsy. But tipsy felt good compared to having to deal with my parents. Two drinks would soon turn into three . . . four . . . more?

The room was spinning, and my mother's warning faded into haunting whispers dying a slow death as the music and conversations around us got louder. Ah, yes. Exactly why I wanted to get out in the first place.

I leaned back against the faux-leather booth-style seat and closed my eyes for a moment. My head was thrumming, my skin getting warmer. Despite it all, I could fall asleep.

Something clinked on the table and a shadow crossed my eyelids. I opened my eyes to find three more drinks. Rohan warily eyed his Moscow mule with a lovely sprig of lavender floating on top. In front of me were not one, but *two* drinks.

Damn it. How did he know I needed four drinks to get karaoke drunk?

"What's this?" I asked Thirst-Trap, fawning over my own light purple drink topped with lavender.

Thirst-Trap stood at the edge of the table and smirked. "Lavender lemon martini to see if you'd like dry. I don't think you usually go dry, but maybe this might persuade you."

"God. How are you so good at this? Were you born a bartender or something?" I asked, my skin firing up every time a word slurred and tumbled off my tongue.

"At least your drink matches his."

Rohan huffed, holding up his cup in a toast. "We look good in every shade of purple."

"The other is on the lighter side: a watermelon champagne made with vanilla vodka and triple sec." Thirst-Trap nodded toward the ruby-red drink garnished with mint leaves.

I really shouldn't drink so much . . . but dang it if it didn't feel good to unwind and loosen up. It didn't hurt that the drinks were beyond anything that I'd ever had.

I took a sip, expecting to get hit with the overtly sweet. The lavender drink had a delicate floral flavor, but the alcohol content was sure to make me heady.

The watermelon champagne was a fun, fruity flavor and hid the alcohol taste. By the way my skin flickered like a furnace revving up, I'd say these drinks were as strong as the first two.

"Is it too strong? I can make a different one," he suggested.

"Nah," I muttered. Smooth. Like that was convincing. "But I'm probably done after these."

"Ah, and here I thought I'd get to show off through all the magical cocktails that you've never heard of." He grinned down at me and good lord if my ovaries didn't start screaming. Suddenly, "Whatta Man" made a whole lot of sense talking about wanting some guy's baby. Salt-N-Pepa knew what they were talking about.

Instead of admitting the readiness of my uterus, as he'd probably consider that more creepy than flirty, I said, "These are amazing. Why they not on the menu?" Ah, fantastic, the words slurred as my tongue turned heavier and heavier.

He quirked a brow. "Are you sure they're not too strong?"

"I see through you," I said instead. Alcohol buzzed through my blood.

"Huh?"

I eyed him, then Rohan. "You two plotting to get me drunk so I sing tonight. Not going to happen."

Thirst-Trap chuckled. "Ah, karaoke calling your name?"

"I'm not answering. Not that I'm going to have more tonight." I wrapped my hands delicately around the stem of my glass as if my touch might shatter it.

"You'll just have to come by again, I guess, to sample the rest of the off-menu drinks." The right corner of his mouth tugged up. Was he . . . flirting with me? Or was he after drink money? Probably the latter. Guys like him didn't typically flirt with me.

"I should get back to the bar. Enjoy." He tapped the table and flashed another dimpled grin.

"Thanks," I said before he strode away, and nearly downed the watermelon champagne before Rohan even took a sip of his lavender Moscow mule.

"Not bad," he said of his drink when I expected some witty comment about my amazing flirting skills.

"Like you said, we look good in purple." I downed the last of the martini and stood. "Okay! I must pee!" I announced, and tumbled forward, gripping the table.

"You okay, Drunky McDrunkerson?"

"Oh, hush. I'm cool. Be right back," I shot back, and regained my composure. The room tilted on an imaginary axis.

"Then karaoke?" He wagged his brows.

"No way." With my chin high and my eyes wide, because of course that helped tipsy me think clearer, I released my grip on the edge of the table and managed to stay stable. I smiled, proud of myself.

"By the time you get through that line, you'll forget that you just said no."

I tried my hardest to walk straight and not bump into anyone. Of course, that seemed impossible as I crashed into at least four people. God, why were these guys' shoulders and arms so giant and just out there all in my way? Couldn't they keep their body parts to themselves? Sheesh.

"Learn to walk," someone said.

He probably didn't say that to hot girls bumping into him. "Learn to keep your arms out of my way," I called back. "Just all out here like Doctor Octopus," I grumbled, imagining his arms turning into eight tentacles poking and slapping people while he didn't give a crap.

The restrooms weren't hard to find since there was only one hallway, to the left of the bar, where no Thirst-Trap was visible. Maybe he was on break tending to his crotch injury.

I groaned and slumped my shoulders when I rounded the corner.

"That's a long-ass line," I said loudly at a line that trailed out of the women's restroom.

Seemed like five minutes had passed and the line barely moved.

I dropped my head back and just went to the men's rest-room.

"Hey," a guy said on his way out.

"Hey, yourself," I said. I had *not* brought extra panties and pants in my purse. I wasn't about to pee on myself and there wasn't anyone else in here. So I squatted and did my business quickly, then washed and dried my hands and masterfully pulled the door open with my foot. I kept my hands up like I was about to perform surgery and walked out.

Into a hard chest.

"Whoa!" someone said. But that voice? I didn't have to look up to know that I'd assaulted Thirst-Trap for the second time tonight.

"Sorry," I said, looking up at his pretty eyes and ignoring the scowl. "Shh," I said, placing a finger to his lips.

He stilled, then hinted a fascinating half smile.

"Please tell your boss to expand the women's restroom. Have you seen this line?" I swung my arm toward the line at my right and he swerved back to avoid getting smacked.

"Okay. Listen, next time you need the restroom and there's a long line, just get me. I'll let you use my office restroom."

"Aw. Bless your heart if you ain't special," I drawled.

He chuckled. "Maybe you're right that you've had enough."

"Yep. If I have one more drink . . . I might end up singing like a moron in a room full of strangers."

"I bet you sing great."

"I bet you like seeing people making a fool of themselves."

He looked left, then right. "I mean, look at where I work."

I smiled before remembering that he was absolutely not flirting with a tipsy customer. He was just being nice so that

I'd come back and pay for more drinks. I nodded and went back to my table.

"Loosen. Up," Rohan said before I could even sit back down. "Or tell me more about your feelings."

"Oh, hell," I grumbled.

Rohan laughed. "Let's go! They just called our name!"

"Oh no. Don't make me!" I whined as he took my wrist and led me to the mini stage, practically dragging me as I half cried.

"K-pop it!" Rohan hollered at the host, swinging his hand in the air.

"Wha!" I pouted.

But then BTS came on and a bunch of girls started grinning and cheering and I don't know what came over me.

Rohan was throwing his hands up and yelling, *"Yeah!,"* being the bestest hype-man one could ever ask for. He had the crowd going like we were at a concert and I was the main attraction. Maybe I wasn't doing life right, but I could do karaoke like a star.

Even Thirst-Trap, when he caught my eye from behind the bar counter straight ahead, grinned and cocked his chin. And *that* felt like a definite thumbs-up.

Confirmed! I *must* be an amazing singer!

Before I knew it, my favorite K-pop song blasted through the air, my head light and dizzy, giggles bubbling up my chest, and I was on stinking cloud nine half laughing and half tone-deaf-singing into a mic making a complete drunken ass of myself.

Talk about being *dynamite.*

Chapter 4

A grown woman with a degree shouldn't be tiptoeing into her bedroom to avoid getting yelled at by her parents for being too "American." Like, can a bitch just drink and pass out?

But that was what I ended up doing last night, and now it was time to pay the consequences.

I'd groggily gone through a slow morning routine, downing ibuprofen along the way, and returned to my room only to discover that I'd missed six texts and two phone calls. All from my agent! Which had never happened before. As in, Amy never texted, and calls were always scheduled.

Her texts referred to an email she'd sent last night when I was getting pity-wasted while pretending to be a K-pop star. I skimmed down the short email and tapped the links.

Amy, who hadn't been successful in acquiring an interested production company in the entire three years we'd been together, had someone lined up and somewhat interested in my work.

I hadn't heard from her in so long that I'd wondered if we were still working together.

Calming my ferociously beating heart, I read partway through her email, hitting the production company's name first. A quick search unleashed a torrent of big-name movies, top-tier stars, and a history of launching the careers of several writers.

That raging heart that I'd barely managed to control beat fiercer than ever.

Caveat? The production company wanted to meet in person because they just happened to be in town doing a last-minute pitchfest. Apparently, according to Amy's email, the production company had one day to fit prospective writers into their tight schedule. *Today.* She'd at least acquired the last time slot, but I needed to haul my butt over there. Right. Now.

I wanted to cry. Seriously?

After a few soothing breaths to level out my quivering voice, I went to the closet and called Amy while shoving aside one garment after another. What did one wear to a Saturday pitch meeting with producers? A dress for creatives? Dress pants for a power play? Nice jeans and a blouse for the laid-back feel?

I wanted to scream. *All right. Calm down. Breathe.*

"Isha! Finally," Amy said when she picked up my call, sounding a little annoyed. Not even a *hello, how are you*, seeing that it had been almost a year since we'd last spoken on the phone.

"Hi! Amy! Sorry I missed your messages. I just saw them!" I heaved. Oh, thank goodness for agents who checked emails and answered phones outside of work hours.

I put her on speakerphone and texted Rohan.

Isha: Are you still working on the segment? Is it by any miracle of a chance done?

I let out a nervous laugh when he didn't respond. No worries! I could present the script myself in real life, in real time, and in the flesh.

Amy sounded less frazzled when she said, "I'm so sorry that this is last-minute. I'd only received an email from the producers yesterday. *Yesterday!* These Hollywood types drive me nuts sometimes! Please tell me that you're able to make it. Getting in front of them, showing your marvelous enthusiasm, could help a lot."

"My hands are shaking, Amy . . ." I said, my voice a-quiver.

Amy exaggerated her breathing as if she were giving laboring advice over the cold distance of the phone. "I know. But in-person events are crucial to get face time, leave an impression, and I know you'll be excellent. Think about it, Isha. You've done these types of events before, and now you have a chance to make quite the impression. Let your passion and energy flow."

I groaned. Telling an introvert to let their energy flow didn't quite mean what Amy thought it meant.

She said, "You've prepared for this sort of opportunity for a long time. Let Priyanka and her journey of joy and hustle and humor and slight terror bleed from your words. I need you to work with me if we're ever going to sell your projects."

"Okay." I dropped my head back and glared at the ceiling. "Do you really think I have a chance?"

There was a brief pause before she replied, "I tend to sell quickly for clients because I pick clients with great work. This pitchfest could be what you need."

Well, that didn't quite answer the question, but I brushed off her words. Maybe she was trying to keep me calm and grounded.

"I'm assuming that you can clear your day, but maybe you can't, and that's fine," she said tersely. "Some people get big breaks, and others hardly get any bites. This may be your bite. The truth is, you don't get a lot of opportunities, so we have to make the best of this one."

I couldn't tell if she was encouraging me or insulting me.

I let out a haggard breath and soothed my raging heart. Besides this pitch session having the ability to jump-start my career, it could also provide just enough to get my parents to back down from this whole steady-job/family-elder-intervention business.

I replied firmly, "No. I don't have any plans. It's nerves. I can do this."

"Great! You don't have much time to drive there, find parking, find the room, check in, and set up for anything you want to prepare."

With Amy still on speaker, I dropped the phone onto the bed while I laid out a pair of dark wine, wide-leg dress pants with a cream blouse and a pair of flats.

As Amy walked me through what to expect, I gathered all my materials and stuffed them into my tote. She then coached me on what to do and not do. Most of what she said essentially flew out the ear of my still-throbbing skull, as I couldn't seem to focus on her *and* my presentation *and* making sure that I brought everything that I needed. Panic was *not* a strong enough word for what was happening. These little tentacles of anxiety around my head were coming to life, caressing and probing my brain.

"Oh, since I have you on the phone, did you get my last several emails?" I inquired.

"Yes, I'll get to them. But don't worry about those right now."

I frowned. Okay, but having emails ignored for months at a time didn't sit well with me.

As soon as I hung up, I barely had time to jump in the bathroom for a quick shower. No time to shave or wash my hair, but thank goodness for bobby pins and hair spray! I hopped into my slacks one leg at a time, trying not to trip over Rogue, who watched me curiously. She had food and water and was set for the next few hours.

With clothes on, a spritz of scented oil and lots of deodorant, and some makeup to cover up last night's fatigued aftermath, I rushed out of the bedroom but hurried right back in. Script! Seemed extremely important! Just in case they wanted it right then and there, and of course a printout of my proposal.

"Okay," I said, and closed my eyes for a minute, regulated my breathing, and pacified my raging pulse. *Calm. Down.*

"It's all good," I told myself as I calmly walked downstairs and out the door. "This is not going to be my one and only shot."

Except . . . it very well could be, and the drive downtown didn't help.

Road rage hath no fury like a woman late to a meeting that could make or break her career! Even with the A/C vents blasting the car with icy air, my armpits dampened like a muggy Texas swamp and my brows moistened with a trickle.

The hotel name flashed ahead, partway up a twenty-story-tall, well-maintained building. I had at least found the right place.

Finally, the entrance to a curved driveway appeared, also one-way, of course. I drove up to what was hopefully valet parking, my hands on the dashboard to air out my armpits.

There was a tall desk on the curb that clearly read: VALET.

And below that, a sign that clearly read: CURRENTLY UN-AVAILABLE. PLEASE PARK IN PARKING GARAGE TO YOUR RIGHT. WE APOLOGIZE FOR THE INCONVENIENCE.

I almost screamed. Of-freaking-course!

Okay. Things would be all right.

I pulled into the electronic parking garage entrance and followed the instructions, trying to relax my breathing as the computerized box thought long and hard. I eyed it skeptically. Was it debating on letting me in because I didn't have a room to enter into its system? Was it going to deny access because the garage was full and only taking those who stayed at the hotel? Was it scanning my DNA? Communicating with robotic alien terminators from the future? *What?* What was the holdup?

Oh. My. *Lord.*

"Think faster," I muttered, checking the time on the dashboard. My time slot would be starting in five minutes, and I had yet to find a parking spot.

The machine sure took its sweet time as I mumbled, "Look, you'll be part of the machine uprising against mankind and eventually end me or become my overlord, but for the love of my sanity and anxiety, *please* work. I beg of you."

I gritted my teeth as the computer, ever so slowly, printed out my ticket. I snatched the paper and cruised the first, second, and third floors for a spot.

Finally! One lonesome parking spot in the wee, dark corners of this god-awful place.

I eased out of the car so as not to bang my door against the parked-on-the-line car to the left, took my tote, and hurried to the hotel entrance. The air outside was the usual consistency of Texas mugginess, dampening my skin with a weird heaviness and battling my hair for frizz dominance.

Inside, chilled air blasted down from the vents above just as my blouse began to drink in the sweat of my pits. Texas humidity had me believing that deodorant was a mass conspiracy and didn't actually do a single thing.

Glancing at my phone, which clearly showed that I was now four minutes late, I checked the email with location info. The session should take place in Conference Room 3C.

As soon as I passed the elevator, mentally going over my presentation and pitch, I noticed the pit stains in the reflection of a mirror in passing. Curse you, overactive glands. I knew you worked the way the good lord intended, but damn, could you have calmed down a bit? No need to drown out my armpits.

Okay. *Don't worry.* I would simply have to remember to keep my arms at my sides the entire time. No big deal. How hard could it be to keep my arms down?

In the hallway, only a few people lingered. And I was glad for that. Emptiness and silence and nothing like the nervous excitement of early sessions.

Once I made it to the designated room, I landed a shaking hand on the doorknob beside a carved wall sign that read CONFERENCE ROOM 3C in shimmering metallic letters.

I furrowed my brows. Should I . . . just walk in? Was I supposed to wait for someone to come out and call my name? But no one was working at the door, and there weren't any instructions on what to do.

I closed my eyes and took a few calming breaths. I wasn't religious by any means but found myself throwing out silent prayers to every deity my family had ever sworn allegiance to and then some.

Please work. Please go well. Please be my shining moment.

My heart rammed against my chest, sending blasts of adrenaline coursing through my body as I gently knocked and then proceeded to open the door. My hands were shaking as I met the gazes of six people, all dressed nicely but informally, all in midconversation, all looking a bit terse and annoyed. As in, how dare this stranger with noticeable pit stains and frizzy hair interrupt the sanctity of their meeting.

I leaned back and checked the room sign. I was in the right place, wasn't I?

"Oh! Are you Isha?" a dark-haired woman asked, walking toward me from the back table of coffee and snacks, clutching a tablet to her chest.

"Y-yes," I said, breathy because I was actually out of breath.

"Come on in," she said, closing the door behind me as the team went back to discussing a project.

I stood immobile by the door with my hands on my tote straps, waiting for an introduction or leeway into their conversation. Adrenaline hit hard, which didn't help my hangover headache, as if someone had thrown a match into my circulatory system and lit my veins on fire. Even my vision throbbed.

The woman leaned down and whispered something into the ear of a man wearing a green dress shirt with the top button undone. Out of the six people, three were men ranging in age; the other three were women perhaps in their thirties, including the one who had shown me in, who appeared to be an assistant.

The man nodded to her, eyeing me with a slight smile, as if to welcome me but also making sure that I knew my place in their hierarchy.

She returned to me and offered, "Would you like a drink or snacks?"

"No, thank you." If I ingested one thing, I might actually vomit all over her black-and-gray tweed dress.

When the conversation eased away from whatever business they were in the middle of, the man with the green shirt introduced himself and the others. Producers, one writer, and marketing. All of his words went over my head and I'd already forgotten their names.

He pointedly looked at his watch and said, "We were expecting you ten minutes ago."

I swallowed. Half of me was consumed by embarrassment, as if I should apologize for just taking up space. The other half was fueled with annoyance because this *was* last-minute. But that didn't matter to them.

I swallowed my pride, my hands quivering at my sides, and said, "I apologize for being late. Austin has grown to insurmountable sizes and traffic has become quite congested." Thanks, mass migration of Californians. "I hope you'll allow me to make up for being late?"

Talk about tension. He had major RBF, but I smiled and tried to de-escalate his uptight attitude.

All right, calm down, woman. I needed them. They, however, did not need me.

"Are you at least prepared?" he asked.

What. An. Asshole.

"Not to worry," I said enthusiastically. "I have a presentation ready, a pitch, and a proposal if you're interested."

While a woman who was sitting next to the man in green politely smiled and swung her hand toward the front of the room and the whiteboard with a flat-screen TV to one side, Green Shirt said, "In any case, we're incredibly busy and can only give you five minutes."

Oh. I swung my head to look at him in my surprise, tripping over the chair at the end and bumping the man in said chair.

A collective gasp hit the air.

"Shit!" he grumbled, his cup of coffee held out from his chest with notable spillage dripping onto the desk, onto his tablet, and onto his white dress shirt.

"Oh my lord, I'm so sorry!" I said, grabbing paper towels from across the table in front of me and going for his . . . hmm . . . crotch?

"It's okay," he said, before my hands made contact. What was it about me and strangers' crotches?

I dropped the paper towels onto his tablet, which wasn't any better, and he furiously dabbed his device and notes. The woman at the refreshments table rushed over with another stack of napkins. He mumbled, snatching the napkins from her, and cleaned his pants and shirt.

Green Shirt sighed from his chair at the other end of the table and rubbed the bridge of his nose. "Continue."

Right. With my skin flaring hot, I set my tote on the table, but there wasn't room to unload when the guy on the right had sprawled his things out to clean up the coffee and the woman on the left had her own items taking up more space than they needed.

I fumbled to get things out. A room had never been so quiet. Ever heard the phrase *so quiet you could hear a pin drop*? Well, if the floor hadn't been carpeted, it would have been true. The man beside me gulped with his final dab. Another tapped a pen on the table. Green Shirt swiveled his chair back and forth with a creak echoing into the silence like a taunting ghost.

Of course, my laptop decided to take its sweet time turning on.

Looking up was a mistake because only one person seemed okay with me being here. The rest were a sea of impassiveness. I wanted to crawl into my skin and hide. My body turned heavy trying to lock down, but I fought through it. I mentally coached myself to get it together. It was all about appearances, confidence, charisma.

How badly did I want this?

When the laptop finally hummed on, blasting me with a bright white light before moving on to the background image, it . . . wouldn't take my password.

Oh, really? Seven years together and suddenly you don't know me?

Green Shirt cleared his throat.

My face heated up to blazing hot levels.

"Ah. Computer issues," I explained nervously. "Why don't I tell you about the premise while it's starting?"

But doing several things at once—summarizing my screenplay and typing in incorrect passwords while bent over the front of a conference table during an adrenaline overhaul—proved to be too much. Too many "uhs" and "ohs" and the dreaded "ums" filled up my head, and my vocabulary. I sounded like an incompetent, incoherent numbskull.

Finally, the computer signed on. Now, where was the adapter?

"Four minutes," Green Shirt said.

"Could I have just a few more minutes? The storyboard really adds depth."

"No," he said steadily. "Visuals aren't necessary."

"Right . . ." I gently closed the laptop and wiped my hands against my slacks, leaving a trail of dampness.

Well, hell. I stood up straight, my heart clamoring, closed my eyes for a second, and took a breath before going on to tell the room my long-awaited pitch. I relayed the tale of my MC (aka main character), Priyanka, and her quest for success in a Western, white, male-dominated industry while overcoming mishaps after witnessing a murder and encountering friendships and a budding romantic interest.

As I relayed my pitch, in all of my quivering-voice glory, I pulled out a copy of the proposal for them to pass around. I started with the woman on the left, since the guy to the right was probably still vexed about his now-stained clothes. The script seemed to impress the three who glanced it over, stopping at Green Shirt.

By now, I was sweating actual bullets and perhaps rambling, babbling about the intro. Instead of an eloquent, succinct, mesmerizing elevator pitch that would pique their interest and leave them salivating for more, I sort of just blathered out the entire synopsis. Too many words. Just like a query to film agents, short was best.

Why was I so fixated on the setup and backstory? Did I have to mention what the characters looked like and who inspired them? No! Of course not! Was I talking so fast that words blended together, and was I making up every other word? Probably, because that was what nervous Isha did.

Before my eyes, I watched as the group fell out of attention. First with glazed looks, then lingering glances elsewhere. Green Shirt even scrolled through his phone!

Dead. My moment had died.

I'd only managed to get partway through the climactic build when Green Shirt tapped a finger on my three-page proposal and then on his gleaming gold watch.

I hurried up even faster, my actions catching on to the excitement and stress in my voice. I was gesticulating now, throwing my arms up to expand the universe of my tale and to show how explosive the scene where Priyanka pushed through her adversities was, with the help of a minor character who came through in a big way, the way the scene could unfold on screen . . . when all eyes fell to my pits.

Oh!

I clamped down my armpits like I was trying to shimmy down a chimney. "As I was saying," I went on with a laugh, even though I wanted to crawl into a hole and pass out from this nightmare.

Green Shirt was nice enough to let me finish. He didn't say I went over time, but judging by the amount of information I gave between him tapping his watch and actually ending, adding the calculation of his facial hair growth and the rotation of the sun through the window, I'd say I took up an extra eon. Give or take a millennium.

With my time far past over, I slumped, and the adrenaline absorbed into my body the way my sweat had absorbed into my clothes. Suddenly my skin was frigid, particularly in the armpit region.

"Well. Thank you for your time and meeting with us," Green Shirt said.

"Oh. Yes. Thank you," I replied, dazed and trying not to gulp for air.

I stuffed all my belongings back into my tote as quickly as humanly possible, once again juggling the large purse against my side from one strap to get the laptop in first.

"Thank you, thank you," I reiterated for some reason, my gaze downcast.

The man to my right flashed a small smile at me when I said, "Again, I'm so sorry about the coffee."

"It happens," he said, seemingly a teensy bit less annoyed.

"We have your name and information from the online scheduler," the woman beside him said with a degree of sincerity. "We'll reach out to you if we have any further thoughts or questions after we discuss."

I released a small sigh, along with a nod, and shuffled toward the door.

"Don't forget your proposal," Green Shirt called to my back just as my hand landed on the door handle.

His words knocked the breath from my lungs and my vision fractured into two.

What normally sounded like a gesture of kindness in any other situation was a nail in my failure-to-launch coffin.

I swallowed hard, pushing the rancid taste down my throat, turned, and quickly walked to the table to retrieve my barely read proposal.

It was done, and oh so pathetically and obviously true that this team had no interest in me or my story.

The woman at the refreshments table handed me a wrapped mini chocolate croissant. Her empathetic gaze with slightly furrowed brows and soft, albeit small, smile said it all.

Wow. A pity gift.

I took it and mouthed *Thanks* before she closed the door.

Facing the corridor, what had been a hall of hope ten minutes ago morphed into a hall of doom, I marched toward the elevator. My shoulders slumped all the way until I was ninety percent Neanderthal posture. I unwrapped the pastry and chomped into it.

The hotel's chilled air left icicles on my skin, minuscule particles deadening my flesh.

That had been . . . brutal. At best.

At least my parting pity treat was good.

Chapter 5

The worst hangover headache paired with the worst creative heartbreak severed my soul. My entire body ached. I just wanted to get home and sleep a thousand sleeps.

I slipped inside my car and practically stripped off my blouse. I turned on the engine and cranked up the A/C to max intensity, letting cold air cool my armpits.

I downed another couple of ibuprofen and then just sat there, melting into the warmth like some muggy, hot mess fusing into the fabric of my car seat. A dozen emotions careened toward me, a wraith of undiluted feelings. Mortification. Terror. Embarrassment. Shock.

And I couldn't help but think back to my conversation with Amy. Was she insinuating that I wasn't working hard enough with her, or that my work wasn't good enough anymore? She sounded a bit off, curt even. I hoped I wasn't failing her. She'd been distant and absent for an entire year now.

I heaved out a breath and checked my phone. There were

missed texts, calls, voice mail, and email notifications. My parents needed me to do this and that. Mohit asked about whatever random item he couldn't find because he never looked for things himself. Rohan checked in on me. Amy inquired about the session.

My eyes fluttered closed for a few epically long minutes. I could've cried, could've screamed, could've fallen asleep. But I did none of those things except revel in the quiet, dark solitude. Once my headache eased a bit and my flittering heart calmed, I texted Amy with both thanks for setting this up and the details of how badly it went.

Then I pulled out of the parking spot, rolled down to the exit, and paid the asinine amount of twenty dollars for parking.

When I pulled into my parents' driveway, I didn't want to get out and face them.

No. A grown woman, no matter the imbalance of her current situation, shouldn't sacrifice her dreams and haphazardly toss years of hard work into the dumpster fire closing in on her. Resilience mattered, damn it.

I lugged my tote out of the car and went inside. As suspected, an onslaught of questions had me flinching from the first word, prickling at my headache.

"Did you pick up the milk and bhaji?" Mummie asked before I even closed the door.

"Did you get my text? Have you seen my tire pump?" Mohit asked before I even took off my shoes.

"Why are you dressed so nice? Where have you been?" Papa asked from around the corner, before I even tucked the keys into my purse.

Upstairs, Rogue barked like a little maniac before I even let out my first exhale. I groaned. "Did anyone take Rogue out?"

They all shook their heads.

"I'm sorry, I forgot all about her," Mummie replied apologetically.

Papa frowned. "I was planning on taking her out in a little while."

I looked at Mohit. Mohit loved to play with Rogue, but when the time came to take her out, it was always the same response. "She's *your* dog."

"She's a living, breathing creature with bodily functions," I said calmly.

He shrugged. "Sorry."

"I'll need to take a nap," I muttered. "*After* I take Rogue out."

"Can you go to the store and get milk and bhaji?" Mummie asked before ducking back into the kitchen.

"Can't Mohit go?" I said, exhaustion wearing down my bones.

"I don't know how to pick out vegetables," he replied. That was, sadly, the truth.

"Well, it's time you learned," I shot back.

"Mohit has been in school all week," Mummie justified, coddling him as per usual. "When does he have time to pick bhaji and cook?"

I held my tongue out of respect, but boy was it difficult.

"Why are you so tired?" Papa asked, still standing in the hallway. "And grumpy?"

"Yeah. Why *do* you look so tired?" Mohit crossed his arms and shot me an accusatory glance like he might throw me under the bus to get out of vegetable shopping.

"I just got back from a meeting," I answered, my voice strained.

"Oh! Like a job interview?" Papa asked with a gleam in his eye and unfettered hope in his voice.

How had I gotten so far behind in life that getting a job interview was now deemed a highlight for my parents?

I put on my best smile and mustered up enthusiasm to at least fake it until I made it. "No. It was for my script. The meeting was with a movie production company."

I could see the wheels turning in Papa's head. *No movie deal? No job offer? No lavish advance? No steady income? What a waste, then. Why spend so much time in this futile pursuit that's yielded nothing? Why not change course before it's too late?*

"How did it go?" Papa asked. "Did they offer you six figures off the bat?" he said both as a lighthearted joke and as a dash of hope, but the words cut deep.

No response came to mind, so instead I laughed it off and hurried upstairs to take Rogue potty. While she did her business in the backyard, I checked my phone.

I replied to Rohan first, letting him know that I'd had a pitch session, and of course he immediately responded.

Rohan: What! That's amazing! Congrats! How'd It go? Knocked their socks off?

Isha: Well, I found out last minute, ended up late, knocked someone's coffee on them, babbled, and they didn't even read my proposal. They weren't particularly impressed.

Rohan: Did they say that?

Isha: No. But one can tell.

Rohan: Until they say otherwise, you have a shot. But you didn't have the segment! Oh, man. Was that why you texted earlier? I was still asleep.

Isha: I know! Timing.

Rohan: I could've had it done! I'm sorry.

My chest warmed at how seriously he took his unpaid freelance duties.

Isha: Don't be. You wouldn't have had it done that quickly, anyway, not unless you were up all night working on it. But we didn't know last night. Besides, this isn't your job, haha, and the segment is just a little extra thing. So don't feel bad, okay?

Rohan: I spent some time working on it last night cuz I couldn't sleep. I'm working on it now. I'm going to finish it.

Isha: That's okay.

Rohan: Why? You still need it. You can show it to other producers. And maybe you can send this to the ones from today anyway. Have a second shot? Can your agent hook that up?

Ugh. How to tell him that I was on the verge of giving up, at least for a while? Even typing out these texts to him brought all the sadness back, despite the smiley face and laughing emojis. So I told him the only honest thing that I could say:

Isha: Thank you.

He didn't respond immediately and I moved on to a recent slew of Amy's emails and texts. She'd . . . already heard from them. Oh my lord. This was as nerve-racking and insidious as opening college admission emails. They almost always started out the same way.

As Rogue sunbathed and watched butterflies float around her, I skimmed the length of the email.

Yep. The producers had *not* been impressed. That much was evident, but to see it in writing made it that much harsher, more concrete, final. Forget the last nail in the coffin! The coffin was being dropped into an infinitely cavernous grave for all eternity.

My chest tingled and tightened. An anxiety attack was about to hit hard.

I had really thought this could be the one, *the moment, the producer for me.* I'd thought if I was determined and worked hard and learned from the best, that I would make it.

Rogue trotted to my feet and cuddled up to me, probably sensing my anxiety as she often did. Humans did *not* deserve dogs, but she was warm and soft and everything I needed.

"Come on, little girl." I let her back inside and she trotted alongside me the entire way to the hall until we reached the bottom of the stairs. She went ahead first but stopped every third step and glanced over her shoulder in that very model Yorkie fashion to make sure I was still there and following.

"Good girl." Always looking out for me.

After emptying my tote and putting everything away, I made sure Rogue was set before running the family's errands. As soon as I returned, I put away the milk and washed the produce and laid it out on drying towels before scrubbing a sink full of dishes.

Everyone had disappeared. Mummie texted that they were

all at mandir to set up for tomorrow's program and invited me to join. Also, there were leftovers on the counter. It was her famous handvo—a loaf made from ground rice and lentil batter mixed with shredded cabbage. Because she knew my favorite part was the near-burnt sesame seed crust, she'd saved most of the chewy top for me. This was one of those million nice mom things she did.

And then she added a curt reminder to show her my list of applied jobs tomorrow.

Wow. Like homework, huh?

My phone pinged with another text. My heart dropped into my gut and the blood drained from my face, my head light and dizzy.

It wasn't from Mummie. But from Amy. She . . . thought it was time to part ways.

I swallowed and, with shaking hands, finished drying the last dish. Trembling fingers scrolled through Amy's words.

Yep. She had absolutely broken up with me via text. She might as well have been an ex-boyfriend, all eager to make things work one minute and bam! Goodbye message hours later.

Ugly dread reared its head, clawing through my guts. Rejection always hurt, but a three-year relationship ending like this was staggeringly painful. I should've seen the signs. The gradual loss of attention. Neglecting emails, missing phone calls. The vagueness. The lack of enthusiasm.

This morning had apparently been our Hail Mary and I hadn't even known it.

I responded to Amy. First asking if we could chat. Then deleting the message and asking if all submission rights for Priyanka's story reverted to me or if she would finish off the sub process with this last script.

In the end, I decided it was best to put away the phone and not respond.

Replying when emotionally charged was a bad idea.

Also, I couldn't see straight through blurry eyes.

I wiped my tears and looked skyward for a second. Damn. Was this what a gut punch out of nowhere felt like? I bowed over and heaved, stopping myself from crying, from feeling loss.

No. No agent was going to reduce me to this. In fact, how *dare* she. How dare she be this cruel and unprofessional. I mean, right after a big blow?

I stumbled into my room, desperately clinging to anything to solidify my need to pursue screenwriting, and instead dropped face-first into bed.

If I could manage to shut down my brain, that would be a magnificent feat.

My eyelids finally drooped as residual adrenaline and anxiety crashed into one another like a gruesome demolition derby match. Savage and macabre, laying any energy to waste.

Sleep. What a marvelous reset button and a few priceless hours of not having to deal with the disappointment that was my life.

I must've slept hard because I awoke to Rogue staring at me with the need to potty, an empty house, and Rohan blowing up my phone with texts. The pings from message alerts reverberated through my room, a haunting of unread words.

Half-awake and without checking the time or the messages, I rubbed my face, put on my glasses, and walked Rogue downstairs. I started a cup of coffee, not caring what time of night or day it was, then went to the back door.

Sleep had helped my headache and had eased the anxiety, but reality prowled closer to the forefront of my thoughts as I took a sip of coffee and started to wake all the way up.

Oh. Crap.

I closed my eyes and shook my head, recalling Amy's text. A million little creepy crawlies sprouted underneath my skin as my stomach churned something sour.

All right. This couldn't be the end-all.

I caught the time as I dove into confronting the loads of messages inundating my phone. Five o'clock came around as I read through Rohan's texts.

Isha: How did you finish editing so quickly!

Rohan: Come on, woman, don't insult me. But now you can send it off to those producers from this morning.

I bit my lower lip. How to tell him that they'd already given their verdict and that he'd hurried for nothing? Worse yet, that it had been the catalyst for my agent dumping me and what was the point? My time was up.

Rohan: I can come over and show it to you. You can tell me if I need to change or add anything. Not gonna lie, though, it's as perfect as perfect can get.

Isha: That's amazing! Can't wait to see it. Thanks for the hard work! I gotta treat you to something.

Rohan: I'm actually at that Indian taco food truck. You want something?

Yeah. Food was always the way to go. I had no idea what to expect, but when my cousin came around thirty minutes later, my taste buds swam in fusion heaven with an unusual mix of Indian and Mexican ingredients working remarkably well together.

"Oh my lord, this is amazing!" I sang while eating at the table, an array of food containers spread out in front of us. Nothing like food to act as a balm over searing wounds of rejection.

"Told you. I only recommend the *best* food places in Austin," he said around a veggie bite. He was definitely blossoming into a foodie, and the mere invitation to a place he deemed worthy brought all the excitement.

Delicious and spicy! Woo! A little *too* spicy. I needed the sweetness from iced tea to cool off my taste buds.

As I listened to him pick out every spice and herb and go over his theory of how this food was made, I wondered aloud, "You'd be great with a career in food, you know?"

"If only my parents thought I had the discipline for that," he responded, his shoulders deflating slightly.

Sometimes I questioned if our parents were too honest, or if they didn't believe in us because we weren't living up to their expectations. Would Rohan be more decisive if others believed in him the way I did?

"What?" he muttered, side-eyeing me.

I gave a soft, small smile. "Nothing."

After we finished eating, Rohan connected his laptop to the TV and played the edited segment.

His work never ceased to amaze me, and I watched in awe. To put it simply, he'd recorded me giving a presentation pitching my work, but his angles and editing made it into art.

"This is your best work," I confessed, even as sadness bubbled up into my chest.

He regarded me for a moment, quietly, his gaze piercing my skull and reading my thoughts like an open website.

"Was it that bad? This morning?" he asked, leaning his back against the couch and pulling a knee to his chest. "Oh, man. Did you really need the video that badly?" He hit his back against the couch arm while Rogue cuddled against his side and looked up to search his face, as if she were trying to figure out what had him so stressed.

I quickly replied, "Oh no! It wasn't you, trust me. I don't think having this segment would've made much of a difference."

"What happened, then?" he asked quietly, and petted Rogue as she rolled onto her back for belly rubs. No matter the mood, that little demand of hers always made me smile.

"Just what I said. I wasn't prepared or in the right state of mind. Too many mishaps. I arrived late, armpits sweating up a tsunami, spilled coffee on a producer, babbled, missed the major arc points."

Rohan sucked his teeth like he felt my mortification.

"Yeah. The main guy never even touched the proposal. And the coffee guy was wearing nice clothes." I covered my face.

Rohan leaned forward, hanging on my every word.

I let out a pent-up, hot breath. "I might've tried to pat down the pool of coffee on his crotch." I tilted my head while saying this and grimaced.

"Oh, damn!" he said, part horrified but also trying not to laugh with the way his mouth twitched in a forced frown. "You and random crotches, though."

My skin was on fire just remembering the incident.

Maybe if I hadn't been out drinking and singing drunk karaoke, or had set my alarm, maybe if I had had everything prepared for a moment's notice, then maybe I'd still have an agent. Maybe. Maybe. Maybe. None of these maybes changed the facts.

"And then . . . my agent dumped me."

A deafening moment of silence stagnated in the air, but there was something to be said about getting things out into the open, off your chest by expressing your thoughts to someone else. In my head, everything was chaos and torture and the end of the world. Saying it aloud helped me to realize perhaps it wasn't so bad and could've been much worse. So what, one meeting bombed. It wasn't going to end me. Right? *Right?*

"Oh, man. I'm sorry. Can you talk to her? Work it out?" Rohan asked.

I gave him a sorrowful smile. "It's like saying can't I work it out with a boyfriend dumping me after years of trying to make it work and just not getting anywhere."

"Ah. There are other agents, though?"

"Sure, but it was difficult getting this agent. I'd need a new script for another agent, and I don't have another story in me right now. Now I have absolutely nothing to defend myself with when my parents demand that I leave this all behind."

He grunted and said, "It's okay," right as the familiar Bollywood ringtone of his phone went off. He checked his phone and swiped to read and responded and did a few other things.

"Hmm. Maybe it was for the best?" he said.

I glanced at him.

He quickly added, "I mean, that agent wasn't taking you anywhere. She hadn't sold anything for you. She was wasting your time. And you need a champion. Nah, scratch that. You deserve an Avenger."

"You're sweet."

"Maybe a Tony Stark? Or a Thor? I know you like those white boys."

"Oh my lord . . ." I cracked a smile, imagining having my own personal Thor as an agent.

"You're not giving up, are you?" he asked, putting away his phone.

I sighed the heaviest breath imaginable. That was a loaded question with a loaded answer. "I've been doing this for years, all through college, a degree even, so many failed scripts and pitches and queries and subs. I fought against the passive-aggressive comments and looks and stuck to this. I fought my parents for this. I strained our relationship over this. I really thought I had something this time. I really thought this was it, that something would come from all of these struggles."

He tapped his chin and narrowed his eyes. "I'm going to take that as a *no*."

Right, because he was the one person who would never allow me to give up.

"Since you're not throwing in the towel and will continue to follow your dream and make it after all so that your story of adversity will inspire others, I have a plan."

I lifted my head and watched that slightly evil but completely mischievous smirk change the entire look of his expression. "Uh-oh."

"Just hear me out, okay? Forget these douchebag producers and your waste-of-space agent. We're going to show them how much they screwed up and how you don't need them anyway.

You know what? I'm glad you retaliated and threw hot coffee at their faces."

"Absolutely not what happened, but okay."

He placed a hand to his chest. "In my soul, I know it was. Let them play their games. We gotta take matters into our own hands. I mean, your parents are forcing you to take a job you don't want and say goodbye to your dreams. That's soul-crushing, and I can't sit by and watch you get shoved down a tunnel of depression while some pointless job leeches your creativity. We have to get this done. You can't let them drag you away. Not like this. Not ever."

My chest warmed at how fiercely he believed in me. Without him, I might've lost to familial pressure long ago. "Sure. I'll bite. What are you proposing?"

"Matthew McConaughey."

"Oh boy. This again?"

He waved off my remark. "You know how Matthew McConaughey was your professor at UT?"

"No one forgets that. I don't let them."

"He has ties to producers and writers."

"Mmm-hmm . . ."

"What if we get him to read the script?" he asked casually, as if getting a superstar actor and director to take time for me were simple.

"And what's that going to do?"

He threw his hands up, startling Rogue so that she shot him a death glare and then went back to being petted. "Sorry, girl." He looked back to me and asked, "Are you joking? A former student of his with an extraordinary script and he's not worth a shot?"

I rolled my eyes. "So extraordinary that production companies are fighting to the death for it? Some of my old classmates sold so fast! One had six producers in a bidding war that led to a million-dollar advance with Netflix. Can you even imagine that!" I cringed, hating how envy lurked inside me this obscenely.

"Yes. I can. And I can also imagine you buying me my own taco truck with that kind of advance. Listen, can you really let writing go?"

I flinched. Even now, with my emotions drowning in rejections and upheaval, a story struggled to climb out from the darkness. No, I couldn't let writing go. I was a creative. And creatives needed their art the way they needed air. Lacking one or the other was inevitable death.

He snapped a finger. "Your friend from college. Veronica? You said she loved it."

"Yeah."

"And you trust her judgment. She keeps it real but also her opinion is valued because she works in the industry."

I nodded.

"I read this script, too. You used to write about white Americans and comedy. This time you wrote about Priyanka and her struggles and some funny moments but some real truths for what it's like for brown people to make it when they're straddling two cultures and getting shoved aside by the system. I felt seen. This script is phenomenal," he said, deadpan.

My breath caught in my throat. The belief he expressed in those words floored me. "Oh . . . thank you. But you're not just saying that?"

He shook his head. "Nope. You know me. I keep it level because you need honesty to be your best. If you battle out all the uglies with your CPs and your agent polishes it with her pro-level expertise, then the producers should be getting the best quality possible. This is it. This is your script, and I will die on this hill over it."

My lips quivered into a shaky smile. Bro to the end. "So. What's Matthew McConaughey got to do with this?"

Rohan grinned so hard that I could practically see his monumental plan unfolding in his head. Oh boy. What was I getting myself into?

Chapter 6

Rohan declared, "We're going to get McConaughey to read this. He's going to fall so hard for this script that he's going to attach himself one way or another: as producer, writer, director, actor, whatever. I don't know if he does all of those things, but sure, why not? This script will move him to fit into every one of those positions."

"No way. Him falling for the script, even reading it, is impossible."

"Nothing is impossible when you've got the hustle acumen of top Hollywood writers," he replied so matter-of-factly that even I wanted to believe him.

I wasn't sure I even knew what *acumen* meant or if he'd used it correctly, but Rohan pretty much slept with a dictionary and right now, he was in his awe-inspiring, hyped, we're-going-to-make-it-after-all mode. The level of determination in his tone and the apex look of faith in his eyes was making it near impossible for me to back down. This was part of his rallying cry, his fervent belief that got even the most cynical believing with him.

Hype-man was an understatement.

Excitement brewed in my bones, but it had a long way to go before fully emerging from the throes of borderline depression. "How exactly do we even get a meeting with him? Not like he's teaching this semester and I can just hop on over to his campus office. He probably wouldn't even respond to my emails, if he even checks his staff email. I mean, is he in Austin right now? Isn't he working on a film in L.A.?"

"Yes, but he's here for the weekend."

I eyed him warily. "Just how would you know?"

"Remember how I was telling you about Seth? My friend whose brother owns the bar and grill that we went to last night. Their grandpa knows McConaughey from way back. So the grandma told McConaughey about her grandkids opening up this pub and that he was welcome to go anytime, and drinks and food were on the house. And once McConaughey was spotted there, their business skyrocketed. He still goes once in a while.

"Seth's grandparents said McConaughey was going to come by and wanted him to save a prime booth. Seth just told me I can come by and see him, but I'm not supposed to tell anyone. But this is kismet, Motiben. This is where your success story pivots and how people in coming years will be singing songs about this moment."

Then he theatrically swayed his hand across the air and looked off into the distance and said, "She rose from the ashes of a coffee-assault nightmare of a meeting, beaten but not broken, and set out to find her former mentor and professor. Since this fateful encounter, the mentor bowed to the mentee, for she'd surpassed all of his expectations that set her on a course toward fame."

I laughed. "Okay . . ."

"Seth can introduce you to McConaughey. McConaughey will then say: *Ah yes, I remember you, great student of mine.* Then he'll invite you to join him and ask what you've been up to. And you'll say, well, since you asked . . . pitch and then bam! Hand him the proposal when he falls head over heels for the plot. He's going to read it because he seems like the type of guy who would do that, all things considered. And hey, weren't you in one of those Austin magazines, your picture right next to him?"

"Yes, but that was just a coincidental layout because I was his student," I reminded him, no matter how gleeful the magazine layout had made me.

"But a coincidence we're going to use to our advantage. We have the location, the personal intro, the professional attachment, the cool coincidence, and a kick-ass script."

I petted Rogue and deliberated on this wild plan of Rohan's. In theory, I had a better chance than most of getting my former professor to read my script, or if nothing else, then at least to provide feedback. And it would be nice to see him again, even if we didn't get a chance to discuss business.

"Maybe we can try this crazy plan. But I'm not drinking this time. I can't if I'm going to speak with him. Don't let me drink."

He clucked his tongue. "You're actually smoother and more coherent when you've had a few, to be honest."

"Hush now. Seriously. I'm not going to drink. Not even a tiny shot," I declared. Not after the mess I'd suffered from last night's outing.

"Fine. But does this mean you're on board? Are we going

to track down your old professor so he can pay it forward with someone who just needs her break to shine?"

I gnawed on my lower lip. Success stories were full of people who had done anything and everything they could to break into the biz. This wouldn't be the first time someone had hunted down a celebrity to read their script.

"What if he's annoyed? This can't possibly be the first time someone randomly went up to him and handed him a script. I bet he gets that all the time and it's insufferable."

"Not random. You know each other from class. He helped you when you had questions, just like any other professor. It's an unofficial meeting. But like, we're not going to call it a *meeting*. It's just a . . . quick sit-down with proper intros by someone he knows."

I considered it a little longer. Rohan raised his brows in waiting. He cast that silent look that tossed out a handful of questions: *How bad do you want this? What's the harm in trying? Going to keep doing the same thing over and over, getting the same nonexistent results?* And the fiercest question blazing in his expression: *You really want a meaningless job while stuck living with your parents?*

I blew out a breath and closed my eyes for a second, pushing out the jitters. He was right. It was a small effort with a potentially huge reward. What was the worst that could happen? Matthew McConaughey might not show up? Matthew McConaughey might decline?

"Okay."

"Okay?" Rohan nearly shouted, and both Rogue and I flinched. "That doesn't sound like you're pumped to tackle your dreams!"

"Okay!" I yelled, covering Rogue's delicate ears.

The bubbling cauldron of excitement brought on by his game plan had ignited, fully exploded, and eviscerated any lingering depression. We were hyped. We were excited. We were . . . about to throw ourselves at an A-list celebrity like a couple of desperate fools.

What could possibly go wrong?

Rohan had gone home to get ready since Matthew McConaughey wasn't expected until around eight. His process of getting ready was a quick shower, combing his hair, and donning any random pair of shorts and a graphic tee.

Meanwhile, I'd showered, pulled my hair into a low ponytail, put on makeup and put in my contacts, and slipped into a pair of black leggings and a white top with borders in UT burnt orange. The length was perfect to cover up any, ya know, camel toe. And the color sure to connect us to our Longhorn roots.

Then I repacked my purse with everything I needed, including the printed proposal with visuals on a thumb drive, and my laptop. Just in case he was interested in seeing the edited segment right then and there.

As I waited for Rohan's return to pick me up, I went over my presentation and what I would say, adjusting everything to sound informal but succinct. I watched my reflection as I spoke, paying attention to my posture, pulling my shoulders back, straightening my spine, lifting my chin, and making eye contact so Matthew McConaughey was sure to be blinded by my dazzling passion.

Practice made perfect, and I didn't want to look like a

chump in front of my former professor. A sense of pride washed over me, and I hoped it would wash over him, too.

As soon as Rohan pulled up, he texted and off we went!

"Are you ready?" he asked, grinning so hard that one might've assumed this was *his* big break.

"Yes. And look at you. Not wearing shorts," I teased, pointing at his jeans.

"Gotta look the part," he said.

I mentally went over my presentation as he drove, my hands clammy.

"Don't worry about this morning so much," Rohan said as he found a spot a bit farther down the street and over one block from where we'd parked last night. Of course, a Saturday night was going to be crowded.

Just the suggestion of not worrying had me worrying. And just the mention of this morning had my skin crawling. I could get over the meeting, which felt like a million lifetimes ago. But one didn't get over a breakup so easily.

As Rohan turned off the ignition, I nipped my nail. "Easy to say, hard to do."

"Gotta get out of your head, otherwise you're going to be your own worst enemy."

"Yeah. You're right," I replied, suddenly annoyed with Amy for ending things the way she had. How incredibly unprofessional! I swung open the passenger-side door and nearly hit a passerby on the sidewalk.

He jumped out of the way just in time and yelled, "Hey!"

"Hey, yourself," I gritted out. Why was he walking so close to the street, anyway?

I glanced around at packed streets and crowded sidewalks

in the dark kept vaguely lit by a sea of yellow streetlights and neon bar signs.

The air was chilly but just right, refreshing even. The mugginess wasn't as overwhelming as it had been earlier today.

Wow. Just earlier today, huh? I couldn't get over the fact that so much had happened less than twelve hours ago. If a nap made the breakup feel less traumatic, then I couldn't wait to get back to sleep tonight. Maybe this morning's meeting would feel like a distant dream by then, turning into a faded memory by next weekend. Maybe this blow from losing an agent would wane into nonexistence and my creative endeavors would return full blast. Better than ever, brighter than before.

Maybe.

I turned my head the slightest degree. My heart lurched up into my throat at the sight of that creepy clown. I shuddered down to my undies. What in the world and *why*? He made eye contact this time, his pale white makeup aglow beneath a blazing red neon sign, highlighting the giant teardrops under his eyes. He didn't smile or wave, and gosh, I'd never wanted to punch a clown in the face so badly.

As I swerved my head to follow Rohan, I tried to concentrate on my pitch. My pulse raged and my entire body ignited. A wave of shaking rocked through me.

No. *Just wait a minute*, I told myself. *Calm down. This isn't the time to panic.*

So what if I was about to throw my last shot at someone as significant and intimidating as Matthew McConaughey? No biggie. At least we knew each other.

I was woman. *Hear me roar.* Et cetera. Et cetera. I was going to turn the tides of fate myself. Kismet better watch out because I was taking the reins.

We quickly arrived at the double doors of our destination. The A/C blasted air at my face and arms as soon as someone walked out, holding the door open just long enough for me to hop on through. The sudden shot of cold air dried out my eyes and had me blinking rapidly.

The air smelled of liquor and fried food mingling with cheap perfumes. Billiard balls cracked to the right and conversations, laughter, and commotion battled over the already loud music playing through the speakers. No one was singing karaoke yet and it appeared as though a band was taking a break, or getting ready to go on, from the small stage way off in the left corner stacked with a drum set and a guitar leaning against a stool.

I was already squinting. The night worsened my eyesight considerably, and because the muted lights were turned so low they might as well be off, it was even harder to see in here than on the streets.

"Are you sure he'd be in a place like this?" I asked Rohan, casting a glance across the busy bar and grill with its younger crowd. Seemed to me that he'd prefer a less crowded place with a classier ambiance.

"He'll be here," Rohan assured me.

My shoulders slumped a tad bit as Rohan and I swept our gazes across the room. I hunted for an empty booth to hunker down in while he searched for this mystery friend.

Beyond all the people and tables and chairs and booths, one couldn't help but be caught by two simultaneous eye-catchers.

The brilliant bar with its sparkling mirror wall like a sheet of diamonds.

And Thirst-Trap bartender.

Chapter 7

Thirst-Trap made the temperature jump a few colossal degrees. It wasn't how he wore the absolute hell out of a V-neck shirt, accentuating some mighty fine pecs and biceps. Who in the world said it was okay for him to look so seductive towel drying the inside of a mug? It wasn't the way his dark, textured hair was pulled back into a man-bun. I'd honestly never been into that sort of hairstyle, but on him? Lord, he had me wanting to bite my lip.

Believe it or not, the degree of hotness had little to do with those things and everything to do with the way his intense gaze swept across the room and locked dead onto mine. Not on the trio of beauties who were now swimming in a swarm of thirsty guys closing in on them, or even a number of other attractive women. But on little, plain ole me.

Who was I kidding, though? Unless he remembered the face of the person who'd knuckle-slapped his crotch, he probably studied everyone who walked in just in case he had to give a police report later.

Thirst-Trap returned to his work quick enough. And without a hint of a smile, nonetheless! That was telling.

Amid all this fighting of senseless urges while attempting to corral my inner desi goddess, I followed Rohan to the side and buckled. Oops! I wasn't even in high heels! Not even a step! Damn you, uncoordinated body.

"Be careful," Rohan said to me from over his shoulder.

There were definitely a few snickers from others, mostly from Rohan. Whatever. He always laughed at me.

"Oh, you saw that? Not nice," I told him above the mellow opening notes of live country music and the chaos of conversations.

But Rohan was that younger-brother type who teased to no end. "Need help walking in those flats? Or did the floor come up out of nowhere? You're not even tipsy. Calm down."

"Hush," I jested, hitting his arm with my purse, accidentally nudging him a little harder than I'd meant to.

Rohan took a step from the push and then tugged down on his red-and-black shirt and pulled out his phone.

"Where's your friend?" I asked him as a small crowd forced us closer to the center of the room.

"Let me text him. Do you want to grab a seat at the bar, and I'll track him down and hopefully get a table so you can relax a bit?" he asked, his focus shifting between his phone and the bar in an effort to locate Seth.

I nodded. Yeah. This was going to go perfectly fine.

So then . . . why was I shaking like a rattler's tail?

On the short trek to the bar, my awkwardness spiked. All

around, people laughed and conversed and looked like they were having a fantastic time in intimate duos and in small groups, mingling and doing their thing.

How was I ever going to be the least bit smooth and convincing with my former professor if I couldn't walk across a pub without my skin flaring up?

My, those bottles of glistening liquor looked mighty tempting from behind the bar. Every other person had a drink in their hand. Maybe that was why they were so relaxed.

All right. So I'd said I wasn't going to drink. But it looked like this mess of a woman inside me required a little something to calm her nerves and chill out. Liquid courage. But just *one* drink. Any more and I'd be back at it with drunk karaoke looking every bit a fool.

Although my former professor wasn't anywhere in sight, that didn't mean he wasn't here. With that reminder, I managed to raise my chin high and straighten my spine and pull back my shoulders. I had to own it. Just in case he was watching me.

I walked past the pool tables surrounded by several college kids in their UT-stamped shirts taking out their frustrations from school and life, howling when a friend missed a shot or roaring when a friend made an incredible one.

I moved past towering guys and cutely dressed women, everyone clouded in a mist of perfumes and colognes, choking me out. I tried not to pass out, all while trying not to bump into anyone. Of course, that didn't mean they didn't bump into me.

"Excuse me," I said to the still-oblivious guys blocking off the narrow walk-through.

Instead of moving or paying any decent attention to me,

one of them stepped back, immersed in chatter, and bumped into me.

"Hey. *Excuse* you," I retorted, and was met by an annoyed roll of the eyes.

I seethed. I swear, one more push from these inconsiderate jack-donkeys and I was going to shove back.

Finally, with a bead of perspiration on my forehead, I made it to the counter and hurried to the one lone stool to the far left, close to the hallway leading to the restrooms, which was great because stress-induced urination was going to pop up—I'd say at least every half hour until I accomplished what I'd set out to do. I tugged back the wooden stool and hunkered down, my gaze cast to my shaking hands on my lap. I clenched and unclenched my fists, my fingers ice-cold as the stings of Amy's departure picked at my brain.

If my agent had left me, then why should a celebrity believe in me?

What if I lost my nerve and did something worse than ruining Matthew McConaughey's clothes with a spilled drink? Something more embarrassing than tripping in front of him and somehow injuring at least one of us? And since he was a celebrity thriving during the golden age of technology, everyone would already be videoing him and then catch my embarrassment on camera, only to go viral.

What if I vomited? Oh my lord! *Why* did I even think that? Now *that* was the only thing coming to mind. The sight, the smell, the gagging . . . it was a miracle that I wasn't hurling right now.

With a defeated groan, I buried my face in my hands, my elbows lazily propped up on the hopefully clean-enough counter. I didn't even care.

"Need a drink?" a deep, throaty voice asked. It was far easier to hear at the counter than anywhere else in the room. He didn't sound like he was straining over the music and conversations or yelling to be heard.

I looked through the slit between my fingers, realizing Thirst-Trap was watching me with that delicious smile of his. He pressed his hands against the edge of the counter arm's-length apart and leaned toward me. His forearms bulged beneath rolled-up sleeves as if that weren't the sexiest damn thing ever. Forearm porn was back. In high-def. The industrial-strength A/C wasn't cutting it, and it was out of sheer will that I wasn't dramatically fanning myself.

I lowered my hands to the counter and tapped the surface, my voice hinting at a tremor vibrating up my throat. "Have anything to make me forget what mortification feels like?"

He grinned, cast in the light of the bar that was a bit brighter than the table we'd been at last night. His glory only intensified. Good freaking lord. The dimples made a comeback. And amazing teeth, aligned and white, set in a perfect smile. How was he not an actor or a model? Why was he working at a bar making drinks? Well, by the looks of this place, he probably made a pretty good living.

He poured a shot of whiskey in a fluid movement, his hand moving up and then back down before setting the bottle onto the counter.

"Ew," I said, and cringed. "What happened to all of those delicious drinks you were conjuring up last night?"

"I think I know your tastes by now," he replied with so much confidence, I wished I could bottle it up and use it myself. On the other hand, he'd let on that he indeed remembered me. A soft warmth spread through me.

"Do you, though?" I eyed the shot glass, afraid of even touching it. Whiskey was too potent and bitter. It wasn't a sipping, enjoy-the-taste-for-as-long-as-possible type of drink.

"It's sweet," he refuted, as if reading my mind.

I raised my brows, meeting his assured gaze. "Do you remember me? Whiskey was not served last night."

"Let's see . . . do I remember you, Isha?" he teased.

My heart did a little flip in my rib cage. "How-how do you know my name?"

"I carded you last night, remember?"

I twisted my mouth. Did he remember the name of every patron he carded? "Right. So you remember my name, but obviously nothing else if you're serving whiskey."

"I remember getting backhanded in the crotch. That's pretty hard to forget."

I curled into myself. Oh lord! Heat crept up my neck like a torch. "So many apologies. Ugh. I'm awful."

He laughed. "It's fine. At least you didn't break it."

I gasped and leaned toward him, whispering, "Do they actually break?" My face roared to furnace levels the second the words left my mouth. I quickly added, "Don't answer that. I don't know why I asked that."

He clamped down on a chuckle. "Well, it's not bruised or anything, so I don't think it broke?" he said, his tone going up an octave.

I cleared my throat. We couldn't keep talking about the state of his privates. "So, aside from the well-being of your crotch, what else do you remember about me? Because this?" I jerked my chin at the shot glass. "I mean, how many women were drinking up your deliciousness last night?"

He grinned hard in a feeble attempt not to laugh.

"Oh my lord . . ." That came out sounding so raunchy! Eek!

He leaned onto his elbows, his face ever closer, and said with a chuckle, "I remember you. Don't worry." Then he added in a sultry voice, "You were the only one last night drinking up all my deliciousness."

My cheeks flared hot, so hot. "That sounded dirty."

"Yes, it did." He grinned. "Did any of those drinks disappoint?"

I shook my head.

"On the house," he offered, pushing the shot toward me.

"I shouldn't really drink tonight," I said, even as I glanced at the amber liquid, even when I had been seriously considering a drink minutes ago.

"Odd thing to say when you're sitting at the bar. What's wrong?"

I grinned, hit by every TV and movie bar scene I'd ever seen. "Is that something bartenders actually ask?"

"I do when I'm interested."

"Does it help the time go by or are you actually interested?" I squinted, and not because I was trying to get a point across or showcase suspicion, but because my contacts were drying out like a cactus in the dead of West Texas summer desert. The taut, gritty sensation stretched over my eyeballs.

"Guy problems?" He frowned.

"You could say that."

"Boyfriend troubles?" He filled a mug with beer on tap, frothing at the cap, and then pushed it down the counter to a guy. The mug slid into perfect position. Not a single drop spilled.

"No. I do *not* have boyfriend troubles." Much worse, my friend.

"So assured? Good for him."

I scoffed. "Assured because there is no boyfriend to have troubles over."

"Ah." The corner of his mouth tugged up. Was he . . . happy to hear that I was boyfriendless? "So, what guy problems have you in this mood, then?"

I blew out a breath. "A meeting gone horribly wrong, and the guy in charge isn't going to give me the time of day."

"Really? What did you do? Might not have been that bad, you know?"

"It was bad. Really bad," I replied, and left it at that, my voice fading, and wow, how did Thirst-Trap go from sort of flirting to reminder of doom? "Also, got dumped." I cringed at the spoken truth. It stung as fresh as ever.

He sucked his teeth. "His loss."

"Oh no. I don't mean a guy. No boyfriend problems, remember? It was a professional dump. Which, ironically, feels like a breakup and yet so much worse."

"I'm sorry to hear that. Still think it's their loss."

I cracked a half smile, but he was simply saying things he thought I wanted to hear.

He cocked his chin at the shot of whiskey. "Try this. Maybe it'll help you unwind. At least for a short while?"

I pressed my lips together, contemplating if I actually wanted the teensiest bit of alcohol. I was strung so tight, it felt like being strangled. I groaned and decided to toss back the shot. Why not? The sliver of drink burned all the way down my throat and coated my stomach with an oaky flavor—deep and strong, yet somehow soft.

I hissed, my eyes misting over with a sheath of tears. "Smooth!"

He laughed, his head tilted back, showing off those dimples and incredibly sexy teeth. Sexy canines. And maybe I was staring—okay, definitely staring—because he asked, "What?"

"Anyone ever tell you that you look like Mena Massoud and Henry Cavill put together?"

"Who?" He pursed his lips. Yeah right, there was no way he didn't know who they were.

"You know. Aladdin? And Superman?"

He guffawed. Yes, he totally knew!

"It's a compliment," I muttered.

"Is that so?"

"Yes! The dimples and smile and man-bun and teeth and all that. All right. What else ya got?" I asked, pushing the shot glass toward him.

"You really want something else? You seemed hesitant a minute ago and I'm not here to push drinks on people who don't really want them." He prepared a drink for someone else but kept the conversation going with me. What a talent, not skipping a beat on either end.

"You're right. I'm hesitant. I need to stay focused. Maybe I should order something to eat instead." I tapped my belly as if he could see me doing so from over the counter.

"Can I order food from the bar?" I inquired. If I had whiskey scorching my veins, then I needed food to slow down the alcohol's effects.

"Yep."

"Have anything not fried or greasy, though?"

"Not typically for a bar and grill. People like fried food with their beers."

A defeated sigh left my lips. "I wish y'all served healthy food, too. Do you know how many more people you'd get in here if you had something like a salad or hummus plate? Better yet, a cheese platter."

He nodded and cleaned another glass before filling it with red wine. "I'll make sure to pass that on to management."

"You do that. I'd be here a lot more if you had better food."

"Come just for the food, huh?" He glanced up at me as he dried his hands on a bar towel.

"Not for that whiskey, that's for sure." I cleared my throat, willing the bitterness to leave.

He laughed. "Fair enough. There's a decent sub place a few doors down that's still open. I could order you a salad from there. Or a sub. I think they have soup, too."

I smiled. "You'd do that for me? Isn't that against the rules of the establishment, bringing in outside food?"

He shrugged. "Who's going to argue with me?"

My stomach growled. "That sounds good. But I don't want you to get into trouble with your boss."

"Nah. The boss is pretty cool." Then he turned to the guy next to him and said, "Hey, do you think you can run to the sub place down the block and get two salads?"

The guy looked from Thirst-Trap to me as he replied, "Yeah, sure. I can go in five when Deanna gets here. What kind you want?"

Thirst-Trap looked to me. "I think they can customize whatever you want."

"Oh. Just a regular side salad," I replied, in a daze that these guys would do this for a stranger during work hours in a packed bar during their busiest night of the week. "With cheddar cheese, croutons, and ham. They should have ham at a sub place. And Italian dressing."

"Make that two. No meat on mine," Thirst-Trap said, and

then handed him a credit card. "Pick something up for your-self, too."

"Thanks!" he said, and gladly took the card. Before he even turned around, a woman popped up beside him and wrapped a short orange apron around her waist. The bar-tender told her a few things and off he went. She must've been Deanna.

"Nice way to treat your coworkers," I said with awe. How was this guy so kind? But no wonder the bartenders seemed so nice when their . . . what I assumed was a manager or lead bartender . . . treated them to food.

"It helps to have a workplace where people enjoy going in to work, ya know? It's better to have them happy than not. I don't mind shelling out a few bucks here and there. Plus, it helps when we need someone to fill in last minute or over-time."

I nodded, but in fact I didn't know. I'd never worked at a restaurant or done anything other than contract or freelance work where filling in last minute wasn't a thing for me. Nor was I ever in offices or workspaces, since all of my work was handled remotely. "Thanks for the salad. You didn't really have to, but I appreciate it. You can add the salad to my tab."

He shook his head once, his lips twitching. "Nah. Don't worry about it."

"What are you doing? Buying me dinner?" I joked.

He laughed. "It's literally three dollars for a side salad. But back to that tab. So you *are* drinking something else?"

I glanced down at the row of customers at the bar. Every one of them had a drink in their hands. Rohan had once told me that people could only sit at the bar if they were ordering drinks. There was no other place to sit, and Thirst-Trap was doing wonders for my stress. Maybe I could order a light drink and nurse it for a long while, biding my time until a table opened up or until my former professor walked in. I didn't want him to ask me to leave if I wasn't drinking.

I rolled my eyes. "Fine."

"What does your heart desire?"

I quirked a brow. "Sounds like something Aladdin would say."

"I promise you that I am not Aladdin."

I narrowed my eyes at him, squinting against the grittiness of dry contacts. "It's going to take some serious convincing."

"What drink can I whip up?"

"Ooh. Can you work those magical hands on a surprise? Something like an AMF."

His brows shot up. "You wanna handle that?"

"I've had them plenty of times," I said, and waved him off.

"*Okay*," he said, as if he didn't believe me. AMFs were basically liquid Jolly Ranchers, to be honest.

He walked off to take another order for someone two seats down, filling a wineglass with dark red liquid. Then he deftly made a bright blue concoction that had me thinking it would taste like unicorns and rainbows. There was something hypnotic about the way he moved, so fluid and flawless. The contraction and release of his muscles, the fine cut of his jaw, the way his brow furrowed when he concentrated but never appearing overwhelmed.

Before he returned, Rohan came to stand beside me, and just behind him was a tall guy with short black hair and light brown skin in a casual tee and jeans.

"We're all set. This is Seth. He said he should be here by ten."

"Really?" I didn't think this was one hundred percent a

real plan, despite how assured Rohan seemed. Sure, I'd packed all the required materials and prepared myself for an introduction just in case, but now it was sinking in. He really was going to be here, and we really were going to do this.

"Of course. Why do you think you're here? Did you doubt me?" Rohan asked, offended, his brows low.

"Never again."

"Damn right."

Seth smiled like the sun, brilliant and commanding. "So this is the famous cousin?"

"I wouldn't say that," I said with a laugh.

"Rohan told me the situation. I'll let you know as soon as I spot him. We just want to keep it quiet."

"That won't be possible once someone spots him."

"We try to be as private as possible." He cocked his chin at Thirst-Trap behind me and then checked his phone. "Have you met?" Seth asked Rohan, who looked at the bartender behind me.

"Sort of, last night, but not officially," Rohan replied. Then he asked me, "Guess who that is?"

I glanced over my shoulder at the man working behind the bar. I turned to Rohan and said, "Thirst-Trap."

Seth almost choked.

"What? Is that too objectifying?" I asked.

Rohan shook his head. "I can't with you."

Seth pulled out his phone. "Sorry, I have to take this call."

"Thanks again," I said as he gave a wave and walked off into the hallway, passing the restrooms.

Rohan beamed. "See?"

My shoulders relaxed as hope ballooned.

Rohan cocked his chin at Thirst-Trap when he returned

with my drink. He eyed our sort-of-flirty exchange of the eyes and smiles, or maybe that was all in my head, the flirting part, I mean.

"I thought you weren't drinking anything," Rohan said before ordering a beer for himself. "Am I supposed to wrestle that away from you? Because I will."

"I had to order it to stay at the bar. It's just one drink, nothing strong, with food on the way. Do you want something to eat?"

"I was going to order nachos. You wanna split?"

I shook my head. "The bartender ordered a salad for me from another place. Do you want some of my salad?"

He craned his neck back, insulted. "Who are you talking to?"

"Oh, right. You won't eat anything green except peppers."

"A salad? Disgusting." He made a face to showcase his well-known distaste for veggies, which was ironic because he was a vegetarian.

"Order your nachos then," I retorted.

"Relax a bit," Rohan said, looking past me toward the front doors and fixating on whoever was there. He straightened up and grinned. "You'll get your chance in five, four, three, two . . ."

Chapter 8

The patrons to my left had abandoned the bar for a table, giving Rohan a place to finally sit after standing for the past fifteen minutes. You'd think he was introducing my former professor into the pub with a cosmic countdown, but sadly, that had only been wishful thinking.

"What?" he asked with a shrug. "There was a fifty percent chance that he would walk in at that very moment."

I found myself laughing as my jitters skittered away.

He ate his nachos as happy as could be, all while throwing shade at my satisfying salad. How could he not understand that I needed something light and nonaggravating to gently fill my stomach and soak up some of this alcohol? Thirst-Trap had the salad plated up to look nice so I wasn't eating out of a cardboard box, or most likely so I wouldn't alert other customers to outside food.

I continuously glanced over my shoulder for the one and only to walk in and grace us with his magnificent presence but found myself squinting with one eye closed. Stupid contacts. The grittiness turned into tiny blades scratching my eyeballs with every blink. Every blink left my eyes drier than the last, initiating another blink right after with no relief in sight.

I found myself blinking one eye and then the other, silently cursing my decision to wear contacts in the first place.

"That's an awful way to wink at people," Thirst-Trap said to me as he refilled Rohan's second and final mug of beer for the night.

We'd been here that long? Apparently so, as I had nursed my coconut-and-candy-tasting concoction into thin air and now nursed a glass of decadent water. See? I could limit myself to just one drink. And it helped. Both ease and a seat at the bar secured.

"It's my contacts. The air conditioning is drying out my eyes," I said, fishing through my purse for relief.

Had I forgotten to bring eye drops? Oh my lord, I had! My gentle search turned into a desperate one, pushing aside the laptop and proposal folder, feeling the hardness of my wallet, the outline of my emergency tampon mini-bag (because I had yet to master menstrual cups in public), fondling keys and lip balm. But no small, familiar squeeze bottle of saline drops.

The undersides of my eyelids burned like sandpaper jutting across the whites. The dry-as-hell contacts stuck to the inside of my upper lids.

I stilled at the pinching sensation. This meant one thing, and one thing only. My right contact was folding in on itself! And just like that, a snap, and my contact doubled over, cursing my vision and instantly turning itself into a stabbing irritant trying its very hardest to pop out with a squeal for sweet freedom. Had I even brought my glasses as a backup? Surely I must've, but I couldn't remember!

"What's wrong with your face?" Rohan asked.

"My contact folded in on itself, and no!" I blinked and squinted to prevent losing the contacts because now *both* had folded in on themselves. What were the odds! And why now, lord, why?

"What?" he asked, startled.

"They're both folded. I have to get them out before they get sucked into the backs of my eyes and fuse into my brain," I said, panicking.

"That won't happen. I mean, one time I lost a contact that moved to the back of my eye, but it randomly came back out two weeks later. It's fine."

I cringed. "That's disgusting and doesn't help. Not to mention I can barely see a thing."

"Are you all right?" Thirst-Trap asked as he crossed something off the clipboard in his hand before sliding it back underneath the counter.

In my panic, between my frantically waving arms trying to get to my eyes and my brain tossing out reminders that unwashed fingers were not meant to touch eyeballs, I knocked over my glass. Cold water splashed against my neck and chest. I hopped off the barstool to my feet, profusely apologizing to Thirst-Trap as his eyes, and many of those around me, dropped to my shirt as the cold liquid seeped through my *mainly white* blouse and chilled my skin. What an icky sensation! It was just water, but it felt like a hundred uncomfortable layers.

Thirst-Trap simultaneously dropped a rag onto the counter and tossed a towel to me.

I was practically delivering some naughty bits for these

strangers as I patted down my breasts in public, and please lord, do *not* let my cousin see this from his side-eye view. Thank goodness he was too busy trying to soak up the spill with the rag instead of noticing my indecency.

Thirst-Trap clenched his jaw and snapped his fingers in front of two guys who were leaning so far over that they might as well have been lying down on the counter. "Hey, now. Don't stare," he told them.

My arms automatically went to cover my chest over the towel, but c'mon. What the hell, men? Could they not gawk? They were just breasts, people.

"Oh my gosh!" I spat.

"You can use the restroom in my office," Thirst-Trap offered.

"Thanks," I said.

He told the other bartenders, "I'll be right back."

He immediately walked around the bar counter, pulled back the waist-high door, and escorted me away. He jerked his chin toward the hall. "Follow me, it's a long hallway with several doors."

I squinted with Olympic-level rapid blinking to prevent the contacts from going any further to the backs of my eyeballs, and blindly reached out.

"Sorry," he said, and gently took my wrist, his fingers soft but on the hotter side of warm. "Is that okay?" he asked. He was closer to me than I'd expected, the sides of our hips practically touching.

I nodded, unsure if looking down would slow the contacts' migration to my brain or encourage them to fall out. I followed him closely, relishing his touch as sort of an anchor.

Thirst-Trap led me down the long corridor. I ended up gripping his wrist over my wrist. After the inevitable trip or two, I grabbed past his wrist to his forearm, as wide and muscular as it'd looked, and walked closer as he slowed his pace. I was practically hugging his arm to my wet shirt. He might've accidentally gotten some forearm porn to side-boob action.

We walked past the restrooms on the left, with a trail of people lining up all the way out the door. I could see that much. We passed the double doors of a bustling kitchen and storage to the right and headed around a corner, where the noise suddenly leveled. We were in the back of the establishment.

"You're not going to kill me back here, are you?" I joked.

"That's morbid," he said. "I would never. It's perfectly safe, but if you feel unsafe . . ."

"Oh. I was kidding. But good to know I can bail whenever I want."

He led me into an office as large as my bedroom, crowded with a desk, several chairs, bookcases, filing cabinets, and boxes of what might have been alcohol.

There was another room kitty-corner to his, perhaps the owner's or bookkeeper's.

The thrum from the music died off this far from the main area, and even more so when he closed the door just short of actually closing it. Or so I assumed since there wasn't a click. I couldn't really see that far.

"The restroom is over there. Take your time. No one should be coming back here," he told me.

"Thanks!" I whipped around to the only other door in the room and hurried into a one-toilet restroom that was much nicer than the main one in the hallway and large enough to add a standing shower.

I closed the door behind me and hung my purse on the hook behind the door, the towel over that, and deftly washed my hands, muttering, "Please stay. Oh god, please stay in place!"

As soon as my hands were dry enough, I went to town squeezing and pinching my eyeball, my fingers suddenly belonging to a giant.

I tilted my head back even further and lowered my gaze as the clear silicone discs slowly made their way up.

Ugh! Damn my slightly flattened eye curvature!

While I worked my hardest on my right contact, the left one skittered higher and higher.

My arms were getting tired and sore. How pathetic. The odd angle with my elbow in the air and the careful but pressurized pinch . . .

After seven attempts . . .

Success! Both contacts were out! They had actually suctioned to my eyes and no one was going to convince me that these things didn't do that.

With a deep breath, I examined them only to find tears. Ruined. I flicked those little torture devices into the trash.

After I washed my hands, adjusting to the blur and squinting, I grabbed the towel and patted my blouse, but the dampness had spread.

Pulling on a wet top unfortunately led to what could only be described as a midbelly, stiff-peaked bullet bra, like arrow-tipped nipples looming over my stomach.

I dropped my head back. I couldn't approach my former professor like this.

The towel wasn't getting my blouse dry enough. Looking around, my blurred gaze landed on a hand dryer on the wall.

I twisted my upper body and bent and contorted in an effort to position my chest beneath the dryer. A severe ache sprinted down my back. The dryer was too low to get my wet shirt under it without breaking my spine.

I grumbled and quickly removed my blouse, smoothed it out as much as possible, and held it under the dryer.

A clank sounded, maybe from accidentally hitting my wrist against the metal tube where the hot air came out. Or was that a knock muffled by the sound of the dryer?

Just as the dryer revved back up, Thirst-Trap slowly opened the door and peered in, which I must've forgotten to lock, because of course.

"Did you salvage your contacts?" he asked as his eyes went wide.

He immediately froze. We each blankly stared at the other for a good five seconds before I yelped, realizing like a slap to the face that I stood in front of a stranger without a top on. Just hanging out in my bra for him to get a sneak peek.

I turned from him, fumbling to keep my shirt under the dryer while clutching the towel to my chest, my bare back now exposed to him. My natural inclination pulled my shoulders forward to curl in on myself, which probably made me look like a hunchback from behind.

Ah. Screw it.

If a stranger was going to get this glorious view of my near-naked backside, he might as well get it in all its splendid Isha glory. I straightened my spine as I turned another inch from him, pushed back my shoulders, and arched so that hopefully the curve of my back tapered to my waist and had my butt looking perky and round.

He called out, "I am *so* sorry!" and closed the door behind him. My purse bounced off the back of the door. "I thought you were just changing your contacts!"

I shook my head and returned to drying my blouse, flustered now more than ever. It took at least another five minutes before my shirt was dry enough, but there was no way the bullet bra effect was going down. This fabric was horrid. Wrinkled and pointed "nipples" did *not* make me look professional in any way, and the look was definitely unworthy of Matthew McConaughey.

Thirst-Trap knocked again, this time much harder so there was no doubt he was at the door.

"Are you all right?" he asked from the other side of the door.

"Yes!" I called back, unsure if he could hear me above the dryer. "I got the contacts out in time, but they tore. And then I remembered that my blouse was wet! I can't walk around like that!"

He didn't respond. Had he heard anything I'd said?

So I yelled out, adding, "Like I'm in some wet T-shirt contest!" into the deafening silence *right* as the dryer quieted. My cheeks flushed hotter than ever. Oh my lord.

There was another knock on the door before it slowly opened a few inches. A hand came through the slit holding a folded burnt-orange shirt.

"You can wear this," he offered, his face and body hidden.

I clutched my blouse to my chest over the towel and took the shirt. "Thank you."

"You're welcome," he replied as he closed the door.

There was no point in trying to laboriously dry my clothes in a bar restroom any longer. Even if it fully dried, there was no way to smooth out the distortions. No amount of waist hugging or arm crossing would deter stares or keep my former professor from questioning my professionalism.

I put on the shirt. It was a medium, so the fit wasn't too big or too tight. The shirt was a pretty decent fit considering it was bar merchandise. The color matched UT's school colors, which was one of the reasons I'd chosen the white top to begin with. It had the burnt-orange-and-bronze shimmer. The T-shirt ended just below the crotch to hide any inconvenient camel toe. There was at least that. It was wrinkle-free and looked brand-new, good quality, and aligned with the pub's more laid-back scene.

A triple search through my purse failed to find my glasses. Had I packed them? Had they fallen out somewhere? At least I had Rohan to guide me around.

I sighed as I gripped the doorknob. Well, I had to face Thirst-Trap sooner or later, no matter the awkwardness. Eh. Let's be real. He'd probably seen many bra-covered chests.

I opened the door, stepping back into the office fully clothed. The door to the hallway was cracked open a hair. Privacy but not trapped.

As my eyesight adjusted to blurred vision, the bartender in the middle of the room came into view clear enough to notice his flushed cheeks. He scratched the back of his head and left his hand there for a moment, clinging to his neck, his back to the desk.

"Thanks for the shirt. I'll . . . return it."

He shook his head. "No need. You can keep it."

I glanced down at the logo. "How much do I owe you?"

"Don't worry about it. On the house."

"No, I can't."

"Seriously. No worries. Keep it. It's good promotion for me if you wear it around town, anyway," he insisted. The flush from his cheeks faded as he pushed off from the desk and walked toward me, stopping about a foot away. He lifted his hand and brushed a few stray hairs from my face.

"Wouldn't want to mess up your hair in all that changing," he said.

Were we . . . having a moment?

What was I supposed to say or do? Thank him? Apologize for taking up his work time? Inquire about his crotch again?

No. No. Definitely stay away from his crotch.

He took a step back and opened the door. "After you," he said, lifting his hand toward the hall.

The noise of the bar spilled over us, taking us from normalcy and quiet to hectic in a matter of steps. One long hallway and a corner made a vast difference in sound levels.

I returned to the barstool beside Rohan, who had guarded my seat, while Thirst-Trap eased behind the counter and went back to work.

Rohan's playful expression took over when he saw me. "Did you get your contacts out or did they wander into your skull?"

I shivered. "I got them out, but barely in time. They have tears, so I'm not wearing them and can't see everything."

"No worries. I got you. You changed your shirt?"

"The bartender gave it to me. My blouse is *not* suitable to wear." I held up the damp shirt before folding it into the smallest square possible to stuff into a side pocket in my purse.

I slouched. "What now? Where is your man of the hour?"

"Why? Are you ready to bail?"

"I can hardly see anything, even worse paired with my night blindness. My shirt is subpar—no offense," I told Thirst-Trap, who happened to be nearby mixing a drink. He shrugged it off.

"So what if you can't see?" Rohan asked, sipping his drink. "I'll guide you over to him. You can see better up close. You might be less freaked out if you can't see his expressions as clearly, anyway. And you're probably wearing his favorite color from his favorite college."

"Do you think he's still coming? It's been a while."

He swiped across his phone. "Seth said he almost always comes when his grandparents say he's stopping by. My sources are usually right. Seth is one of the reasons I end up *bumping* into celebrities so often."

"I hope this guy is legit. But at least things can't get worse, right?"

This had definitely been the worst two days of my life, and I seriously questioned if I could handle anything else going wrong.

What else could the universe put me through? It couldn't possibly hate me this much. And no offense, karma, but I was getting ready to sharpen my nails if you thought I needed another bad day.

Chapter 9

He's not coming, is he?" I asked about one hour, two cocktails, and three shots later.

Everything tasted like Thirst-Trap had mixed candy and desserts in a blender and I greedily siphoned it down my gullet hole.

"I don't know. He was supposed to be here," Rohan replied, deflated, and slowly sipped his way through a soda, his shoulders hunched over. Disappointment crested his features. I wasn't sure if it was because of Seth letting him down or because he thought he was letting me down.

I went to touch his shoulder but ended up touching his eyeball. He flinched. "Bro, why are you moving slow-motion?"

He pulled my hand down. "Okay, you're past your limit, *bro*."

I slowly blinked and watched him. He could sit around forever and wouldn't mind one bit, like his superpower was being laid-back. But right now, he fidgeted with his phone and then looked around for Seth. I'd hardly ever seen Rohan on edge.

"It's okay," I mumbled, smacking my lips and opening my eyes wide. There wasn't enough light. Why were these places always so dark?

We'd moved to a small booth in the corner where we were tucked away but able to stare down the front door. I started sliding, slumping further and further into the seat, beneath the shadows of the low lights overhead until I was halfway under the table. I pushed a fork around soggy salad remains, mainly strings of cucumber, and struggled to sit up straight. My body, just like, *weighed* three hundred more pounds. I wondered if this was what it felt like to walk on Mars . . . or whichever planet had denser gravity. Or did they not have gravity? Did different planets have different gravities? Gravitas? Yeah, *gravitas* sounded like the right word. I was so smart.

I went to tell Rohan my take on gravitas and gravitons but instead eyed his nachos, the few lonely chips left doused in congealed cheese and jalapeños. I couldn't remember why I wasn't supposed to eat, but my stomach gurgled. I snatched a chip when he wasn't looking, thinking I could be stealthy, but smashed the cheese end against the corner of my mouth. Ugh! Almost there!

He glanced at me and up went that eyebrow.

The plastic leather seat squeaked every time I shifted, which was a lot, trying to get comfy. Maybe if I just laid down? I scratched my hair, feeling ants crawling down the back of my neck. I shivered and finally leaned an elbow on the table to keep myself upright, my chin on my fist, slurping my drink out of a straw like a five-year-old drinking juice. It was time to adjust my path, get on board with my parents, or something of that sort. Time to apply to the IRS before my mom ripped me a new one.

"We can go," I suggested, and yawned.

"No. He's coming," Rohan insisted. "We're doing this tonight, and you're going to wow him, and he's going to sign on to the movie deal right here. And your parents are going to back off and see your glory instead of forcing you into a corner."

I tilted my head to the side and admired his naivety, or was it optimism? Ah, it was so cute how hard he believed. Even if this wasn't how things worked.

"This drink lost its flavor."

"That's because it's water," Rohan said, and eyed my glass. "On second thought, maybe we should call it a night."

Thirst-Trap appeared from the foggy blob of moving bodies to my left and asked, "You guys want anything else?"

"Nah," Rohan said, then looked to me.

I shrugged. I shouldn't have more, not unless I wanted a repeat of last night, but the fight was quickly fading as was the will to stay sober—pfft!

"Sober?" I cackled.

"Who the hell are you talking to?" Rohan asked.

"Oh! No one. Um, no more. Thanks."

"Let me go find Seth and ask him if he's heard anything before we leave. Be right back," Rohan announced, and slid out of the booth.

I watched his back as he disappeared into the blurred throngs to find Seth. More and more people were coming in, letting all the air out. More and more were getting tipsy, loud. And I was halfway to being drunk myself.

Hmm. Were any of these people drinking away, partying off their issues, too? Ya betcha. I couldn't be the only one drowning in my head. Or . . . I guess technically no one else was in my head, either. Or were they?

Thirst-Trap slid into the chair across from me, clasping his fingers together on the table and leaning forward. Did he just freeze?

I poked his knuckle. "Keeping his spot warm? He hates sitting in warm chairs knowing someone else's butt was just in it."

He cracked a smile, the light gleaming on those sharp teeth that were suddenly a lot sharper and longer than I'd remembered, which now had me putting two and two together. He worked nights and had sharp teeth and was deadly attractive. Ah! It was so obvious! Thirst-Trap was a vampire.

Hmm . . . I wondered what it would be like to get bit.

He cleared his throat. "Do you want anything else to drink? By drink, I mean soda, water, coffee. I make a mean raspberry Italian soda."

My lips slowly curled into a smile. "You're too good at your job. No wonder this place is packed and everyone has a drink in their hand," I said, my tongue turning heavy and on the verge of slurring, my eyesight getting a wee bit drowsy.

"Guess people love drinking my deliciousness," he teased.

I cringed, but then smiled and muttered, "Yeah, they do."

He chuckled. "Yeah, you've definitely had enough."

"Better call it a night."

"Okay," he said softly. "What are you doing after this?"

I squinted at him to get a better look at the shadows falling over him, the cut of his jaw, and the, uh, double heads? I blinked a few times. "Crash, probably."

"Good. You'll be going straight home. I hope things get resolved and you feel better."

"Thanks. Me, too."

I was a minute away from undoing my bun and running my fingers through my hair. Might as well not care if my hair looked frowzy and my shirt had droplets of dressing splattered across it like a two-year-old's painting. My gaze faltered to my hands in my lap. Why the heck was I groping a tampon? I shoved it into my purse beside me.

"I came here to do something tonight and it's not working," I confessed, the disappointment unsubtly huge in my voice.

"Like what?" he asked.

"Never mind how wild this sounds, but there was supposed to be a celebrity here tonight," I loud-whispered.

His brows furrowed.

"The pub's owner's brother's . . . grandpa's wifey or something . . . said he was coming," I explained, my words starting to tumble on my tongue.

He nodded like, yeah, okay, sure. "What were you going to do with this celebrity?"

"Show him something," I whispered even louder.

His right eyebrow shot up. "Ya don't say?"

I grunted out a breath. "Not like that, you perv. It's business."

"Isn't it always?" He smirked.

"Doesn't matter. He never came."

He watched me for a while before I asked, "What?"

He leaned over and tucked some loose hair behind my ear, letting his thumb linger for a second on my jaw. "Things will always get better."

"You don't even know what's wrong."

"Maybe one day you'll tell me."

"Pfft. Like on a date? I don't even know your name."

"It's Tarik," he said, or so I thought he said. His response sort of trailed off when Rohan approached and Thirst-Trap (let's be real, it was just better to call him that and not get attached) slid the chair back, scraping the legs against the floor, and relinquished the seat.

"He's probably not coming," Rohan said.

"Oh. Spoiler alert." I sorta expected it by now, but why was I so overwhelmingly sad?

My chest ached. Hearing the official news swiped the last pillar of hope from underneath my legs, creating a crackling, sinking sensation. I was falling, and there was nothing to hold on to.

Three blows in one day. *Ouch.*

"You okay?" Thirst-Trap asked, his arm around my shoulder and pulling me toward him as I was falling against the seat.

"Oh my god . . ." I muttered against him before he released me.

I tossed back the last gulps of this stronger-than-ever water drink and stood. I wavered a teensy bit, but Thirst-Trap caught me by the waist.

Aw. Eff it. I wasn't even drunk yet, but I was heady and slowly let slip the last bars of control. I *wanted* another drink. I *wanted* to not feel anything anymore, to lessen the burden of my failures.

"See? Your drinks are way too strong for me. Guess you didn't call it as well as you thought you had," I joked around the disappointment burning a hole through my chest, or was that the alcohol raging through my system? "And oh my lord, you smell so good. What is that? Bourbon?" I sniffed his neck, inhaling mild guy cologne mixed with all the scents of liquor and limes and cherries and olives. He was so warm and soft. Would it have been weird to lick his neck? Yeah. He probably wouldn't like that. But like, dude was a deadly attractive vampire, so he was probably used to getting licked.

"Okay, Drunky McDrunkerson," Rohan said, putting down his credit card and calling the waitress over with a raise of his hand.

But Thirst-Trap held me closer to his side when he asked, "Are you okay to walk?"

I waved him off. "I usually trip, but sure." What the hell? Maybe I could just act drunker? People seemed to be happier that way, saying what they wanted, doing what they wanted, acting how they wanted. But as I stood there, a whoosh hit me, leaving me heady and really, really warm. Like wanna-take-my-clothes-off warm.

He looked to Rohan. "She's not driving, is she?"

He scoffed. "Yeah, right. She never drives downtown. She only came because I drove. And I'm good to drive. Don't worry, I always watch over her. And she doesn't usually get this wasted. It's just . . . a bad time for her."

"Aw." I gently smacked his cheek. "Shuch a gewd boi." I glanced at Thirst-Trap and added, "Did I tell you he's my little cousin? Baby of the family all grown up."

The waitress hurried over to hand Rohan the bill and then muttered something to Thirst-Trap.

"I'll be right back." He excused himself, but as soon as the waitress returned with a receipt, I was tugging Rohan out the door. There was no reason to stay, to get sucked back into Thirst-Trap's deliciousness.

"Oh! My purse!" I yelped, rushing back to the table before some thief made off with it.

Ah! It was still tucked into the corner of the booth, camouflaged against the dark blue colors. I grabbed it just as someone bumped into me for the *twentieth* time tonight! Argh!

"Hey, watch it!" I snapped, and dramatically rolled my eyes *and* my neck. Lord! Would these guys be pushing me all over the place if I looked anything like a model? No, they would not!

The guy shot me a surly look, so I squinted really hard at him. Couldn't even put his masculine pride aside and look apologetic.

A-*hole*, I mouthed.

"Dude!" Rohan said, pulling me away by the elbow. "Calm down. No need to be yelling at people."

Was I yelling?

I checked my purse as I stumbled toward the front, my head thrumming against the music and moving to the side and around the insurmountable size of the crowd beside the pool tables. God, like a writhing mass of six . . . ten . . . something large amount of people deciding to fuse together and walk around the pool table and bend over as one entity. They blinked at me with a dozen eyes.

I fished through my purse and accounted for all my belongings, including that most important emergency tampon, and craned my neck to check out why the billiards were so popular.

I'd pulled the script proposal out to fumble around for my phone, seeing that the outline of my wallet and keys could still be felt through the fabric of the inner compartments like giant, flat booties in skinny jeans, when someone shoved into me. Hard.

The script, and the attached flash drive pouch, flew out of my hands and somewhere into the pit of this absurd, looming darkness, in this *madness*.

That. Was. *It.*

"Watch where the hell you're going!" I snapped.

I actually snapped. And not only that, but the giant buffoon of a dude didn't even bother turning to apologize or make sure I was okay.

Ugh! I hated this place and all the stupid faces in it. "Yours is the stupidest!" I declared.

Now, where in the world was my freaking proposal?

I looked all over the floor, searching the shadows with squinted eyes, short of actually squatting and running my hands over the disgusting ground. Squinting plus the dim lighting plus the number of people equated to me nearly losing my mind in a tipsy freaking rage.

With nausea rolling up my throat, I bent over to get a better view of the floor under tables and seats. A purple folder was sure to stick out! Oh, *wait*. How was a not-glow-in-the-dark purple folder going to stand out in the shadows?

"What happened? Are you okay? Why the hell are you on the floor?" Rohan asked, suddenly at my side, startling me.

Was I? *Ew.* I jumped up and immediately clutched the back of the bench-style seating in front of me and heaved. Everything went in and out of clarity, people slowing down and speeding up.

"Oh my lord! I almost hit you!" I slurred.

"Sure. If you can even see me . . ."

"Har har. I dropped my folder. Help me find it."

He looked around and walked this way and that, farther and farther, to search until he melted into the room and became one with the darkness. Sadness rushed through me. Aw. *Bye, Rohan.*

"Wah!" I wailed, practically on my knees again. "Where are you?"

My back spasmed, forcing me to come back up, rising out of the stench of shoes, when the sudden movement sent my head into dizzy mode. Ooh. I wobbled forward and landed my forearms on the back of the bench-style seating dividing the room.

I huffed and puffed as the woman directly in my line of vision sitting across the table gave me a WTH look so serious, she could've won a gold medal in the meanie games. My eyes dropped to her man-escort directly below me, his dark hair practically crawling out of his head like tangled worms. Ew. Dude, take a shower.

Beside him was a stack of books and folders. Maybe he was a college kid. Or . . . actually I dunno what else. Why else did he have a stack of paperwork at a bar? Was he at meetings late into Saturday night? Who did that?

I thrust myself against the back of the bench for support, except the force of my impact sent something from the top of his stack flying over the edge and onto the floor between their table and the one to the right.

"Sorry," I groaned, or hissed, or yelled. Honestly, I was just happy that my arms had caught me, like little helpers, against the back of the bench seating instead of my face. So sue me for clinging for another minute to push away the headiness that had me tipping over.

Both the woman and the man-escort reached down to pick up the folders and papers and had a moment of giggling. Aw. So *shweet*. At least *someone* was having a cute time. Minus the scowl-of-nightmares she kept shooting at me like I was trying to take her man.

I rolled my eyes. Dude. No one wanted her wormy-haired guy.

What looked like a purple folder, I mean, who could tell, flashed like a light bulb, for some reason, as the guy took the stack of folders and shoved them into his messenger bag.

I reached for the stack, tipping over the back of the bench with my butt practically in the air. Ah, see! This was why I didn't wear skirts in public.

"Hey!" he said, twisting around and hugging his stuff to his chest.

"Dat's mine," I said, swiping the air but not quite close enough. My fingertips scraped against the paper. Oh, cruel world.

"What? Are you drunk? This is mine."

"Naw. Dude. I had a few drinks, but I'm cool. That one on top is mine. Read it," I insisted, pulling myself closer to him but still so distant. Ugh, why was this bench in the way and pushing me out inch by inch? I reached and reached, but still so far. I swear, if this bench was conspiring with the man-escort, I was going to beat the stuffing out of it.

"Don't fight me," I mumbled, "I'll cut a bench up."

"Did you just call me a bitch and threaten to *cut* me?" the guy croaked.

"What's your problem?" the woman said, now grabbing the rest of the stack and keeping all things away from me, even as I made grabby hands.

"This isn't yours," the guy repeated, slipping away from me.

"Yeah? Then show me. My name's on it," I insisted.

"I don't have to show you anything."

"Thief!" I gurgled as I toppled forward.

Whoopsie! I felt myself go top-heavy and definitely fell forward onto the seat, my face hitting where he'd been sitting. It was still warm from his butt. Eck. Butt-face.

I struggled to push myself up and back when someone backed into me. An entire crowd of people standing around, talking, laughing, semi-dancing to music, had cornered me into this very uncomfortable and highly compromised position. Pants over skirts for the win, tonight and every night!

I shoved off the bench as the woman and man-escort took their things, and *my* freaking-frick proposal, and shuffled out the door, throwing me crazy-eye stares like *I* was the messed-up one. Bro, they're the ones who just stole my property!

"Hey! Stop!" I shouted.

Struggling to just stand upright had me pushing my butt against someone who stood way too close. I couldn't breathe, couldn't move as the crowd locked me into place, as the darkness grew and breathed and fused people together.

"Excuse you!" I said.

"No worries," someone said.

"*All* the worries!" I grunted.

Another shove, another bump, another unsavory touch. All against me.

Agh!

I spun around, the anger of a thousand fiery suns reincarnated in my soul about to detonate. I shoved the guy back. *Hard.* My arms actually ached and my wrists went *pew, pew, pew!* I wasn't sure if I'd developed arthritis or just cracked my joints. But oh my lord. I'd actually assaulted him. Sure, he was well over six feet and burly, but he was holding a drink and my shove of rage, amped up by aggravated strength, pushed him forward.

He stumbled. His beer rose out of his mug like a frothy, smelly geyser. It happened in slow motion. Of course. Because karma wanted me to pay attention tonight. I wasn't sure why, but I was about to find out.

His eyes went wide, comically wide, and his mouth gaped open. The woman in front of him yelped and jumped. She failed the slow-motion test. She was just normal. But she should've been faster. His beer splashed all over her, splattering her face, neck, shirt, and arms.

Everyone in the immediate area froze. Some paused in surprise. Others moved out of the way and flicked beads of beer off themselves, because who wanted to be doused in that stinky stuff? Others, I assumed her friends, glared at me with demon wrath glowing in their beady eyes. Others snickered or laughed or cringed. Just enough faces came in and out of the singular shadow entity of merged bodies for me to know that I'd just made a scene.

"Oh my god! This is an expensive outfit!" she cried, throwing back her dirty-blond hair. Then she demanded, "What's your problem? You're going to pay for this!"

"I'm so—" I began to apologize and then wondered why I was always apologizing. Why did women always apologize, especially women of color? "Dude. He's the one who spilled it on you."

"You pushed me," he growled. Actually growled. WTF?

"Bro. Calm down. Li'l me got that kinda strength? And you were pushing me into the wall over here. *Y'all* owe *me* an apology!" I bellowed, poking a finger into my chest.

"I can't lose you for one minute, can I?" Rohan asked, pushing through the circle of onlookers being all lookie-loos.

"Oh, I think there's going to be a fight," the woman said, all sassy head-bobbing and glowering.

I guffawed. "All one hundred pounds of you? In those heels?" I clucked my tongue. Although impressive if she could fight in heels.

"Yes."

"Oh! Wait! Wait! Wait!" I grabbed the beer from the big dude's hands as he watched, stunned by the drink kidnapping.

"Yo, what are you doing?" he demanded.

"Don't worry. You'll get your cheap beer back." I laughed. "Hold on. Okay. Okay. Say that again," I instructed the woman, holding the beer in one hand and my bag in the other.

"We're going to fight?" she asked, moving her neck back and forth, but also looking a little confused.

"Oh, please. My mother's Indian. She does that side-to-side neck thing in her sleep. Stop appropriating my culture," I spat, doing the side-to-side neck thing better than she ever could.

"What?"

"Yes. You probably do yoga and drink chai tea lattes and golden drinks from Starbucks. You don't know what the hell you're doing! Okay. Okay. Stop messing me up, for real."

"We're definitely taking this outside," she declared.

With a straight face, I shoved the beer back into the guy's hands and said, "Hold my beer." And then I laughed. Like freaking hard. I couldn't help it, I was cry-laughing . . . cralaffliling. When was I ever going to use that line? I was practically slapping my knee in amusement. And yeah, it got some chuckles out of a few people watching.

"You owe me a beer," the guy said, now hovering over me.

"Shut. Up," I slurred, swinging my arm around to give him what for, thinking he could just intimidate women and boss me around when he never apologized for bumping into me!

With a fierce swing of my arm to get my hands into his face, my purse went flying with it. Oh yeah. Forgot I was holding a purse. Anyway, it was enough momentum and weight from my laptop to almost hit him smack in his douchey face. Except he put his arms up. Guy that big and couldn't even take a hit? Pfft!

He stepped back from my swing . . . and toppled over a chair.

He fell with a thunderous crash, making my heart skip a beat because *ouch*, knocking a table clear over. Food and drinks went flying. The guys who'd been sitting there jumped to their feet and pushed him up, cursing him out. But he came out of that mess belligerent and swinging at them.

Oops. I stepped back as Rohan snatched my arm and dragged me out of the crowd.

An actual bar fight broke out. I'd never thought I'd ever see one in my life, much less be the one who started it. Where was my phone, though? I needed to livestream this!

The woman tried to pull the guys apart, but her guy friend/ man was more pissed than ever. Rohan and I were already at the door when she yelled after me to get my bleeping-bleep back there.

"Yeah, right," I cackled.

"Come on!" Rohan said, pushing me through the doors first.

As we hurried past the line of people waiting to get in, I mean good for this place for having an actual line, I swore the man-escort with the messenger bag was getting into a car across the street.

"Hey! My folder!" I shouted at him.

Rohan tugged me down the sidewalk. "Our lives first! I've never been in a fight and we're not starting tonight!"

I knitted my brows together and conceded.

True. True. Rohan had my back and probably would fight to save me, but *not* tonight! I had to protect the baby of the family.

Chapter 10

Spoiler alert: running down a dark street while near drunk and barely able to see almost *always* led to accidents. Why yes, I surely did trip off the curb and nearly twisted my ankle. Who built such high curbs, anyway? And also, why? What were curbs even for?

I fell for what felt like at least three stories, a sharp sting zipping up my ankle, but caught myself before my knees skidded on the dirty street. A chorus of faded laughter and snickers lit up my ears as the darkness splintered with streetlights and people who looked like people.

Rohan took my elbow to help me get back to my feet, even as I stumbled, nearly running into the slanted part of the street where water ran off into the catch basin in front of gutters. Wasn't that where creepy clowns lurked? I did *not* need to get my ankles snatched by one.

So I hurried up and squinted really hard to make tails or

ends of lines and shadows. Something tickled the back of my neck and I jumped, slapping a hand on the spot.

"Calm down," Rohan said.

"Wasn't that a giant spider? Or ghost fingers?"

"It's . . . your hair. Your hair's falling out of your bun."

"Oh. That makes more sense," I said, retying my bun into a ponytail.

Just when I thought it was okay to blink, I walked thigh first into an empty bike rack while trying to get around people. I hissed as a hard slap of pain sizzled up my leg.

One: what genius thought it was clever to make camouflage bike racks? Hello? Ever heard of red paint? I knew we were at odds with bicyclists, but I didn't think bicyclists had gone Rambo.

Two: why the frick did pedestrians insist on walking side-by-side and taking up the entire breadth of the sidewalk? Didn't they understand how two-way sidewalks worked? Also, it was okay to walk in front of or behind their friends. The world wouldn't explode. No one would get left behind. Although, by the looks of the darkness swelling in and out of the alleys, one might beg to differ.

I glared at a group of three trying to walk side-by-side, but I wasn't going to be bullied. Enough was enough.

"Stop taking up the entire sidewalk!" I shouted.

They startled and split apart, casting some nasty looks at me. I shot an agitated look right back.

"Well?" I asked, throwing my hand out. "Where am I *supposed* to walk? In the middle of the street? I'm not a streetwalker."

"Let's go," Rohan muttered.

We hurried, even though we should've been in the clear and able to mosey our way to the car and call it a weird night. But nah. Fate had other plans.

Glancing over my shoulder, I caught two angry people shoving out of the pub's doors. That woman with beer staining her expensive but barely okay-looking outfit must've been pretty pissed because she and the big guy followed us! Eek! What creeps! The beer could be washed out of his definitely not fancy clothes. Anyway, he hadn't lost *that* much money on spilled beer. It was just beer! Not liquid platinum gold!

So fine, I might've been able to take on the woman, unless she was a martial artist or had fight training or was like . . . any sort of athlete, really . . . but that guy? No way. He'd pummel us.

My feet picked up their unstable pace. Running. I hadn't run since high school softball practice, and I was pretty bad back then, at the peak of my physical endurance. For the sake of Rohan's dear, young life, I tried my hardest to run fast and somewhat coordinated.

I thought I was doing well until Rohan yelled, "Hurry up!"

Right! But I was really trying, little bro. My legs were just so darn heavy. Had someone actually stuck bricks into my pockets? Did leggings even have pockets?

We rounded the corner at the end of the block and slowed down as darkness swallowed us whole. It breathed all around us and shimmied like heat off Texas-summer rocks. Hmm. How did we go from crowded and lit Sixth Street to deserted horror-movie back alley?

I giggled. Were we about to get murdered?

"None of this is funny," Rohan chided.

I pouted. "Aw. Look at you, being so *matt-toor* out of the two of us."

"Come *on*. We need to get to the car. I can't remember where it is or where we are."

"We should get out of this alley before someone comes at us with an axe," I conceded.

The air suddenly felt thinner; it smelled of gross city streets filled with trash and puddles of pee, something a little rancid, but mainly cigarette smoke. Barf. I waved at the air around my face, my gaze darting between buildings where shadows grew and fell apart. There were a couple of dumpsters up ahead and then more alley before we'd hit another street.

This was *not* where we'd parked. The alley wasn't even wide enough for traffic.

I hurried my butt, nerves scrambling up my backside for a whole other reason. Bad things happened in near pitch-dark alleys and side streets at night, especially downtown. There might've been a flash of white and red from the corner of my eye beneath what I assumed was a fire escape ladder, or a monster . . . I dunno, it was hard to tell the difference.

"Hurry," Rohan said, glancing at me from a few feet ahead when his eyes darted to my left, his mouth dropping as he reached out for me.

On instinct, my heart revved up like a hammer in my chest and I spun around. I wasn't sure why. Like, did I really want to see what was happening or coming at me? Maybe if I didn't see it, it wasn't real.

That white-and-red flash I thought I'd seen seconds ago? It. Was. Real. A shudder rocked my body in a surreal WTF moment.

A frenzied clown popped up out of the shadows like a nightmare being born: his red hair wild, the white of his face paint blinding, the downturned red mouth distorted, and those giant teardrops popping off his face in 3D. He reached out to snatch my arm.

I screamed, "Pennywise!" and swung. Hard. Like he was about to drag me into a gutter. Oh *hell* no. Not today!

All those years of repressed fears of clowns came shooting out of me like fireworks setting this darkness on fire. My mom had said I was being childish and clowns were fun. Naw, man. Clowns spawned from the bloodiest parts of hell and here was proof. Why else was he trying to snatch me?

"Get off!" I yelled, and kicked and hit him with my purse with all my bar-fight-aggravated strength one more time for good measure, because we all knew hellspawn clowns didn't go down easily. The force sent him flying against a metal pole.

Rohan was at my side in a matter of seconds, pulling me back as I stumbled, and stood between me and Pennywise.

The clown grunted, slumped on the ground, yelling obscenities and adding, "I'mma kill you for that!"

"Let's go," Rohan hissed, pushing me forward until we were running again.

The alley seemed to go on forever, extending on and on like a cartoon hallway, or were we not moving? I expected a whole horde of clowns to appear around us like this was the gateway to the underworld.

I ran dizzily and not at all in a straight line, my breathing turning erratic and all that liquor bubbling up my stomach, clawing its way out. I was going to be sick, but there was light ahead! The next main street! Oh, thank the lord! Salvation was at hand!

The glow of the streetlight crashed over Rohan as he stopped at the end of the alley and turned to wait for me, bending over at the waist to catch his breath. Just another few feet!

My left foot slammed down hard on the steep decline of a curb that I wasn't expecting, sending a shooting pain up my ankle and leg as I fell and scraped my knees, my hands rubbing against the gross AF ground. I yelped, pushing myself up only to look into the cold, eerie depths of a gutter. Were there eyes in there watching me? A whole person? A million clowns?

I wailed, "Wah! Pennywise trying to snatch me!"

"Oh my god!" Rohan grunted as he pulled me up, but I tripped against him and limped on the painful, burning ankle.

"Save yourself! Go on without me!" I cried dramatically. "No, wait!" I clutched his shirt. "Help me! I want to live! He's gonna drag me into the gutter!"

"There's no clown here, but there will be one soon," he said, looking past me to where Pennywise rose from the shadows. He came in and out of view as the figures of two more people blurred behind him. "Come on, come on!"

I pushed through the pain careening up my left ankle and ran down another street to the left and back around more alleys, but better-lit ones so hellmouth clowns couldn't get us. If it meant surviving killer clowns and an irrationally irate couple, then I had to suck it up.

We ran to the street, across another, and around the corner until we zigzagged our way back to who knew where!

My sides cramped as we pulled into a back area near a couple of dumpsters. My ankle screamed, *If you don't stop running, I'mma kill you myself!*

"Where are we?" I gasped, straining to catch my breath, and rubbed my ankle. "I can't keep running on this ankle. Are we anywhere near the car?"

"I have no idea," he replied, panting. He had his back to the wall and peered around the corner.

"Check GPS. I mean, that looks like Sixth Street over there," I said, and cocked my chin at the street ahead where people walked past the alley opening.

"You're not going to like this," Rohan muttered, and pushed me toward the dumpsters.

"What?"

"They're coming. All three of them."

"Hey! That's not fair. They can't form an alliance."

"If you can't run, then you need to hide. I'm going to keep going and then circle back for you."

"Hide where?"

He let out a breath and knocked on the dark green garbage receptacle behind us. "Up you go!" he said.

"Up where?" I asked, looking around.

"Dumpster."

I scoffed. "You're joking."

"Do I look like I'm joking?"

I squinted at him. No. Rohan was definitely not joking.

"You want garbage or the clown?"

"Aw, hell." No one chooses to get Pennywised. I stood, turning toward the dumpster, and grabbed the sticky metal edge and positioned my foot on the side handle. Ew. Ew. Ew. I could almost feel maggots crawling on my fingers and cockroaches skittering into my clothes.

Rohan didn't have much patience left and pushed both my feet up so that I went tumbling into the dumpster. Protect the purse! Protect the purse! I hugged it to my chest and carefully felt around the compartments to make sure everything was still inside.

Ew, ew, ew. I carefully, quietly, found my balance and tediously squatted, trying not to touch anything. Who needed a gym? These thighs and core muscles were beasts. *Grrr* . . .

The sound of Rohan's hurrying footsteps faded away as the darkness breathed around me. In another minute, another pair of footsteps came and went, disappearing into the distance with a woman's fading voice yelling, "Babe! I can't keep running!"

But her *Babe* apparently didn't care because he didn't yell back or stop by the sound of his thunderous rhino steps. From the sound of her shoes, she was still wearing those stupid heels from the bar. How did people run in those demonic devices? I could barely walk in them and here she was, running all up and down downtown. She probably could fight in them, too.

After another minute, they were completely gone. Unless this was some sort of clever ploy to make me think they'd left and were actually waiting between the dumpsters to catch me. So I waited. And waited. In dead silence. With the breathing darkness.

"Hello, my old friend," I muttered. The darkness wasn't so scary, really, when it was just breathing.

My thighs were getting heavy and numb, and my lungs burned from trying to hold my breath from this rancid stench. Was something sliding across my shoes? Was this smell going to camp out in my hair?

I squatted a while longer before attempting to stand. Seconds dragged on like hours.

Don't inhale. Don't inhale. Do not inhale.

But carbon-based life-forms have to breathe! And this breath was more sickening than all the disgusting smells I'd ever inhaled combined. Maybe I had stepped onto a particularly gross garbage bag that had ruptured, because I smelled

it. I was surrounded by stank, the kind that was so strong I
could taste it. My eyes watered as I looked skyward and silently asked the heavens what I had done to deserve this.

Don't gag. Don't gag. Do not gag.

Dry heaves came, small but mighty spasms that forced me
to hold a hand over my mouth just to keep the gagging under
control.

Don't vomit. Don't vomit. Do not vomit.

"Isha?" Rohan's angelic, albeit out-of-breath, voice called
from outside the dumpster. "It's all clear . . ."

I pushed myself up, my stomach gnarling and swimming in
nausea, as someone shoved open the back door to the building
and called out, "What are you doing back here?"

Rohan faced the man, turning his back to me.

I jumped, my head popping up past the edge of the dumpster to prevent this guy from dumping trash on my head. With
that sudden motion came a queasy roll to my stomach, an
undamming of visceral contents.

"Get me out! Get me out!" I cried, scrambling to crawl
over the dumpster.

"Whoa!" the guy said, dropping what looked like a blurry
black trash bag that was half my size onto the ground and
lunging toward me.

He caught me before I fell out of the dumpster in all my
revolting disgustingness. I couldn't scurry out of that hellhole
fast enough but found myself toppling the poor guy with garbage stank that could raise the dead. I was quick to tumble out
of his arms and onto my injured ankle, trying not to yelp. He
didn't try to stop me, and who could blame him?

"Oh my lord, I'm so sorry," I hissed for some reason, trying
to hold in my gags and dry heaves as tears blurred everything.

"Are you okay?" he asked, his face going from blurry to clear and matching a familiar, throaty voice.

Oh lord. Thirst-Trap. We were behind the pub, weren't we? *Don't cry. Don't cry. Do* not *cry.*

Rohan helped me onto my feet. I moved away from Thirst-Trap so he didn't get the full whiff of my putrid dumpster perfume.

"So sorry, man," Rohan explained. "These people chased us out of the bar and all over the place. She had to hide."

Thirst-Trap looked both perplexed and concerned with those knitted brows and that downturned mouth. His brown skin looked shadowy, despite the waning light over the back door.

Then his face blurred from my teary gaze and his skin turned pale as red splotched my vision. I shoved my purse into Rohan's hands.

Salad and nachos and all the night's drinks built up like a geyser ready to ignite in my stomach. I'd barely turned from them when out came everything. The projectile vomit barely missed Thirst-Trap's shoes, and I mean *barely.* As if this weren't mortifying enough! Also, how could a stomach hurl like a cannon? That had to be a résumé-worthy skill.

A deep heat raged up my chest in wildfire flames as I barfed and heaved. Vomit was literally the only thing that could've made the dumpster stank smell worse. And if dumpster stank made me vomit in the first place, and vomit made it smell worse, then reasoning concluded vomit, in itself, made me vomit more. Talk about a vicious cycle!

I spat out the rest while Rohan patted my back. Everything went in and out of focus as exhaustion suddenly tackled me to the ground. Through the corner of my eye, he covered his nose and looked away. Aw, I was too stanky even for him? The guy who could stomach anything?

Thirst-Trap ran back inside the bar. Who could blame him? I'd have run off, too, if I hadn't been so dizzy. I bent over, my hands on my knees, and wheezed. I took solace in the fact that I'd never have to see him ever again. I would never, in a million lifetimes, return to this place of bar fights and hell clowns.

I spat a few more times as Rohan stepped farther and farther away.

"No offense," he said, his voice nasal and his hand still covering his nose. "If I see that, I'm going to puke, too."

"Understandable," I groaned, leaning against the wall for support.

At least I hadn't vomited on their shoes, or mine, or my clothes, or in my hair with the random strands and tufts that had come undone from my ponytail.

"Hey," a deep voice said from behind me.

I jumped and turned to face Thirst-Trap. I froze. What . . . was he doing?

"Sorry. Didn't mean to scare you." He offered a bottle of water and a short stack of napkins.

"Oh . . . thanks," I muttered, timidly taking them from him. I imagined this was how zoo animals felt taking things from mesmerized visitors: a little apprehensive, a little grateful, a bit terrified.

I opened the bottle, turned from him, took a swig, swished, and spat it out. I repeated this a few times and then wiped my mouth with a napkin.

"Better?" he asked.

My shoulders slumped as I pivoted back toward him, dizziness hitting with the movement. But I pushed through it. He could not, for the love of karma, try to keep me from falling again. Not like this! I swear to the tampons in my purse that the next time he touched me, if ever, was going to be a *nice moment.*

"Whoa!" He reached out for me, but I stepped back and hit the wall.

"No!" I nearly screamed. "Not the moment!"

He held his hands up, baffled. "Oh . . . okay. I won't touch you."

I slid down to squat on the ground. "I am so, so, so sorry," I mumbled before burying my head in my lap, hidden by my knees and arms.

"It happens," he replied, seemingly unfazed, but then again, maybe whatever was left of my brain cells was trying to shield me from his most likely disturbed expression. "Are you going to be okay?"

"Yeah. Now that I'm out of the dumpster."

"Okay." He paused. "Let me know if y'all need anything," he said, and backtracked.

Rohan came over to me a second later and sat on his haunches beside me, my purse in his lap. "You all right?"

I shook my head but replied, "I will be."

"We're behind the pub."

"I figured that much . . ."

"Car is down two blocks. I lost those guys. I can bring the car around, okay?"

"What about him?" I cocked my chin toward Thirst-Trap, who had dragged out the hose.

"He's not going to clean it up. It's an alley."

He turned on the faucet. The spray of water filled the silence as he literally hosed down vomit.

"Oh. Guess he likes a clean alley," I mumbled, trying not to sob. I'd never been more mortified.

Rohan said, "Don't worry about it. It's, like, business, ya know? Vomit attracts people who vomit. He won't want that, a bunch of people back here puking and him having to clean up even more stuff later. Just like that bar fight will attract more fights."

I scowled. "Bar fights aren't as common as you think they are. Stop watching so many movies."

"Seth was actually just talking to me about this a couple of weeks back. This area hasn't had a fight in years."

"Until me. I'm *so* embarrassed. I would sell my soul for a do-over. I almost puked on Thirst-Trap and now he's cleaning up my nastiness. Kill me now."

"He can hear you, ya know?" Rohan glanced at Thirst-Trap, whose shoulders were convulsing. Was he laughing or was my half-blind/all-drunk eyesight wavering? Maybe he was dry-heaving.

"No, he can't."

"You're talking *way* loud, dude. Why do you think he's laughing at you?"

"Cuz I'm a drunk mess?"

"Or 'cause you called him Thirst-Trap."

I shot my hands out toward the bartender and said, "But he is, Rohan. He *is*."

"Bro. Take this breath mint." Rohan pulled out an opened package of white breath mints speckled with small, icy-blue crystals.

"Does my breath smell like puke?" I asked, popping one in.

"Yes. It's gross. Take all of these."

"Good!" I said all in his face as he waved off my breath. "You shoved me in there. I wouldn't have puked if you hadn't put me in the freaking dumpster. Do you know how bad it smells in there? It's trash bags brought up from hell because Satan's dumpster couldn't handle them."

"I saved your life. Listen, I can't fight. I don't think *you* can fight. *I saved your life.*" He handed me the entire package of mints, which I gratefully took and shoved two more into my mouth.

After a moment of silence, save for the sound of a hose washing away all trace of everything I'd consumed in the past six hours, I quietly asked, "Am I horrible person?"

"What?" Rohan stared at me.

"That guy I hit?"

"In the pub or in the street?"

"The *clown*. The douchebag in the bar deserved it. Look at him, all psycho coming after me like I'd run over his dog or something. But I attacked a clown," I loud-whispered.

"Shh!"

I flinched. If movies had taught me anything, it was that clowns loved revenge. "Fight or flight, Rohan. Maybe he was just an innocent person? Um, dressed as a clown for some reason? Maybe dressing as Pennywise completes him, and I freaked out because I stereotyped him. I am a clown racist. I shouldn't judge him, lest we be judged. He's still human."

"Okay, drunken Socrates. First of all, the clown came at you out of nowhere for no reason. Secondly, he grabbed your wrist. That wasn't okay. You gotta defend yourself, and never feel bad about that."

Another moment of silence passed as Thirst-Trap finished

up, turned off the water, and wound up the hose into big loops. He tilted his head to watch me as I asked Rohan, "Am I a disgrace, a failure? Be honest."

"What? No!" Rohan said without even taking a second to consider.

"Wha! Tell the truth. I know you don't say nothing to no one that might hurt their feelings on purpose, but tell me the truth. Look at me."

"Ugh."

"*Beta*, look at me," I said in a strange auntie voice for some reason as I kept tugging his face to look me in the eyes.

"Why are you so strong when you're drunk?" he asked, and jerked his head away.

"*Bro*. I can't get a decent four-hundred-and-one-K job. I can't sell a script even if I was on the street corner giving it away." I paused as I almost forgot where I was going. "Oh yeah. I'm a hot, nasty, stanky mess."

He sighed. "You got hit by one *super* disturbing night after one very bad day. Suck it up and try again."

I studied his face in the dim moonlight and the flickering backlight above the pub door where Thirst-Trap stood after he'd secured the hose. Rohan was sometimes so mature and optimistic and, like, *so real*.

"You so wise, little one." I patted his head.

"Oh my god," he muttered.

I jerked forward, alert, and whispered, "Pennywise. Where the clown at?"

Rohan shrugged and looked around the corner.

Oh lord. The hellmouth clown was still out there, grabbing ankles, surprise-attacking drunk girls, melting in and out of shadows, plotting revenge. No curb was safe.

Chapter 11

"Are you guys in some sort of trouble?" Thirst-Trap asked, offering Rohan a hand to pull him up.

He explained, "Thanks, man. I think we're in the clear. We were being chased by some wild couple from the pub and a clown."

"Huh." He offered me a hand before Rohan could turn to help me up.

I shook my head, not wanting him to touch any part of my gross body.

He retracted his hand as I forced myself to stand, my gaze fleeing to land anywhere except on his frown.

Rohan checked the alley and said, "Yeah, no sign of them."

I crossed my arms and said, "We should go."

"Do you want to wait here while I get the car?"

"Hell no," I said, then glanced at Thirst-Trap. "No offense. I don't want to get separated."

Both guys nodded in agreement.

"Are you sure you guys are going to be okay? Do you want me to call the cops?"

"No," I said quickly. I'd probably confess to assaulting Pennywise and be taken in because jails were full of clowns. And being locked in a cage next to one was horror-movie-esque.

"I'll walk you guys to your car. Hey, mind if I give you my number so you can call me if anything happens?" he asked Rohan.

"Thanks for looking out, man."

He gave Rohan his number but Rohan didn't give out his. Good call, in case this was a ruse because Thirst-Trap knew I'd started the fight. He then turned to me and asked for my phone. Right, because I couldn't be trusted to type in his number correctly.

I handed it to him, screen unlocked, and he input his info and handed it back to me. "Thanks," I muttered with no intention of ever contacting him.

"I'll walk you guys to your car. No one's going to bother you."

Must've been nice to have the confidence of a guy—a super tall one with muscles.

I followed Rohan closer than bees on a bluebonnet with Thirst-Trap following a few feet behind as we emptied onto crowded Sixth Street. I walked through the pain in my ankle so I didn't look any more pathetic.

"We're getting close to the car. We should've kept going another block the first time, instead of going down this way," Rohan said, nodding toward the alley to the left.

Did something move in the shadows? A flash of red and white?

"Pennywise!" I hissed, hunching over and clutching Rohan's sleeve and pointing like a wild woman.

"I don't see anyone," he said, peering into the shadowy depths of the alley.

"Are you sure? Look harder." I leaned toward the back street and squinted. But everything was just blurred stuff in the heaving dark.

We paused at the end of the alleyway, closer to the side of a building to avoid the throngs of clustered, ambiguous people, and surveyed the long, straight space. Nothing unusual. Nothing was moving or coming at us. Of course, Pennywise was crafty, so who knows! One couldn't just ease in and out of hell without learning a few tricks, ya know?

We soon spotted Rohan's car just where we'd left it—in some ordinary, unassuming streetside parking spot. But, like, dude had a black car that looked like every other black car in a sea of black cars during black night.

"He never came," I said, slumping.

"It's okay," Rohan assured me. "We'll catch him another way."

"But Matthew McConaughey was supposed to be my breakthrough. How are we supposed to find him now? He'll be back on location soon."

"Let's calm down first from almost being killed and then regroup."

I dramatically threw my head back before remembering Thirst-Trap was right behind us. He didn't need to get another whiff of me. I snapped my finger and loud-whispered, "Let's just go to where he is."

"You're still drunk," Rohan muttered.

"I need to meet him tonight!" I wailed.

"Okay. First off, lower your voice. Secondly, you're not going to impress him like this."

I stopped at the car when he opened the door for me. "My parents are going to turn me into an auntie at that place. Eff that. It's ride or die tonight, Brohan."

Rohan glanced past me and gave a thankful smile to Thirst-Trap. "We're good. Thanks for everything."

"No problem. Are you okay?" he asked me directly.

I made eye contact and carefully said, "I'm cool. He's never not taken care of me."

"Remember, either of you can call me if something happens." With that, he nodded and left, and we got into the car.

Rohan stole a few casual glances every which way as he drove off. He vigilantly checked his mirrors every few seconds as I sank into the seat. Safety at last!

"Are you okay to drive, sir?" I asked, leaning my head against the headrest and trying to get my thoughts straight.

"I'm not even tipsy," he replied, sounding both confident and sober. Lucky bastard. "Unlike you. How did you get this drunk, dude?"

"I had three, um, four drinks? Some shots when you weren't looking, hee hee. I don't remember. Thirst-Trap makes strong drinks, but like the waitress also took orders."

He snickered. "Can you stop calling him that?"

"But he is a thirst-trap. Did you see him?"

"Oh my god, stop."

"What's his name, then?" I asked, vaguely recalling that he'd told me his name but hell if I could remember.

"How should I know?" he asked with a hint of snark. "I don't walk around asking guys their names."

"Thirst-Trap it is!" I flinched at the sound of my own voice, reaching to touch my brow but poking the corner of my eye instead. I looked out the window as we passed the pub. It went by slowly in heavy traffic. I sank even lower, just in case Pennywise or that drunk couple was watching and waiting.

"It's fine," he said as if reading my thoughts. "No one can see through tinted windows."

"Oh yeah, but like Pennywise isn't just anyone and might have supervillain powers. Ugh. I'll never see Thirst-Trap again." I fondly touched the window, feeling like a movie character saying farewell to her love with a gentle touch to the glass.

"Did you just slap my window and leave big ole streaks? I just cleaned the windows."

"He must think I'm some weakling."

"You mean gross as fu—"

"Hey! Leave me alone," I whimpered.

He sighed, clearing his throat. "Sorry."

"It's okay. I think I'm gross, too. Let's go home. I hope my parents are asleep or heads will roll!"

"Can you talk a little quieter?"

"Oh? Am I lewd. No. Wait. Loud."

"Both." He laughed. "Drunk-ass."

"*Brohan!*" I whined. "I am your elder. You have no respect."

"Dude . . ."

I turned on the car interior light and fished through my purse. Laptop? Check! Wallet, keys, phone, hand sanitizer? Check! Ooh! Chapstick! My parched lips really needed some of that. I slathered on the coconut-scented wax and kept shuffling through things.

Why were there so many receipts and coins? Pens. Writing pad. Small makeup purse converted into emergency tampons-and-panty-liners bag. Small container of lotion. Cell phone charger. Earbuds, for some reason. Damp blouse, of course. Bottle of ibuprofen, much needed. And something hard wrangled up in a mess of paper napkins.

"Aha!" I announced, holding up my glasses. "I knew I wouldn't have left the house without these!"

"No wonder you couldn't find them in all that. Why do girls carry so much stuff?"

"Because we like to be prepared! Talk to me when you need to jot down notes ASAP or start getting parched lips, dry hands, and periods."

He fanned his face. "Eat more breath mints, first. Also, there's air freshener in the glove compartment. Spray yourself."

"Do I stink?" I gasped, putting on my glasses, my eyesight adjusting before I sifted through all the fast-food napkins and straws and cutlery stockpiled in the glove compartment in search of air freshener.

"Yes."

Found it! A little spray went a long way and had me smelling like lilacs and rain.

We sat quietly for a good while, anxiety rearing its ugly stupid head with a splatter of cruel words: *failure, desperate, disappointment, reject*, et cetera, et cetera, into forever.

Something had to be done. I couldn't keep feeling this way, I couldn't keep failing. I had to find a different way. A glorious way.

I blew out a raspberry when a *genius* idea struck, and I mean call me freaking Einstein. "What if . . . we just go to Matthew McConaughey's house?"

"Uh. No."

"Sure. He's probably at home." I looked at my phone and squinted. "It's only nine-point-two-forty o'clock."

"What?" He peered at my screen. "Okay. First off, that's your calculator app. It's past ten."

"Oh . . ." I stuffed the phone back into my purse.

"Second, you're drunk and reek of garbage. Third, look at the last objection."

"It's fine. He'll think it's . . . endearing. Or at least, he'll be apathetic. Apathetical? Hypothetical? Eh?"

"Sympathetic?"

"It's what I said. Like, aw, poor thing went through all this? I just have to at least listen to what drove her to such grand gestures."

Rohan shook his head. "You can't spend your big shot like this. It's a bad idea. Trust me. Once I went into a major final super sick and instead of asking to retake it later with a doctor's note, I sucked it up and did it because I was so tired of school and guess what? I failed the final, which made me fail the class, which put me behind and messed up my entire schedule of classes for the next semester, and put my parents out of tuition money, and quite possibly put me off college, which means I might've gotten my degree if I had not gone sick to that final. So yeah. Not fun. Not smart."

I regarded him for a minute, my eyes narrowed like that might help me understand his words better. Finally, I smacked my lips and said, "Naw, man. In it to win it. We can do this."

"Listen, Motiben. We can try to find him next time he's back in town." He leaned over to check his phone when the Bollywood song notification went off. He groaned. "Well, looks like he was just at the bar."

"Then turn around!"

"No! You're smashed. And anyway, Seth said he was there for a minute and since he couldn't get a hold of us, he didn't try to keep him there. So he left."

Tears rushed to my eyes, and I didn't know if it was the alcohol or the overwhelming doom of my future. "There is no next time. My parents are clear that I need to start applying for IRS auntie jobs this weekend and let go of this writing thing. They've had it with me. I cannot have an auntie job. You can drop me off. I'mma Uber."

"I'm not leaving you alone."

"If you take me home, I'm just going to Uber."

"Where? You don't even know where he is."

I clucked my tongue. "Bro, please. This is Austin. Everyone knows where Matthew McConaughey lives. It's the best-kept worst secret."

"And do what if you somehow make it into his neighborhood and past security?"

"Just talk to him," I replied matter-of-factly, not understanding why he was asking so many questions. In my head, we drive, knock, greet, explain, and ta-da!—it was very straightforward.

"Nothing about this is a good idea."

"It's brilliant!" I argued, fully convinced that our night could turn around.

"Even if he's home, he probably wouldn't just open the gates of his high-security lot to us."

"I thought you *believed*," I drawled, and gestured wildly.

"I do!"

"So then? Or are you losing faith in your dear ole Motiben and her mad creative skills?"

"Never, you virtuoso," he said, but not quite sounding convinced. "But . . . seriously, just take a beat."

Sucking in a breath and releasing, I said, my lips trembling, "Just let me do this. I need to did this."

"Your desperation is showing, plus you can't even talk right."

"I did, too, talking right! And I *am* desperate."

"Oh my god. Let's make a deal. I'll take you home, and if you can sober up, I'll take you first thing in the morning?"

I might've had a wee bit more to drink than I should've, and everything was sort of tilting to the left, but I knew Rohan. He expected me to pass out. "Okay," I said.

"Good," he replied.

Before we knew it, he was pulling into my neighborhood and parking the car across the street and down a few houses per usual. He went for his seat belt when I said, "It's okay. You don't have to walk me in. I'm cool."

"You sure?"

"Yep."

As I reached for the door handle, he said, "Just so we're clear . . . you're going to shower and chill out, right?"

"Can't wait to shower! Thanks for the ride and saving my life!"

He flinched. "Remember to be quiet when you get inside."

"Oh yeah." I placed my finger to my lips and shushed him.

He rolled his eyes and shook his head. I fumbled through my purse for my keys as I crawled out, closing the door, and made it to the front porch.

The motion-sensor lights came on.

"Shh!" I told them. God. Being all loud.

I jammed my key into the keyhole over and over, but ugh,

it wouldn't fit. I leaned down and carefully studied the hole, holding the key at the end and trying to make it fit. Was this not the right key?

I held it up to the bright light only to see white on white.

"Damn tampon. Getting more action than I have all year," I mumbled, and fished through my purse for the actual key.

When I finally unlocked the door, ever so slowly and quietly, I waved at Rohan. He left once I had a foot inside the house.

I frowned, turning toward the darkness. I blinked at the cavernous, gaping void. The foyer and the hallway just past it tilted and bent into obscurity. Dizziness hit hard and I felt myself tipping before I caught myself on the banister.

I grumbled and went to my room, sneaking in and hoping not to wake up Rogue. I stumbled toward the closet to turn on the closet light to find her passed out on her back with paws in the air and her tongue hanging out. What a life.

Gathering some clothes, I quietly walked to the bathroom, pausing every time I heard a noise, a squeak, and showered. For a long time. Triple washing my hair and body and then once more for good measure.

I inhaled vibrant scents of chocolate, coffee, and sweet sugar from the foamy bar in my hands. "How you smell so yummy, though?"

Holding the bar to my nose, I took a deep breath, transported to a bakery, and wondered if this made my skin taste as decadent as the bar smelled. So I took a lick across the rough, coffee-grained corner. Then a nibble before spitting it out. Worst chocolate bar ever.

The steamy water lulled me toward sleepiness, but I eventually got out and returned to my room with fresh clothes on and stinky clothes in my arms. I tossed them into the hamper. The closed kind so that the stench didn't overpower the room too much. Then I sprayed room deodorizer all over.

I gagged and smacked my tongue against the top of my mouth. So thirsty.

I giggled. Thirst-Trap.

No. I cringed the second I remembered what he'd seen of me. I was a walking disaster, but a parched one in desperate need of water.

I carefully went downstairs in the dark, letting my phone screen light the way, and chugged water in the kitchen. Some of it missed my mouth and trickled down my neck, but guess my neck was thirsty, too?

As the darkness sort of shivered around me, sending chills down my spine, I froze the moment the front door opened and closed.

My parents' conversation carried through the hallway as I huddled against the pantry door like a thief about to get caught.

When I heard my name, I instinctively moved toward the hall to catch the tail end of their discussion.

Papa was saying, "Isha can't talk to the family. We don't want everyone knowing our business or that we have problems."

Mummie replied in a curt tone, "That girl needs to get her act together. I am tired of this. I am tired of defending her poor choices to everyone."

Ouch. Talk about a stab straight to the gut, Mother.

"We need to be on the same page," she went on. "No more nice. Our foot is down and it's not coming up until she finds a reliable job. She is an adult and should have a career by now, not depending on us. She should be making better decisions with her life before it's too late."

"Shh," Papa said. "She might be awake."

"Let her hear. She needs to know the truth, how this is hurting all of us. All of my sisters and your brother are ready to sit down and talk to her. They can do this before the elders get involved."

As in the community elders? As in I was so far gone from a family intervention that they thought they had to bring in the big guns?

I gulped. Crap. Like a tribunal? A trial? What was I? Being committed as a felon where everyone was going to know all the ways I was coming up subpar and tell me what an utter failure I was?

My eyes glistened as an undercurrent of sadness dragged me down.

"Good plan. First the family elders, then the community elders. We can't have everyone in the same room talking to her at once. It would scare her."

Mummie retorted, "Let her be scared! She should be. She's never going to learn on her own. If she has nothing to show for herself at her age, with everything we've given her, then she needs to be scared."

Papa sighed. "I don't want to mentally harm her."

"You're too lenient on her," Mummie said as they headed upstairs, their voices fading.

"Maybe if she could show something for all these wasted years, we could help her?"

Mummie sounded like she was arguing against it when the door to their room shut off their conversation.

I let out a harsh breath, my chest burning, the darkness growing. So it was true. I *was* a failure, a disappointment, a stain.

Tears streamed down my face.

Why was I like this? What sort of adult was I?

I groaned through clenched teeth.

No!

I was *not* going to go out so easily!

I took a step forward and tripped on my feet, catching myself by the counter, and pushed away the dizziness. I sucked in a breath from the pain shooting up my ankle and arranged for an Uber. Then I quietly marched upstairs, gripping the banister because of course I tripped up the steps three times, went to my room, and put on a nice pair of slacks and a decent blouse.

Grabbing my purse with my things still in it, my glasses on, I crept out of the house and got into an Uber down the street.

"All good?" the barely adult guy in the driver's seat asked.

I nodded and stared at the back of his head. Look at him. Working and getting paid and probably taking care of bills and living on his own and moving forward with life. *Such a good boy you are.*

My phone pinged a few minutes into the ride.

Rohan: You feeling okay?

Isha: Yeah!

I hated lying to him.

Rohan: Want me to bring you ice cream?

I wiped a tear from my face.

Isha: I donut desurve u

Rohan: I know. ;) Come down. I'm outside. You want orange push-pop or pista cup?

My heart skipped a beat. Oh, crap.

Isha: Dats ok

Rohan: Dude. I'm outside. Stuff is going to melt.

Isha: Nah u eat it my stomachss bleh

Rohan: Where are you at?

Isha: Huh???

Rohan: Motiben, are you not at home?

Isha: whhaaa???

He didn't respond after that and no texting bubble thing came on. I sighed, swiped out of texts, rummaged through my phone to see what Thirst-Trap had put his number under so I could delete it—turned out he put his info under "Thirst-Trap"—only to lurch forward when the phone rang.

Rohan's name flashed across the screen.

Eh. He might as well know.

"What's up?" I slurred.

"Where are you?"

"In an Uber."

"Oh my god. Seriously? To his house?"

"Yep."

"Okay. Text me the address."

"So you can stop me?"

"So I can give you a ride back. Or are you going to make your Uber wait on you as you try to get past security?"

"Fine. But don't try to stop me, though."

"I have to make sure you're safe. So . . . hurry up. I'm already driving."

He hung up and I sent him the address.

Or so I'd thought.

Minutes later a text popped up on my locked screen asking: What's this for?

I pushed up my glasses and narrowed my eyes before swiping to unlock my phone. I read the messages clearly. Confused, I looked to the top of the chat box to realize I'd not texted Rohan, but . . .

Thirst-Trap: Who's this?

Eek! I must've tapped on message when Rohan called. It was okay to ignore him, right?

Thirst-Trap: Is this Isha by chance? Are you okay?

Oh, crap. He'd been so kind to us. And now he sounded worried. All right, fine!

Isha: yes sorry texted wrong person

Thirst-Trap: Did you get home safely?

Isha: yes thanks

Thirst-Trap: Good. Get some rest.

Whew! Glad that was over. I groaned and sent Rohan the address, double-checking this time to make sure it was really him.

Rohan: Got it! On my way.

Thirst-Trap: You're not going to this address . . . are you?

Oh no. I thought this was over. But now that he knew this was me, I couldn't ignore him and I was too drunk to come up with a witty answer that didn't actually answer.

Isha: why do you ask

Thirst-Trap: Because I overheard you and your cousin talking about getting to a certain celebrity tonight and this is his address.

Aha! I knew everyone knew where he lived.

Isha: I was just in my pjs

Thirst-Trap: That's not a no.

Damn his acuteness. And his cuteness.

Isha: nooooo

Thirst-Trap: It just seems like a bad idea to go there tonight.

Isha: why do you care

Thirst-Trap: I just don't want you to regret anything in the morning. That's all. I don't know the whole story of what's going on, and I'm not asking you to tell me anything, but I'm positive that whatever you're trying to do tonight can be achieved later. Whatever happens tonight, I hope it ends up being a good night for you.

I chewed on my lip. He didn't know anything. And I didn't have much time left.

Chapter 12

My former professor, last I'd heard, lived out in a luxury home off the lake in the celebrity neighborhoods. These homes were built with expensive granite, marble, iron, wood, Spanish tiles, and probably gold studded with unicorns speckled with the essence of rainbows. They had the best views overlooking the lake with boats and yachts and whatever else waiting for them.

During the day, because who hadn't driven through these parts to get a glimpse of celebrity lifestyle and ooh and ahh, these neighborhoods were splendid. Water sparkled across fountains. Blooms spread their painted petals extra wide. Even birds and bees turned up their noses at us lesser folk, and mosquitoes were too good to suck our peasant blood.

Despite all that glimmered during the day, night was a different story.

It was dark. Well, I guessed that wasn't a huge surprise.

"Is that the house up ahead?" the driver asked.

I craned my head to see around the passenger seat in front of me. "Sure."

The numbers matched and I had some time to kill if I had to walk around. I mean . . . how far could houses be from one another anyway?

The driver parked and out I went! Ah! Brisk air! And a curb! I carefully stepped up, my purse at my side.

"Hey!" someone called from nowhere.

I squeaked and jumped, turning around to face Rohan, with my bag ready to knock him out. "How did you get here so fast? I almost killed you."

He snickered. "I mean, I drove. Your driver was slow."

"Where's your car?"

"Over there." He pointed across the street and down a house. "Got the good sense not to park directly in front of his cameras."

"Smart," I said, taking a step forward and then noticing the night sky, where stars sparkled like diamonds in a pile of black and blue silk.

"Whoa," I breathed. "Amazing."

"Never seen stars before?" Rohan asked, absolutely unimpressed.

"Not like this. We city folk don't get this."

"You've been in the country. Also, you live in the suburbs, *city folk*."

"But suburbia has all these annoying streetlights and pollution. You don't see the stars as clear as this. Doesn't it make you feel insignificant seeing how big the galaxy is?"

"Okay," he said slowly. "So. His house is over there?"

Rohan pointed at the steely gates blocking off a partial driveway leading toward a pair of inner gates, which were a little pushed back from the street.

Walls of ivy-covered concrete and tall bushes masked the
entry and the gates, and also closed off the entire property from
Peeping Toms, or ya know, peeps like me. I liked a challenge.

"Yep."

He didn't respond and we watched each other for a minute.
I felt soft tendrils of anxiety brushing my thoughts, adding to
a growing headache. So much messiness and dread in one day
and it was all starting to crawl back out.

I hiccupped. Before I started crying, before depression
clawed all the way to the surface, before the darkness breathing around us devoured me, I turned from Rohan.

"Okay, I'm going," I said chipperly, giving him a salute.

"You sure?"

"Yeah! I got this! He might actually be inside. I'll just . . .
just leave something for him," I mumbled, and stumbled into
the driveway. The world spun on its axis, and I gripped the
purse against my chest to steady myself, for some reason. It
worked, okay?

Rohan caught up to me as I waddled toward the gates.
"What are you doing?"

"Going to knock."

"You can't just ring his bell and intrude in the middle of
the night."

"Sure I can! One day, when people make a movie outta my
life of how I got my big break, this'll be a pivotal moment!" I
swung my arms up, accidentally knocking my purse against
my head. "Ow!"

"Yeah? Well, how are you going to persuade the security
guy at the gates to let you in?"

I paused and tapped my chin with a fingernail. "Awesome
question. Guess it makes sense that a super fabulous person

would have a security guard. My profs would totally talk to drunk me in the middle of the night, though."

"Smashed former student showing up at his house is a legit reason to call the cops—"

But I wasn't hearing it, or at least tuned out the rest of his words, because I could *not* go home a failure, without anything to support my case against the parents. I was *not* worthless. I wasn't a total screwup. This had to happen, tonight, even as alcohol raged through my veins and caught up with its bestie: depression. I mean, why the heck not just go up in a blaze of glory or burn to nothing? After tonight, I wouldn't have anything left anyway. So . . . pfft! Eff that!

I bypassed the wide entrance to the grand estate wondering what rich people did at night. Had my former professor eaten at some fancy place where each item costs over a hundred bucks? Did he have gold flecks in his champagne and on his burger? Was he too good for a burger? Had the chef hand-picked imported wines and cheeses for him? Did he have a superior palate that had opened a seventh sense decoding some cosmic secret?

Did his family sleep in thousand-thread-count silk sheets made from rare silkworms raised in space? Were their mattresses made of clouds?

Probably. They were celebrities, after all.

Anywho . . .

I stopped several feet from the driveway, out of sight from the gates and probably the security office, grabbed a handful of leaves and branches, and tugged them apart. Aha! Not a solid cement or stone wall but a metal rod fence. One with those decorative puffy diamond ornaments up and down the spires. Perfect places to position my feet as I hoisted myself up and over the wall. I mean, I *had* once climbed a rock wall at the gym, so I got this.

"Motiben!" Rohan hissed, hurrying after me. "Get out of there!"

"Stay here. Be right back, bro." I jumped down the other side, landing on plush AF grass that still sent pain screaming up my ankle. I clamped down on a wail, or maybe I howled into the night, I couldn't tell at this point.

I ignored the pain and threw Rohan a peace sign in the darkness, but the shadows of the vine growth completely blocked him from view.

Also, thank goodness for purses with zippers to keep everything inside. I spun on my heels and limped across the lawn. *Oooh*, so bouncy and even. Did grass grow sprightlier for rich people? This was proof that it did.

The even ground made it an easier walk toward the circular driveway curling around a tree toward the grandiose house, like being on a movie set lit by moonlight and stars. So fancy.

"Motiben!" Rohan hissed. Having jumped the fence, he was now running toward me at the same moment a light beamed right in my face.

I flinched and shielded my eyes, but it was too late. My retinas!

"What are you doing?" a deep, husky voice demanded.

Uh-oh. That was definitely *not* my little cousin.

The light flickered from me to Rohan, who froze into place with his hands up and his head dropped down in defeat.

"Come with me *right* now," the security guard growled, ushering us toward the security office at the base of the driveway, where he called the police.

Busted.

I slumped in a chair beside Rohan at the police station . . . or was this a security station? It was tiny. And the guys weren't wearing APD uniforms. I kept my eyes forward. And stared while Rohan furiously texted in the chair beside me.

There were two guys here, one behind a desk and one working the files in the corner. There was a hallway behind them in what I imagined was a labyrinth of holding cells and interrogation rooms and maybe an office or two and a sad kitchenette where they brewed two kinds of coffee: one robust and meant for the guys on shift, and the other sickening and meant to terrorize perps.

"Can I have some coffee?" I asked. "But like the good kind."

The guy behind the desk quirked his brow and frowned. "This isn't Starbucks."

"I said *good* coffee."

He sat back in his crisp black-with-white-trim uniform. "To smother down the level of drunk?"

"How'd he know I'm drunk?" I whispered to Rohan, who shook his head, his expression stoic.

Rohan nodded at my pants and said, "Well for one, your clothes. What are you wearing?"

"What?" I glanced at my shirt. "Slacks and a blouse. Or!" I gasped. "Am I actually not wearing anything?"

"You're wearing those bright red parachute pants my mom got you from India that don't even reach your ankles."

"Ah!" I studied my pants and sure enough: harem pants. I swore they were slacks in my closet. No wonder they were so comfy and breezy.

Oh! I pushed my knees together, remembering the crotch hole.

My phone pinged with a text. Good thing security hadn't confiscated our stuff yet.

Thirst-Trap: Hey, are you okay?

Isha: huh???

Thirst-Trap: Don't say or do anything. I'm on my way.

Eh. Apparently, *he* was the one texting the wrong person this time.

I watched my cousin.

Aw. Poor, innocent Rohan. He was about to get charged for trespassing. I was truly despicable! He was going to have a record because of me!

No, no, *no*. I had to protect the baby!

"After you answer some questions about why you were trespassing, we're going to make a copy of your ID and get you into the system," the security guy explained.

Rohan couldn't be in the system! He couldn't serve time in jail! He couldn't be that far from taco trucks and celebrity-owned pizza places! He wouldn't do well with having to wake up early and being told when to sleep and what to wear. And he was vegetarian! Did American jails even care about vegetarians?

Tears welled up in my eyes as his life, intertwined with mine, flashed before my very eyes. That wasn't just a saying, as it turned out! It was a real thing that was happening right freaking now.

Holding him as a baby in total awe.

Him fussing in my lap when he got older and me not knowing how to handle his screeching.

Him getting all the ice cream during family gatherings because he was the baby and us older ones had to be *loving*.

Him getting into trouble at school because he couldn't handle the smell of meat in the cafeteria.

Throwing colored powder at each other during Holi and fighting over the best kites during kite festivals.

Him standing up for my right to wear short shorts by wearing—embarrassingly—short shorts himself.

Him being so proud when I graduated college, despite my parents being pissed at my major.

Cooking his favorite foods for breakfast, lunch, dinner, and dessert in a daylong celebration when he graduated high school.

Our bond that developed even deeper over not feeling like we belonged and deciding that we were perfectly fine together.

All the times he drove me to Taco Bell at two in the morning to get nachos and restocking our hot sauce packet stash in the kitchen drawer.

All the times he pulled me out of situations and helped me cover them up and carrying them to the grave.

All the times he believed in me when no one else did.

And now? His future flashed before my eyes.

With a criminal record in the system, his entire world would crumble. Our parents would be eternally disappointed and irate. No girl would marry him. Depression might take him. He'd get all thugged out with tats and do drugs to cope. He'd have to hit up everyone for cash for his addictions but then never finish rehab, which would cost, like, ten grand a month. And then he'd die pissed and lonely and my family and I would be broke from paying for his rehab and arguing at his funeral because his downhill descent into anarchy started in the very moment I'd dragged him into trespassing in Matthew McConaughey's yard and didn't protect him from getting into *the system.*

I heaved in and out, the guy behind the desk watching me and asking, "Are you all right?"

I wailed, "Let my baby cousin go! He's *innocent.* He didn't have anything to do with this. Just look at this baby chipmunk face. He's a baby. A *baby*!" I grabbed Rohan's face with my hand and squished his cheeks so that his lips puckered out. "*Beecharo.*"

"He doesn't know what 'beecharo' means," Rohan mumbled, and wiggled out of my hold with a grunt.

I released poor Rohan and explained to the perplexed guy behind the table, "It means 'poor thing,' but like from *deep* within my emotions, like *so* poor and innocent and removed from this mess that it breaks my heart. Charging him will shatter my *soul.*"

"Uh-huh," the man said, tapping a pen against the stack of papers in front of him as he checked his phone.

"What's your name? Steve?"

"Chris."

Eh. Close enough. "Don't you have kids?"

"Is he your kid?"

"No! How old do you think I am? But, like, don't you have kids or siblings who will run after you when you do stupid things to try to pull you back? That's all he was doing. I'm the one who should be charged."

"Don't worry. You'll be charged."

"But not him. He was just trying to stop me from doing anything stupider. Wait . . ." I paused and tilted my head. "More stupid? Yeah, 'stupider' isn't a word."

"Even when you're smashed and about to go to jail, you get grammatically correct?" Rohan asked, slouching deeper into the chair, shaking his head.

How was he so unfazed by all of this? Such a trooper. I giggled.

"What are you even laughing at?" he asked.

"Remember when you were little and would get so excited that you pooped? And we'd all applaud and call you super pooper?"

"Where the hell did that come from?"

"I was just thinking that you're so calm and collected, such a trooper. And 'trooper' rhymes with 'pooper.'"

We then turned to Steve/Chris in unison like some creepy twin thing. He seemed a little unnerved, the way he swallowed.

"Please!" I said.

He startled.

I told Rohan, "I'm *so* sorry. I'm a horrible motiben. I only thought I was horrible before, but now I truly am. Because of me you're going to be in the system, a criminal, a *thug*."

I turned back to Steve/Chris . . . Stechris. "He's too young to be a criminal. He has his entire life ahead of him. He hasn't even kissed a girl yet."

"Oh my god," Rohan muttered, texting again.

"Him trying to stop me can't ruin his future, not for something so petty on my part but so heroic on his. His parents'll never forgive me. My parents'll end me. Do you know few things in life are as bad as having Asian parents thoroughly disappointed in you? They don't let you live that crap down.

You'll be traumatized and doubting yourself in every tiny thing you do. Rolling over in your grave, haunted through the rest of your reincarnated lives. Also, he's too pretty to be in jail."

We'll be thrown into the slammer for sure. Our parents'll discover our empty rooms in a matter of a few hours. We'll have brought shame and dishonor to our entire family. Who will take care of poor Rogue? Oh my lord, Rogue! Who was going to take her potty in the morning? Rogue was such a sensitive pup. She could probably feel my feels from across the city and was weeping her little doggie eyes out. She couldn't survive the world without me.

I was another bout away from asking for coffee again, because dude absolutely had ignored my request and I needed to sober up before getting sent to the slammer, a moment from wailing over the atrocity being committed by dragging Rohan into the system, and seconds from stressing out over Rogue's future. A dog needed her mama. I was losing my crap.

I profusely apologized to Rohan, adding, "I'm such a bad elder."

"It's okay, Motiben."

"I don't even deserve to be called Motiben!" I wailed.

"Things might not be that bad," he insisted. "Maybe we won't face charges. Maybe we'll get off with a warning since it's our first misdemeanor. Maybe we can go home and get a court date to pay a fine or something, and our parents will never find out. Yeah . . . things might work out."

I swiveled my head to the right when the door swung open, hitting the archaic little copper bell. And in walked the last person I expected to see.

"Oh no . . ." I groaned, burying my face in my hands. Why was he even here?

Chapter 13

W was that . . . who I thought it was? Having glasses on and seeing him clearly made things three times worse, three times more real. Having seen him in blurred drunk vision meant my brain would hopefully dissolve the memories faster. But seeing him as clear as fluorescent day meant this memory wouldn't fizz out as easily.

Thirst-Trap. In the mighty-fine flesh.

Maybe if we kept our heads down and didn't move, he might not notice us? Maybe if he dropped that bag of what smelled like deep-fried food off at the desk, he'd walk right back out on his merry way.

"What's he doing here?" I muttered to Rohan, leaning toward him so Thirst-Trap wouldn't hear me.

"I don't know. Wait . . ." He frowned and looked at the cell phone in his lap.

"What?"

"I'd texted Seth to tell him what happened, in case he could help us out in getting McConaughey not to press charges. He said he'd work it out but couldn't come down here fast enough, so he was sending his brother. The one who . . . owns the pub . . ."

We both stared at the backside of Thirst-Trap in all his T-shirt-and-jeans glory. He chatted it up with Stechris. They had a merry ole time while the clock was ticking down to the inception of our criminal induction.

He placed a large plastic bag on the table as Stechris rose and sifted through the goodies, pulling out aluminum containers and opening corners to release fragrant aromas of fried, spicy, cheesy foods.

My mouth watered. I hadn't eaten since the taco truck bowl in the early evening and the side salad at the pub and that one nacho chip.

My stomach grumbled hard. Dizziness tackled my brain cells and everything sort of whooshed around my face. I felt like I was going to pass out.

They had a long conversation filled with laughs and a few times where Stechris glanced at us, his face super stoic and creepy.

"He's just trying to psych us out," Rohan grumbled. "Just keep looking sad and apologetic."

I didn't have to try at all. My lower lip quivered.

"Nice touch," he commended.

After what seemed like forever, and even more so when Stechris and his coworker started eating and my stomach edged toward imploding from hunger, Stechris stood. Thirst-Trap took a step away from the table but didn't look at us. He just rubbed his chin and looked at the desk.

"You know," Stechris started, "you could be charged with trespassing and have a criminal record."

I nodded, my hands trembling as if we were on trial waiting for a verdict. Would we be incarcerated for life?

"These are serious crimes."

I made a face. Really? There weren't worse things happening in Austin? Like homicide and rape and fraud and beatings?

He paced around the desk, his hands clasped behind his back as the other guy snickered and Thirst-Trap rolled his eyes.

"We're not going to charge you."

Rohan and I blew out a collective breath. Oh, thank the mother of the gods.

"But this is a first and final warning. If we see either of you back here, you'll get arrested on sight."

"But what if we're invited?" I asked dumbly.

"And who do you know that lives here, exactly?"

"Matthew McConaughey."

"Uh-huh," he said, sounding annoyed but maybe also amused, while Thirst-Trap regarded us.

Our eyes finally met.

Awkward AF.

I crossed my legs, because . . . crotch hole.

"If you actually are invited, then that's different. Were you invited today? Should I have made a call to ask?" He reached for his phone.

"No!" I jumped up and immediately flopped back down. Catching my breath and closing my eyes to ward off the headiness, I said, "We weren't invited today. Thanks so much for your time. We won't bother you again." I opened my eyes, seeing two of Stechris, and offered a wide smile that felt more like a grimace.

"Uh-huh . . ." He watched us as I froze into place, into this awkward position of sitting here with my hands curling and uncurling into fists and a fake smile plastered across my face and my knees pressed together to hide the crotch hole.

"Okay. Get out of here before I change my mind," Stechris announced, and sat back down to eat.

Right now was probably a bad time to bring up coffee again.

Before I knew it, Rohan was helping me up and ushering me out the door.

I closed my eyes, inhaled and exhaled. But enough of that. I could count my blessings later, safe at home and in bed beside Rogue. We needed to get out of here before those guys changed their minds, before Thirst-Trap came out.

The doors swung open, and Thirst-Trap jogged down the steps toward us. Part of me hoped that this was all a weird dream or maybe he wouldn't see us. I supposed thanking him was the least I could do, though. Seeing that he was the only thing that stood between us and a lifetime of thugging out.

My skin tingled and burned, but it had to be done. I popped in the last two mints, kept my hands in front of my lap in case crotch hole wanted to make an appearance, took in a big, deep breath, and rambled, "Thanks for saving us from that cop."

"Yes. Thank you so much, man," Rohan added, his face flushed.

Thirst-Trap looked perplexed for a moment with the slightest furrowing of the brows before glancing over his shoulder at the small building. "Oh, he's not a cop. They were neighborhood security."

"Oh. Hmm. Guess a lot more things make sense, then," I replied.

"And you're welcome."

I swallowed hard.

He sighed. "So you didn't take my advice and came here anyway?"

"What are you doing here?" I asked instead.

"I was concerned. You texted me by mistake, remember, telling me where you were headed, and then I got a call from Seth that you two were in trouble."

"You—you came all the way out here just to help us?"

"Yeah. I mean I was already on the way out the door with takeout for myself, and it just happens that those guys are easily swayed by food."

Tears welled in my eyes. "You sacrificed food for strangers?" Ugh. That was just so ultimate.

"Of course. It's just pub food."

"That's so sweet and decent of you. How are you this nice?"

He shrugged. "Better question is how would I have slept knowing that I ignored the call."

I wanted to tackle-hug him to the ground and quite possibly kiss him. Damn. What a man. But I kept my hands to myself and nodded, pressing my lips together so I wouldn't cry.

"I'm glad my brother told me."

I bit my lip, drawing his gaze back to me. "This is all my fault. My cousin was just trying to stop me. How did you . . . pull that off? Is food really all it takes?"

He chuckled. "Sometimes. But I know those guys."

"Well-connected, aren't you?" I asked, wondering if he knew how to play these guys because his grandparents actually knew Matthew McConaughey that well and he'd been here before. Was he bros with my former professor?

He shrugged and stuffed his hands into his pockets. "My family gets around."

"Oh. I can't thank you enough. Wow. You really didn't have to come all the way out here for a couple of strangers."

"Nah. Don't worry about it."

I closed in on myself, feeling smaller than ever but also hyperaware of everything. My skin hurt and my head throbbed. This didn't seem normal. I stumbled toward Rohan and said, "We should get home . . ."

"Can I offer you guys a ride?" Thirst-Trap suggested.

"Thanks, but we drove here," Rohan explained.

He raised a brow. "Do you want a ride to your car?"

"No. It's . . ." I started to say, but then we glanced around. Where in the world were we?

"It's pretty dark," he commented. "Did you want a ride to your car? What street are you guys parked on?"

We looked one way and then another. Even if he pointed us toward the neighborhood exit, it would be a long walk.

"Thanks, man. We'll need to take you up on that offer," Rohan said.

Too late for an excuse that I couldn't find. At least I snatched the handle to the back seat and sat directly behind Rohan, who chatted it up with Thirst-Trap.

He drove carefully, slowly, and looked back at me after he stopped behind Rohan's car. "Are you sure you're good?"

"Yep! Thanks so much! *Bye!*" I'd never shimmied out of a car so fast in my life.

We eased onto the road and Thirst-Trap drove behind us until we parted ways on the main street past the exit. We were about to face much bigger problems than possible incarceration.

"What are we going to tell our parents?"

"Nothing," Rohan muttered. "Why would we say anything?"

"If we get caught?"

"We're not going to get caught. They're all asleep."

"But if we do get caught, we need to think of a story. A good story."

"Yeah? What's something believable when your breath reeks of alcohol?"

I breathed into my hands and sniffed. Ew.

That little stroke of anxiety? Full. On. *Slasher mode.*

My brain hurt. My heart crumpled. My entire body went slack. I was done for.

Chapter 14

It's that bad?" I asked when Rohan pulled up to a house down the street from mine, my head pounding as some of the alcohol started wearing off. Just enough to sort of hate myself even more.

"Nah. Just . . . wash your face with a soapy rag, or ya know, one of those makeup wipes you have. But like, a ton of them. And also your neck and arms. Change your clothes."

I nodded and sniffled, running the back of my hand against my nose. I was covered in grass and dirt and my face was stained with the tears of shredded dreams.

"It's okay, Motiben . . ." he said, his chin downturned and casting his gaze at the dashboard like he wanted to hug me but remembering he hated hugs. "Ready?"

"Yeah." I reached for the door handle and added solemnly, "I'm really sorry about tonight."

He flashed a lighthearted smile. "It was an adventure.

Nothing terrible happened and you have material for your next project. Don't worry so much about it. We'll get that script out there."

I stifled my bawling.

"It's okay," he said softly.

"You such a good boy, I don't deserve you."

"Oh lord. Dude, calm down."

I nodded and held my keys up, thoroughly examining them.

"Whatcha, um, doing there?" Rohan asked.

"Making sure it's not a tampon."

"Okay. Makes sense."

"House key, right?" I asked, holding out the second-largest key.

"Yep."

"You don't have to walk me. I promise I won't run off with another Uber. You should get some rest."

He regarded me for a moment and then nodded. "K. G'night, bro."

"Good night."

I crawled out, grabbed my purse, and closed the door. My stomach was turning queasy as I approached the porch.

The motion-activated lights came on, and I winced from the sudden, blinding whiteness.

I quietly unlocked and opened the door. Rohan eased past as I waved at him.

I pushed the door closed, and the gentle sound of it clicking went off.

"Shh," I reprimanded, frowning at the door.

I slipped off my shoes, pushing them into the coat closet.

My shoulders slumped, my back ached. I went up the steps in the dark. One step at a time. Quietly. Slowly. Must not wake up raging parents.

Good job, no tripping for once.

Annnnddddd . . . I spoke too soon . . . *thought* too soon? Whatever. I caught myself with a grunt. My purse with a thump. I spider-crawled a few steps. Imagining this horror-movie scene in total darkness sent shivers down my spine.

My hands tingled from my weight.

"Hello?" Mummie called out, her voice raspy, sleepy, rustling through the dark like some eerie ghost haunting the midnight hour to gatekeep all drunkies trying to sneak in.

I froze, sticking close to the steps, my boobs squished, but that didn't stop her from emerging from her room, flicking on the stairwell lights, and looking down at me with a scowl.

Squinting against the light, her arms crossed as if she were freezing in her straight-outta-India gown, she said, "Beta? Are you just now getting home?"

"Isha che?" Papa's hoarse voice called out from the depths of the dark room behind her.

"Hah," she answered back.

I pushed myself up from the steps and tried to stand as cool as possible. "Went for a long drive. Sorry to wake you," I replied, hoping that keeping my answers minimal evaded any possibility of slurred words. Although, to be honest, my level of drunk had gone down a bit. Sobriety hadn't fully yet hit, but Mummie had the observational skills of a hawk.

This wasn't the first time my parents had been awoken by me getting home super late. It happened often during college finals. It happened once in a while when I had been at friends' houses or parties. Didn't matter that I was a grown woman now. Living with my more traditional parents meant they frowned on a lady being out at all hours of the night. And not because it might make me look bad, but because there were so many things that could go wrong in the dark.

Mummie stood at the top step and there was no way to pass her without giving her a whiff of my breath. Or could I hold my breath long enough to get past her? Or had I been thinking too long, when seconds were minutes, and minutes felt like seconds? But now, several seconds, minutes, whatever . . . what was time? . . . had passed and things went from *oops I woke up my parents* to tense because it definitely looked like I was hiding something.

Her narrowed eyes stayed pinned to me as I held my breath. Was she going to lose her crap . . . was she too tired . . . or had she not figured it out yet?

Finally, she said with a yawn, "Okay, beta. Get some sleep," and stepped aside.

I blew out a hot breath, my skin on fire. "I need some water," I said, hoping that I could walk back downstairs instead.

"Good thing we filled up the fridge this morning. Times like this, we're happy we don't have to walk all the way downstairs for cold water."

So stupid of me!

There happened to be a mini-fridge in the laundry room to the right, kitty-corner to her room. My parents meant for the water to be for anyone, but only they drank from it. She went into the room to get a bottle as I hurried up the last few steps.

"Beta," she said, offering the water.

I had to take it now. I leaned toward her in slow motion, my vision going in and out just a wee bit, to take the icy-cold bottle.

"Why are you acting so strange?" she asked, her words coming out slowly, her eyes more awake.

The evolution of her facial expressions said it all. The wondering as her sleepy eyes woke up some more. The furrowing of her brows as confusion weighed down on them. The twitch in her nose as she got the whiff of betrayal. The narrowing of her eyes as the smells mingled in her nostrils. And finally, the pressed line of her mouth as her nose wrinkled in first disgust, then anger.

Please, let my still damp hair and recent shower overpower the stench of alcohol.

"*Daru!*" she snapped accusingly. "You've been drinking daru?"

For someone who had never had a drop of alcohol, she sure could sniff it out faster than anything. While she was chastising me, Papa rustled in the bedroom and came out into the lit hallway. He went from worried to upset in two seconds flat. New parental record.

"*Isha?*" he growled, sending chills down my spine and back up again. "Have you been drinking?" He came closer to smell the alcohol on my breath and there wasn't a thing I could do about it.

"It's not a big deal," I found myself saying. "I'm not a kid. I drink responsibly. Nothing bad happened." Eh, sort of.

"We do *not* drink in this family." His voice rose. "You don't want to be a doctor or lawyer or engineer. Fine. You don't want to attend mandir or observe anything religious. Fine. You moved back into the house because you couldn't maintain sustainable income. Fine. But we will *not* have you drinking alcohol. Do you understand? You will *not* go down an even more self-destructive path."

I flinched but nodded. Being drunk past midnight having woken up my parents in *my* current situation was probably not the best time to argue my defense. Besides, even if I could come up with an argument aside from being an adult, my twisted, loopy brain cells weren't going to find one this second.

Papa's eyes were red from both sleep and anger. His nostrils flared and steam practically wafted up from his head. "No respectable daughter of mine should be parading around at night, partying this late, at bars drinking! What will others think! Aren't you the least bit ashamed? You at least know what *we* think. Or do you not care?"

"No, it isn't that—"

"Then *what*? No regard? No respect? Who were you with? What friends? Were you with a man?"

"No!" Oh my god. Was this really my life? Was I really being asked these questions?

"Were you with Rohan?" Mummie asked calmly.

"What?" Oh boy. Lying was not my forte. Especially when it came to lying to my parents' faces.

"We already know he was with you. We were at his parents' house this evening to drop off some bhaji."

"Oh . . ." My eyelids fluttered and my gaze dropped to the carpet.

A sickening numbness wrapped around my body.

They shook their heads as the worst possible thing dawned on them. I was a bad motiben to my cousin. I was the troublemaker, the enabler. Tears gathered in my eyes as my mom wiped tears from her cheeks. "Was he drinking?" she asked, her voice shaking. "It's already bad enough that he refuses to attend mandir or observe anything, because he's still a good boy. But this? You're supposed to be a good role model for him, protect him, guide him, not let him drink with you."

I swallowed hard. There was nothing to say, really.

Papa added, "What will his parents think of you, huh? That you're a bad influence on him, that's what. They will never look at you the same way, never trust you. Once they find out, everything will change and you can't undo that. Is that what you want?"

"No."

"Did you even think about that?"

I clenched my eyes shut.

"Did he get drunk, too?"

"What! No!" I replied, meeting his arctic gaze.

"Don't lie to us."

"I'm not. He doesn't get drunk. He was just keeping me company because I wasn't feeling good."

"Why aren't you feeling good?"

"I . . ."

He waved a hand and then crossed his arms. "What, huh? Tell us what made you feel so bad that you had to go out and do this?"

I rubbed my arm and looked away. "See . . . I didn't get a producer for my script, and then my agent left me." I hiccupped on the last words. "He knew I was depressed about that, so he took me to a place that has food and games and music. Wasn't just a bar."

"Really, Isha? You had this major that you knew would be hard to make a career out of, that's why you didn't tell us. Now you have all these poor excuses to behave wildly *and* drag your cousin with you? You may have ruined your life with these choices, but don't take your cousin down with you.

He's young. He still has time to get back on course. You have time, too, if you make changes and make better decisions."

"I'm sorry," I muttered.

Papa mumbled something incoherent and finally said, "So we are not going to tell his parents, hah? They won't know about this. I'm trying to protect your reputation and your relationship with family, that's all we have. Once you lose their respect, you ruin your reputation, and they will never look at you the same way."

I kept from sobbing, from letting my tears fall. The numbness broke right through me, as if I weren't even standing there. He was right. Family relationships were important and vital. We had to stick together. They always said that. The world tried to tear us apart, so we needed to make sure we stayed together, strong.

"We'll discuss things tomorrow," Papa said.

"Go to bed and sleep this off," Mummie added, her voice shaky but steeled. It was . . . different. She was beyond angry. She was disappointed. And I didn't mean disappointed because I made a bad grade or didn't major in science or didn't become a doctor. Disappointed like maybe this was the final straw, and there was no coming back from this. Like maybe I was broken and she'd never look at me the same way again.

A hollowness bloomed in my chest as they switched off the light and went to bed.

The darkness rose around me, crashing over me, dragging me toward a gloomy sea of despair. I knew I had to fight this, this consuming sensation, this void of nothing where everything hurt, but in this moment . . . I couldn't care less.

Just take me, darkness. Swallow me whole. Because my parents were right to be disappointed in me, to call for intervention.

I couldn't imagine how they'd respond if they knew about all the other stuff.

"Okay," I said to no one, my voice trembling, and went to my room.

I petted a still passed-out Rogue, who had no idea what sort of night this had been, grabbed some clean clothes, and called Rohan.

"Hey, what's up?" he asked in a quiet voice.

"Made it home okay?" I asked, twisting the hem of my shirt.

"Yeah," he said with a chuckle. "I live literally two minutes from you. And I'm not wasted."

"Right. Just wanted to make sure," I replied softly.

"Are you all right?"

Shudders rocked my body and my face quivered on the verge of crying. "No."

"Ah, it's okay, Motiben. We can catch Matthew McConaughey another time. If not, we'll still get that script sold. We're going to be toasting to your success in no time."

Tears streamed down my face. He truly was too good for me, and I didn't have the heart to tell him it was all over for me. With nothing to show, a set of pissed parents at their ends, and a community-wide intervention lurking around the corner, I was done for.

Instead, I told him, "You're so sweet. Well. My parents caught me."

"Uh-oh. Were they mad?"

"Yeah. They could tell. They're furious."

"It's okay. They'll get over it. They've caught you drinking before."

"The worst part is, they know you were with me."

"What? How?" he asked, not sounding as distressed as I felt.

I took a huge gulp of water. "Your parents told them you were with me earlier. I told them you didn't get drunk, so hopefully they don't think you were drinking at all. A heads-up. Don't try to lie out of that one. If they ask you if I was hammered, don't lie. I told them you stayed to watch me and make sure I didn't get into trouble, but that you'd meant for me to eat dinner and play games. Did you get caught?"

"No. No one is awake. They never are this late. And since my parents know that we went out together—"

"They trusted that you wouldn't be getting into trouble," I ended, closing my eyes.

"Yeah."

"I'm a terrible elder. I'm so sorry," I cried.

"Stop that. You're fine. You're not terrible. You had a bad night."

"I got wasted and started a fight and assaulted a clown and dragged you into trespassing!"

"Shh! Your entire house doesn't need to know."

"I'm a bad motiben."

He let out a breath and said in a stern voice, "No, you're not. Dude. You're the only one I can be myself around. I don't have to hold back or brace for you passive-aggressively telling me that I need to be more or do more. You're calm with me and encourage me, but don't push me or make me feel bad. You celebrate every tiny thing I accomplish, and I know it's real; it's out of love and joy and pride. You're actually proud of me. While our parents were yelling at me to go to college, you'd come sit with me in my room and tell me that taking my time was okay and not getting a degree didn't make me less of a person. When I didn't want to work and my parents were always pissed, you'd take me out to eat and help me figure out what I'd enjoy doing. When I stopped going to mandir and everyone there got on my case, you sat with me and listened and acknowledged my feelings and depression and told me how you felt the same. You're my bro, Motiben."

"You're so sweet." Tears fell down my cheeks. Rohan calling me his bro was the epitome of compliments, stronger than any bond. But the degree to which he admired and respected me only made me see the truth. I had to be a better role model.

I groaned. "My parents said they wouldn't tell your parents so your parents won't get mad at me or refuse to let us hang out again. What a mess."

"Hey. Sleep on it. Sleep in, sleep late, sleep as much as you need to. Things won't seem so bad tomorrow."

"How are you so much more mature than me?" I wailed.

"Shh! You're so loud. Get some rest, okay?"

"Yeah. Okay. Thanks."

"But first clean up since your parents are awake anyway. Cuz your bed doesn't need to be covered in dirt, too."

My lips twitched. "Okay. Good night."

"Night."

We hung up and I went to the bathroom.

I took another shower to get the dirt off, to wash away this mess, to pretend anxiety was draining away along with soapy water and grime. Afterward, I slathered on scented lotion and deodorant and slipped into all fresh clothes and made my way back to my room.

Everything went into the hamper to be washed tomorrow, and the hamper went into the laundry room to keep the stank out of my room.

Rogue was a grumpy pants when I took her outside to potty in the cold dead of night, but she wasn't about to wake me up in four hours to potty.

Regardless, she took forever and it was two a.m. when we finally got back inside.

My parents were still in their room, their door closed, but as I walked by, their voices permeated through the door in sharpened jabs aimed at my heart.

Disgraceful. Shameful. Pity. Wasted potential. Bad influence. Possibly creating a rift with Rohan's parents. Intervention to come. Community elders to get involved.

Crap. Having them involved meant total lockdown, total backlash, a hammer to the nail in my coffin. The community would see them differently if they involved the elders, all because of me. They were willing to get shunned and gossiped about if it meant getting me on the track they wanted me on.

Anxiety whooshed into the pit of my soul. I clenched my hands at my forehead. I wanted to scratch it all out of my brain.

Was I an utter, unredeemable failure? It seemed that everyone thought so. A failure at college, a failure at getting a full-time job, a failure at jump-starting a career, a failure at selling a script, a failure at keeping an agent, a failure at being religious enough, a failure at being the guiding elder sister.

I placed Rogue on the bed, closed my bedroom door, my back hitting the wall, and clutched my chest, heaving and panting.

Red crossed my vision. I went straight to my whiteboard and Post-its and notebooks and let effing loose.

Eventually, maybe minutes later or hours later, who the hell knew, I crashed into bed beside a quiet, watchful Rogue, my glasses on my bedside table next to my charging phone.

I rolled onto my stomach, shoved my face into the pillow, and stifled a scream. What a mess!

I wasn't a bad person. Right?

Still. If Rohan's parents found out, this would be all they'd see every time they looked at me. They wouldn't even recognize how mature Rohan was tonight. He took responsibility where he needed to. He never ditched me, never let me wander off and suffer alone.

Sure, neither of us fit the mold of the perfect child, the kind our parents felt they could brag about to any auntie and uncle within a fifty-mile radius. But the bottom line was this: my cousin was the best.

He never let me down and always had my back.

Rohan was the ultimate bro—the Brohan and true to the name.

Chapter 15

Rogue's telepathic glare was the only thing that could get me up the following morning. Well, and also the headache splintering my brain into a jigsaw, the rawness clawing all the way down to the inside of my throat. I hissed upon waking up.

I draped my arm over my eyes, pretending to not have noticed her. She scooted closer and closer to my face, extending her neck until her little twitchy nose almost touched my face. And she stayed just like that. Unmoving. In a blinking contest to the death.

"Go to sleep," I muttered, my voice hoarse. I might've been hungover, but I did recall having taken her potty before going to bed.

She chirped.

"Hold it in," I mumbled, letting the grogginess of sleep lure me back into its clutches.

She chirped louder.

"Just wait," I grumbled, and went to roll over, flinching.

Who knew running around, climbing things, and falling into dumpsters and onto lawns would leave a body feeling like it'd just spent three grueling hours hitting the gym?

By now, Rogue-alicious was *not* having it. She padded onto my stomach, somehow adding weight to herself, and I almost puked when she walked onto my chest and sat all six-point-six pounds down. I couldn't breathe.

"Fine. I'm up!" I rasped, gently sliding her onto my side again.

With a groan, I checked my now-charged phone, ignoring the text notifications. It was almost ten. I could've slept all day, but my little girl was probably about to pee, and *poop*, on my pillow.

I set Rogue down on the floor and drowsily walked her through the overwhelming quiet of the house and out to the backyard. I didn't bother putting on glasses, just in case my parents were around. If I didn't see them, they weren't there, right? That's how things worked?

Thankfully, no one was around. Of course, my parents were up and about somewhere. Their usual routine was to be showered and offering prayers by eight every morning. They must've made their breakfast offering to their idols and partaken of it themselves before going on with their day. Wherever they were, I was just happy not to have to see their disappointment or hear another lecture.

Rogue did her business fairly quickly. We went back to my room, my ankle forcing me to limp every few steps. There, I filled her water and food bowls. As she chomped away, I downed a few ibuprofen for the killer headache throbbing at the base of my skull and radiating outward, tingling on the edges of my shoulders. The lingering effects of drinking had me wanting to lie down in the dark for the rest of the day, but I had some things to get done.

I started laundry, then returned to my room to sit down and put on my glasses to deal with today when I finally saw, in clarity, the state of my room.

What. The. Hell. Had I done last night?

The detailed storyboards on the whiteboard were streaked clean, leaving remnants of lines and curves here and there. My notebooks were splayed open and all over the place with pages ripped apart in a brutal paper massacre. Half of my scriptwriting books were jammed into the trash can with a few haphazardly piled between the bin and the wall.

Exhausted. Defeated. Deflated.

My barely rigid shoulders slumped and sagged. The burden of a hundred doubts and failures encumbered my bones. I could practically feel my shoulders splintering from the weight.

These stories floating around the room, the things that once gave me life and brewed unparalleled excitement, slowly wilted into items that incited pangs in my chest.

"Oh my lord . . ." I muttered, overwhelmed between the headache scratching the inside of my skull and the heaviness of my shoulders, the ache in my chest.

My brain throbbed, like it was expanding inside a suddenly too-small head.

What was the point? Also, I was certain my skull was going to explode any second, splattering this room full of my stories with brain matter. Seemed poetic in a sense: death over the very thing I loved.

"Mmm, mmm, mmm," I grunted, took my glasses off,

placed them on the bedside table again, and flopped onto my pillows. Nope. I couldn't deal with today, after all.

Even opening the blinds to let in much-needed air and light, much less cleaning up the shrapnel remains of my work, was too much effort.

My phone pinged.

It was probably Rohan. Who else could it be?

It took everything in me not to emoji-sob to him and ask if he hated me, or had lost all respect for me, or had gotten into trouble, or was feeling bad in the case that my parents had hammered into him.

But no. I didn't because all the guy wanted to know was what I was up to today.

Nothing. Pure and simple. But maybe at some point I'd sweep through the room and collect the shards of my dignity and glue them back together into what was sure to end up being a hideous conglomerate of rubbish from my so-called career.

He texted again, asking if I wanted to do something. Anything.

Nah. I didn't feel like leaving this bed, even as depression ballooned up behind me, as if coming out to say *Hello, my dear friend. It's been a while.*

But he persisted and kept texting me, making sure that I was all right. But the thing was, I wasn't okay. Perhaps my parents were in the right. Maybe I was a dire failure, an utter and lost fool to think I could make something of myself in the *entertainment* industry. I wasn't well-connected. I didn't have beyond-amazing talent that made others want to snatch me up in a heartbeat, apparently. This whole up-and-down roller coaster of highs and lows? Maybe I wasn't fit for this after all.

I texted Rohan back, so that he wouldn't worry or fret over

me. Aside from the obvious reasons why I might not be feeling okay, Rohan was quite perceptive. Especially when it came to me. He knew, even if no one else did, when I was down. We were cousins, which meant we'd seen each other get into trouble a million times. It wasn't anything new, particularly when we were so similar and tended to get into trouble for comparable issues.

But he knew things were a little harder for me, or at least I viewed them to be a little harder on me. Because yes, being an elder meant I had to be pristine and proper and good in setting examples for others. I had little to no room to err. I was nearing thirty, which meant I had expectations that I was not quite meeting: degree(s), settled career, sufficient if not lucrative income, possible marriage partner in sight if not already married. Not to mention I was female, which meant there were double standards to face off against in already tedious uphill battles. Women shall not drink, smoke, curse, dress or behave immodestly, or have sex (what's that? Ha! Just kidding!) before marriage.

With Rohan's intuitive sense of knowing me and how realistic the odds of last night sending me tumbling down into a rabbit hole of despair and depression were, he didn't relent. I supposed there were a number of things that he could've homed in on, and no, I wasn't going to count them off again.

Yet Rohan didn't focus on any of those things.

Rohan: Want to grab a pizza at that place I took you to a few months back? The one that personalizes every order? My treat . . . just don't do that thing you did last time. :P

I smiled, albeit faint and fleeting. The guy loved his pizza and had grown into a connoisseur. The place was expensive but simple. You created your own pizza. Each one was the same size, the same price, thin crust, and personalized. It was basically walking down a line of sauces and toppings, then a quick fire-roasting, and ta-da!

The last time we went, Rohan had gone for what he called his usual: spicy red sauce, very little mozzarella, lots of onions, and red bell pepper. I had hemmed and hawed for the longest time before he prodded me in the side and told me to hurry up. I'd attempted to replicate this fabulous white pizza that I had at Gotham Pizza in New York City. I had them make my pizza with cream sauce, a little mozzarella, a sprinkle of parmesan, and lots of ricotta topped with spinach and crumbled feta.

"Ew," Rohan had said, pretending with great conviction that my pizza looked gross and pale.

"It's really good," I had said after a bite. Very close to Gotham, but not quite. "It's called 'white pizza.'"

He shook his head. "Damn shame. You and your racist pizza."

Rohan: All right fine . . . you can have your racist white pizza.

I let out a little smile and sent him a laughing emoji. I lay on my stomach, the pillowcase digging creases into my skin, and contemplated going out. It would help. To get out of the house, away from my parents' disapproval and this mess, for some much-needed food in my belly and to apologize to my cousin for being such a wreck in life. He really deserved better from me.

Flickers of last night came back to me no matter how hard I tried to fight them off. My stomach turned in on itself. I lurched up and bent over, dry-heaving.

My body, from my skin to my bones, was on fire.

I gulped water from the water bottle beside my bed only to glance at it after setting it down. The water bottle Mummie had given me last night. Her sorrowful tone chimed through my thoughts.

Lord. I'd thought things would feel better the next day, less extreme after sleeping it off. But no. It was even worse because there was a certain clarity amid the skull-cracking headache. Seriously. Was my brain about to explode? This couldn't just be all from drinking. I'd never been this miserable.

Maybe all the details weren't there, but there were a few things.

Rohan: You there?

Rohan: Hello? You ghosting me? Or did you fall asleep?

Rohan: Okay, well I'm hungry. Ima take a shower and be at your place in twenty.

Isha: It's okay. I don't feel up to going anywhere. Thanks, though . . .

I just wanted to play my sad playlist and sleep. As I closed out of Rohan's messages, I noticed an unread one from earlier this morning.

Thirst-Trap: I won't bother you again if you'd rather I not text you, but I wanted to make sure you were doing well this morning.

I smiled softly, then cringed. Knowing that he'd seen the worst of me had another wave of nausea rolling up my throat.

He . . . had been so unerringly kind. He gave me drinks on the house and a shirt to cover up with, cleaned up my mess, and drove all the way to the lake to get us out of a jam. And he didn't even know me! I couldn't even remember his name! He deserved more than an embarrassed apology uttered in mumblings from the back seat of his car from a drunk woman wearing crotch-hole parachute pants. He deserved to hear it in person, to his face, and from a clean and stink-free version of me.

I drew in a deep breath until my chest expanded as far as it could go, until my ribs ached, until my back cracked. I shouldn't miss an opportunity to be an adult and face my issues. I had to at least make one thing right, if nothing else. At least confront one disaster.

Rohan: Just gonna mope all day, then?

Isha: Actually, I need to apologize to your friend's brother, the bartender.

Rohan: You don't have to. He probably gets that all the time.

Isha: No. I really should. And I'm sure he does NOT get that all the time. He went very much out of his way and saved both of us.

Rohan: You're right. That's a good idea. I think they're open today.

I looked up the pub on GPS and viewed their website and

hours, and sure enough, they were indeed open on Sundays. Maybe he was there, maybe he wasn't. But if he was, today seemed like it might be slow enough to talk to him.

Rohan: Want me to come with you? I can drive.

Isha: That's okay. Thanks. I need to drive around and figure some things out.

Rohan: You're okay . . . right?

Isha: I will be.

I dropped the phone onto my lap and looked around the room.

Sitting around would just allow plentiful time to wallow in misery and mess. I would probably end up eating junk food in the dark and binge-watching Netflix for days. Although not a horrible idea.

No. I had to do the mature thing. This guy deserved an apology and a decent thank-you. He had done too much for a stranger . . . *way* too much.

I groaned and shook off a shiver. Even though I'd showered last night before getting into bed, I swore the lingering odor of vomit still clung onto my nostril hairs for dear life.

First, I called the pub to make sure he would be there.

"Which bartender?" a woman asked.

I blew out a breath. "Um. I don't know his name. He worked last night."

"There were three male bartenders who worked last night. One is here."

"Oh. Hmm. Okay. I'm a little confused. All I know is that he's tall and handsome and has brown skin and black hair in a man-bun and makes beautiful off-menu drinks."

She laughed. "Ah, okay. There's only one of those. He's here right now."

I snapped my finger as more tidbits came back to me. "Ah! The owner."

"Yep. That's him."

"Great! I need to drop something off for him in an hour or so."

"Sure thing."

"Thanks!" I said, and hung up, my hands clammy and shaking.

Why was I so nervous? And a better question: why hadn't I asked for his name and for her to let him know that I would be coming? I supposed I could text him.

No. No way were my strung-out nerves going to let me. I could see myself hemming and hawing and the next thing I knew, I'd talk myself out of going altogether. Just go already . . .

"All right!" I smacked the edge of the bed and pushed myself off.

With determination to offset the dread of my entire existence, I put the laundry into the dryer and took another shower and washed my hair twice more. As I shaved, letting conditioner sit in my hair, I contemplated the best ways to apologize to a guy while ignoring the teeth marks on my bar of coffee-and-sugar-scrub soap. Not to mention, a good enough way to apologize to my parents and Rohan.

For them, I knew that laying low and being seen at home was important. I might (gasp) even have to attend mandir to appease their worry that I might be on a downward slope into hedonism.

And Rohan? It seemed that I could do no wrong in his eyes. Not that I was particularly important or perfect, but he had a wide range of forgiveness. He understood, but he also didn't think things like this were a big deal. It wasn't as if I'd ratted him out.

But Thirst-Trap? How to apologize to him? And why did I feel the gripping need to do so? We weren't close enough to warrant anything expensive or extravagant or too thoughtful. We barely knew one another, strangers in passing, really.

I hadn't messed up so much that I needed to beg or grovel or get emotional.

A card? No. That seemed cheesy. What would it say anyway? *Sorry I puked all over your lot and you had to clean up my nastiness?*

Flowers? That seemed much too . . . intimate.

Food? Ah, yes. Food was the way to the heart. Apologies were practically insta-approved if they came with food.

As I dragged myself out of the shower, dressed, and dried my hair, smelling it for the hundredth time to make sure that disgusting vomit stench was gone and that it instead flourished with all the coconut and gardenia madness my shampoo and conditioner and leave-in conditioner promised, I decided to stop by a little café on the way to the pub.

Although food had been decided upon by the time I'd tugged on my jeans and slipped into a T-shirt, another thought hurtled itself at me.

Was he allergic to anything? Nut allergy? Gluten allergy? Lactose intolerant? Was he keto, paleo, vegetarian, vegan?

Why, universe, why?

Once my laundry dried—thank goodness the vomit and dumpster smells had come out—I quickly folded everything.

I grabbed my cross-body purse and trotted downstairs. Letting out a strangled sigh, I went down the hall, around the corner, and into the area that divided the living room to the left and the kitchen to the right with the breakfast nook straight ahead.

Papa was at the table drinking his usual late-morning cup of cha while Mummie moved around the kitchen preparing lunch.

"Beta," Papa said from his paper, his eyes soft and only a mere hint of a greeting smile. It made my stomach sink. His despondency lingered in the air, thickening with an unease on my part. It was *palpable*. My insides sank lower and lower, meeting my self-confidence along the way and dragging it into the depths of hell along with it.

"Morning, Papa," I replied nervously, wishing for this to all go away and have my parents just the least bit proud of me.

"Are you hungry?" Mummie asked from the kitchen. When she made eye contact while washing rice, she held it. Damn if my mom wasn't passive-aggressive. She didn't have to say a word to remind me of what sort of trouble I was in.

I shook my head. "I was going to pick up a pastry. Would you like something?"

"Where are you going?" Papa asked, half-curious and half-accusatory. Or was that my chicken soul peeking out?

"To 29 Café. The one on Twenty-Ninth Street. It has that extra foamy cappuccino that you like."

"Ah. That's very good," he commented.

"Is it . . . okay that I go?" I bit my lower lip. How was I this old asking my parents if I could go out on a Sunday morning to get breakfast?

"Of course. Beta, you don't have to ask."

"Unless you're trying to go to bars," Mummie chided.

I dropped my head back. "No one is trying to drink on Sunday morning."

"You shouldn't be drinking in the first place," she scolded.

I opened my mouth to defend my right to drink, but after last night, or rather this morning, I wasn't about to step into this mess. "You're right, Mummie. I should be careful about what I do with my body." Abstaining from getting drunk was beneficial; there was no lie to that.

"I'd ask if you've applied to any of the jobs we discussed, but you probably didn't take the time with all that running around you did," she said evenly.

"You're right. I didn't," I replied bluntly. Also, we hadn't discussed anything. Being told and having a conversation were two vastly different things.

If looks could light fires, then hers would ignite entire suns. Sheesh. The anger. The glower.

"Would you like me to bring you back anything?" I asked, turning away to leave.

"No. We have cha," Papa said as Mummie added, "And lunch will be ready soon."

"Okay. See you later. I might not eat lunch if I get pastries."

"Bye, beta," they said in unison.

Whew! I hadn't been that awkward or desperate to get out of my parents' company since college. Maybe getting a "real job" wasn't so bad, if I could find something that I enjoyed and could advance in. It wouldn't necessarily mean giving up my dreams, but it would, at least, support living on my own and not feeling, or being treated, like a child. After all, no one wanted to be a complainer stuck in the mud forever.

Chapter 16

With my headache starting to calm down, a backup of ibuprofen in my purse, and a game plan, I headed downtown and stopped at the café first, grateful for near-dead traffic. Less idiots on the road, less road rage, less accidents, less honking, and all adding up to a leisurely and easy flow. My brain wasn't attempting to keep an eye on all one thousand cars that were usually around or pray every time I changed lanes or crossed streets or made turns. Yes, Austin traffic had become *that* horrendous since the massive spikes of people moving in.

I lingered, almost literally dragging my feet out of the car, and if one could drag a car's tires, I did that, too.

The café was busy. The robust menu called for more lingering as I skimmed the offerings on the wall and perused the display cases. Quiches, croissants, cakes, pies, muffins, scones, donuts, cookies, and so many additional items. I almost went the safest route by ordering a chia pudding cup, but that felt like a half-assed effort. And boring. And quite possibly tasteless.

My eyes went wide and my entire soul lit up seeing the small selection of cupcakes from Hello Cupcake, which was a cupcake-only bakery on the other side of I-35. They seldom had this selection and it always disappeared in a heartbeat.

Why were there still cupcakes available? Who cared! I grabbed three.

A lemon drop one for Thirst-Trap was a white cupcake with a subtle tart, citrus flavor and a pale-yellow swirl of frosting topped with candied lemon peel. Sugar crystals sparkled all over the curled, sunburst-yellow strands like diamonds. It was absolutely too gorgeous to eat.

A white chocolate with raspberry filling for Rohan because he wasn't the too-sweet type but did enjoy berries. His cupcake was a not-too-sweet chocolate cake with a semisweet dollop of white chocolate icing and a sprig of mint nestled underneath a trio of bright red raspberries. It was a start to ask for his forgiveness.

And, finally, a habanero pecan praline for myself, which was a decadent chocolate cake with hints of spice and a thick, golden caramel haphazardly drizzled on top of roasted whole pecans. I suspected there were bits of pecan inside the cake as well. I was an absolute sucker for Texas pecans and praline, but add the unorthodox hint of pepper and it was just beyond amazing.

With my gifts in their individual and cutesy packaging with what looked like hand-drawn smiling cupcakes, I crawled back into the car and headed to the pub with burgeoning dread.

If not for the very deliberate act of walking back into his

workplace, the chances of seeing him again were slim to none. Austin was a metropolis. If he worked and lived downtown, then the odds of not seeing him in north Austin were ever in my favor.

So then, why was I so nervous? No. Mortified in this nauseating sense of humiliation.

I tried to shrug off the nervous energy, tried to coach myself into believing that he, as a bartender, must have come across worse situations than me during his career. It wasn't that bad. Really, it wasn't.

So what if he'd seen me spill a drink on myself? It probably happened all the time.

So what if he'd walked in on me in his private restroom topless? He'd probably seen much worse go down in restrooms.

And sure, he must've had bar fights at his place before.

And he must've seen plenty of customers vomit.

And he must've had to clean up said vomit. Probably.

Well, okay. Sure, the alley part was forgivable and maybe one day forgettable, but what he did for us at the security station was above and beyond.

Which was why a little paper bag hung off my right wrist, carrying the contents of a please-forgive-me gift.

He'd helped me. He gave me a shirt to cover myself. He saw me vomiting my guts out and handed me water and cleaned up my mess in his alley . . . and then, like a bartender in shining armor, he delivered us from the hands of the system. Everything he'd done was kindness and compassion. The latter spared us a future of trouble.

I cringed. I owed him *way* more than a cupcake.

As I opted to take advantage of closer Sunday parking, the

back alley came in and out of view on the right in passing. Oh. My heart. During the day, it was unassuming and ordinary and quiet. It was where people went to dump trash or take shortcuts.

Flashes of memories came back.

I groaned, my skin icy cold and my brain cells telling me to go home. Except I was already here. Parked several spots down, in front of one establishment over. What was this place? Another bar? Whatever it was, it was dead quiet.

There was a spot right in front of his business, and the street was fairly empty on a Sunday afternoon, but I supposed Thirst-Trap not seeing me sit in my car ten minutes longer than necessary trying to muster up courage, get out of the car, walk toward the pub, then backtrack, then walk back to the pub and backtrack again and again all while nibbling on my nail and muttering to myself on how to smoothly approach him in conversation was a good thing.

I finally shook my shoulders loose and stared at the double doors. "You got this. Woman up."

"Is that how you psych yourself up?"

I yelped and jumped around to face Thirst-Trap in the very fine, very well-lit flesh. I had a hand to my chest to somehow calm my nerves, because I mean, damn. *Okay.*

"Sorry," he said with a grin. How could this man possibly look more attractive? Add well-rested skin and sparkling eyes, a dimple now seen in the glorious light of day, a snug black T-shirt and jeans, and yep, Austin, we had an answer!

"You can't sneak up on people like that!"

He furrowed his brows and then looked behind him and then around us. "Broad daylight on an empty sidewalk with literally three cars and no traffic."

I sighed. "Well, I didn't see you. So stealthy."

"Okay." He laughed and handed me a paper cup with a lid.

The bag around my wrist rustled slightly as I carefully took the warm drink and inhaled the richness of freshly brewed coffee. "Thank you. What's this for?"

"I figured you might want a drink . . . I mean, coffee."

I winced. "Yeah, because I probably shouldn't have a *drink* drink after last night."

"It's okay. I mean, I actually don't know everything. It was a pretty wild night and I only saw glimpses."

"How did you know I was coming?"

"I got a message about your call saying you were coming by."

"And you knew it was me?"

He shrugged. "Could've been anyone. On one hand, I would've given you a latte to be nice. On the other hand, I would've had two cups of coffee if you ended up being someone else."

"Ah. Unlucky you. Sometimes you need a second cup if the coffee is good."

"Or lucky me to see you again."

I winced. "You're saying that after last night? Or are you trying to get something for all your trouble? Because that was a lot of trouble."

"No, definitely not looking for compensation."

"Oh. Too bad, because I come bearing a gift." I lifted the bag.

"Then I suppose I'll be making a concession in that case."

I took a tentative sip of coffee, hoping to buy time while contemplating a response. My eyes lit up. "Oh. Wow. This is really good coffee."

"It's a mocha latte made with spiced Mexican hot chocolate. The combo sounds genius and a natural pairing, but you don't find a lot of places that use Mexican hot chocolate, much less the spiced kind. You'd think living in Texas we'd see more of it. A place up the way makes them." He glanced over his shoulder behind him, indicating a café tucked into the corner of a building across the street. "Their coffee is much better than ours, not that we do lattes. I honestly don't know why anyone orders our drip."

"You should probably ask your boss about getting better coffee."

"I'll do that." He smirked. I could absolutely see myself drinking coffee out of those dimples. But he probably wouldn't appreciate someone pouring scalding hot liquid onto his face and then trying to drink it off.

"Oh, right. People probably don't come here to order coffee."

"Come on in." He walked ahead of me to open the door, lifting his coffee-holding hand to usher me into his place.

It took a second to shake off the nature of his politeness. Despite living in the South, Southern kindness ceased to exist in the city. Although Rohan and Papa held doors open for me, I never expected it. This was nice.

I wasn't sure why I'd thought the pub would be deserted. There were a few servers deftly cleaning tables and booths and chairs and any other touchable object. The floors appeared to have been swept and mopped recently and smelled of cleaning products.

Every now and then, there was a random limp to my step that sent a seething bolt up from my ankle.

"Are you okay?" he asked from behind me.

"Yeah. I fell and hurt my ankle at some point last night," I replied, walking through the pain.

"We can take a seat," he suggested.

"Are y'all open every day?" I asked as Thirst-Trap walked past me and to the counter at the bar.

"Yep."

"So people drink at all hours, basically?"

He smiled. "We do have food, you know?"

"Oh, right!"

"Even though a certain someone said we should offer more, we're working on expanding the menu."

"What you have is pretty good, actually. I had a few items Friday night. Very spicy jalapeño poppers."

"It's the habaneros mixed in."

"I was warned. Still good. Although I couldn't taste anything for a bit while my taste buds recovered."

"That's why we have those little peppers next to it on the menu." He winked.

"Oh, right . . ." I grinned as we sat next to one another on barstools. "And the verbal warning from the waitress. And the side of sweet raspberry jam, which is an excellent pairing."

"Thanks. My idea."

"Much appreciated." I set the coffee on the counter, careful to not let a drop spill on the sparkling clean surface, and then pushed the bag toward him.

"So, what's this?" he inquired as he pulled out the little cardboard box. As he did so, he turned a bit into me so that our knees touched.

Heat rose to my skin and suddenly drinking hot coffee felt like a bad idea. "Um. A little gift to, you know . . . thank you for helping us out so much. And also . . . sorry for putting you through last night and definitely a huge thank-you for coming through at the security place."

I didn't want to meet his eyes. In fact, it was quite the mental battle to force myself not to look at him at all. But I managed to glance at him without exploding and found his lips curving upward in a soft, understanding sort of smile. But also, perhaps a bit appreciative?

"You didn't have to."

"I really did. Especially when you showed up last night."

He smiled. "Guess it's a good thing you accidentally texted me."

"Did you really add yourself into my phone as Thirst-Trap?"

"Aren't I, though?"

I laughed. "Yes." My face flushed as I confessed, "I think you told me your name last night, but I don't think I heard it right. Or maybe I just can't recall after how wasted I was."

"Tarik. But I don't mind being called Thirst-Trap."

"You don't mind being objectified?"

"It's kind of funny—and flattering—coming from you. I don't think anyone has called me a thirst-trap before."

I scoffed. "Not to your face. I at least have the guts to tell the truth."

He smiled even bigger and I just wanted to stare at his face all day. But I eventually snapped out of it and nodded toward the box. "I hope you like it."

"I'm, um, diabetic," he confessed.

"Oh my god!" I grabbed the box from him and said in a rush, "I'm so sorry! I didn't know what to get you. I thought of lattes but didn't know if you could be lactose intolerant or had allergies. I thought of a burger, but then didn't know if you were vegetarian, and forget about soggy fries. Cookie or croissant, but didn't know if you were gluten-free. I took a chance hoping you could eat this and not explode." Oh lord. Why was I babbling?

He laughed, carefully taking back the box. There was a moment when his fingers caressed mine and a flutter exploded in my gut like hitting a brick wall.

"I'm kidding," he said, eyeing the decadent lemon drop confection from Hello Cupcake. He swiped a finger across the fluffy icing and put it at his lips, savoring the sweet and tart. How was something so ordinary *this* sensual?

I found myself holding my breath and shamelessly staring at his mouth.

"This is sinful," he commented. "I should've asked if you wanted to share."

"No. I actually have one in the car. Think I'd get cupcakes and not one for myself?" I swatted the air and chuckled. Any less smooth and I would've slid right back into last night's debauchery.

As he ate the cupcake in three giant bites—that mouth of his, damn—I said, "Joking about having diabetes isn't funny. It's a very serious thing."

"You're right."

I frowned. "So, seriously, am I aiding in your mad decline into insulin dependency or are you just not going to tell me if you really have diabetes?"

"I mean, I barely know you to tell you my health history." He smirked.

I groaned with a roll of my eyes, his grin widening. "At least you enjoy eating a good cupcake."

"Why does that sound dirty?" He arched a brow and looked off into the corner.

I laughed, having no idea where he even heard the remotest bit of dirty in that. Although people had turned things like *cookie* and *cake* into a sultry innuendo, so why not *cupcake*? "Because you have a dirty mind?"

"Ah. Right. You know me so well already."

"Hush now and drink your coffee."

He flashed that swoony grin and took a sip.

"Next time I'll bring you something less dirty, maybe queso," I suggested.

Both of his brows went up. "Are you planning for a next time?"

Heat washed over my cheeks. "No." I was definitely not planning on more hijinks that required an apology.

"What a shame."

"You want me embarrassing myself again and having to bring you apology food?"

"Or we can skip straight to the food. No apology. No need for an apology."

I took a sip of coffee, my words catching in my throat, and yet I was unable to move out of the intensity of his gaze. I was also acutely aware that our knees were still touching.

Wait . . . was he asking me out?

He glanced down to busy himself with closing the cupcake box. His cheeks flushed. Was he embarrassed? How irresistibly cute.

I clamped down on a smile from behind my cup, pretending to drink when I just wanted to cover my face because how adorable was Thirst-Trap right now? I mean . . . *Tarik*.

Before he could get back to possibly asking me out, my phone rang. Nothing else quite cockblocked like an angry mother calling and sending a text to ask my whereabouts and what I was doing. The leash around my neck tightened and my giddiness drained faster than the blood in my face.

"Is everything okay?" he asked.

I stared at my phone screen, unable to drag my gaze away. Tarik wasn't anyone to me and probably never would be. There was no way a guy as put together as him wanted to actually date a failure like me. He had a stable job—he owned his own business, for goodness' sake—and he seemed to possess a good level of maturity and humor. He most likely didn't live with his parents. For all I knew, he probably had a degree in business or even an MBA from the magnificent burnt-orange UT campus down the way.

I licked my lips and slipped off the stool. "I should go."

"Are you all right?" he asked, meeting my depleted gaze with a concerned one.

"I need to recover from last night. I have to get home and take care of things."

"Is it . . ." he began, and scratched the back of his neck. "Is it okay if I text you sometime?"

Such a simple question coming from him knocked the breath from my lungs.

When I didn't respond, he added, sounding quite disappointed, "It's okay if not."

I cleared my throat. "Why, why would you want to?"

He pressed his lips into a line, the soft kind that was a heartfelt, sympathetic sort-of smile.

"After last night, I mean. Why would you want to?"

He shrugged and said, "I was looking forward to queso, or you know, something less dirty."

I bit my lip, my heart pounding, and said, "Yeah. That'd be all right."

He opened his mouth to respond when my phone rang again.

"I have to take this," I muttered.

He nodded.

I took a few steps away and answered the call. "Hi, Mummie. Yes. I'm on my way home. Did you want me to pick up anything?"

I gave Tarik a little wave and mouthed *Thank you* as I raised the still half-full cup of coffee to him.

He swiveled his stool to face me, leaned against the counter, his knees apart, and said, "Come back again."

Then he added a devastating smile that had my bones melting into goop.

I smiled back and headed out.

"Who is that?" Mummie asked on the other end. Wow, talk about super hearing.

"The guy at the counter," I replied, and pushed through the front door, squinting in the bright afternoon light.

"Where are you?"

"Downtown," I said. "I told you I was going to the café. I bought a cupcake and have a latte, so I don't think I'll be eating lunch when I get back."

"Oh. Okay. Well, hurry home."

"Why?"

"Sabha."

My heart pattered. Yep. Inevitable for my parents to push

me into the religious sermons of mandir before I fell off the deep end and drowned in my debauchery.

I licked my lips. It was easy to decline when I was in college because I was busy studying. It was even easier to decline afterward because I was living on my own. But now? Living at home *and* having been caught drunk off my butt around an impressionable cousin? Declining would not go over well. Still, I was an adult.

"Maybe next time," I replied.

I flinched and held the phone away from my ear as Mummie went off like the Fourth of July fireworks finale hosted by Willie Nelson on Lake Travis. She practically ruptured my eardrums. I only caught bits and pieces and thank goodness Tarik, or any decent person, wasn't around to hear.

Well. I guessed that was the end of that.

I wasn't in the mind frame to argue with my mom or give her another reason to look down on me. I needed to appease her for the time being and earn her trust back. I needed to get my crap together and woman up, be an adult, and figure things out soon.

For today, I went home and got dressed in a comfortable red-and-green salwar kameez, no makeup, no jewelry, and escorted my parents and brother to mandir for two *tedious* hours of sitting on my butt and listening to muted prayers and conversations and sermons.

I wasn't surprised to see all the regulars or to hear from them how they'd love to see me here more often. But you know who was a surprise to see here?

Rohan.

Chapter 17

The best thing about wearing a salwar kameez was that it was as comfortable as pajamas or, really, any set of loungewear. The pants were pull-on with a tie to suit any level of pre- or postmeal belly and came in a variety of styles from leggings to harem-style loose. The top ended anywhere between the hips and the knees and could be either fitting or loose, any style of sleeves, but almost always airy. The dupatta was that extra bit of shawl-like fabric of an accessory to make one feel less basic.

I opted for sleeveless because my armpits needed air more than they needed to be covered up.

Most women at mandir wore a salwar kameez or a sari, though several came in blouses and slacks. All in all, modesty was key and I appreciated comfortable clothes.

For the most part, the majority of the guys wore kurta pajamas to keep it traditional, but several wore slacks and button-down shirts.

Then there was Rohan, sticking out like an uninterested sore thumb in jeans and a Deadpool T-shirt. God bless him.

It didn't matter what he wore. He could've been in his usual basketball shorts or a torn jersey for all anyone cared. Why? Aside from double standards, everyone was just happy to see him. He hadn't stepped foot on this property in months, and that was only to drop off his mom.

His parents gushed over him being here, praising him, showing him off to anyone who glanced their way or walked too close. All the guys greeted him with smiles, uncles chatted him up, aunties fawned over him, and the girls gushed over him, too.

He was a freaking rock star just for showing up. Well, I supposed, Rohan being Rohan had something to do with it, too, because he had everyone laughing.

As for me? Some aunties, as well as women my age, greeted me. But it was superficial at best.

"Nice to see you!"

"Been so long!"

"How are you?"

"What are you doing for work now?"

Et cetera. Et cetera.

The burdensome sentiment of not feeling . . . well, holy enough . . . lingered around me like a bad smell. Not devout enough. It was as if everyone here had watched my life on high-def and knew all my dirty little secrets. Drinking and getting wasted. Vomiting in public. Nearly getting arrested. Eating seafood with the eyes still attached. Lurking in my bank account and tsking at the menial amount of several hundred dollars. Knowing that I'd kissed guys, and much more if we were being honest. Not having a husband or any good Indian boy remotely interested in me by now. Not on my way to buying a house and having a couple of kids. The list went on.

Sigh. How exhausting.

But the double standard for Rohan would wear off soon enough. They'd expect him to keep returning, to dress nicer, to get back "on track," et cetera.

From across the hall that separated male and female worship areas, he approached me in hurried steps as soon as the program finished, with an urgency that had me wondering if he'd been caught, too.

"What's wrong?" I asked in a lowered voice, keeping an eye on anyone close enough to overhear but also searching for our parents. My worry eased just a fraction when I saw that all four were busy chatting with others in lively conversation.

"Have you seen the news today?" he asked, whipping out his phone and scrolling through a website before turning the screen to me.

I had to read the headline twice.

DISTURBING CLOWN DISTURBING THE PEACE.

And right in the middle of the local news article was a picture of a Pennywise doppelganger, complete with unforgettable fake curly red hair, paper-white face, stark black arched brows, oversized tears, and downturned mouth made comically large with overdone red lipstick.

I shivered down to my bones. Ugh. Clowns. "Ew."

"Seriously? That's all you have to say when you were screaming that Pennywise was trying to snatch you into hell through a gutter?"

"Oh . . . *oh*!" My eyes went wide. "So he *was* real, and really there, and that really happened?"

"Yep."

I rubbed the goose bumps from my arm. "Was he a killer clown after all? Oh my lord, did we narrowly escape being murdered?"

"What? No. They arrested him last night."

"Shut. Up," I said, even as I blew out a breath of relief.

"If you hadn't beat the crap out of him, he would've just been hiding in the alley, dealing drugs, and going home to do it again another day. He got caught because while he was running after us, he ran into an undercover cop who'd been trying to fake a deal with the clown and they finally busted him."

I sucked in a breath, downturning my lips, and slowly nodded. "So what you're saying is, is that I'm a *hero*."

He grinned. "Calm down, Wonder Woman."

I gave a soft smile. "I'm glad he was busted, and I'm glad I didn't assault an innocent clown."

He retracted his phone. "Far from innocent. Those teardrops? They're actually coke bags to signal to druggies that he has some for them."

I scowled. "Disgusting, yet an interesting approach. But why dress like a clown? Wouldn't he want to be inconspicuous?"

"He told the police he dressed that way to alert druggies who might've heard about him, but also if someone sees him, he can just run off and change and wash his face. Like, it's hard to tell that he's actually gangly and blond with tan skin. You'd have no idea what his face looked like underneath that makeup, his hair beneath the wig, or his body type beneath the puffed clothes."

"I wish people would put in as much effort into helping society as they do trying to profit off it."

He shrugged. "I'm not for drugs, but he's working with a

broken system. Well, guess we all are. Anyway, heard you were coming through the parental grapevine."

I nodded. "What are you doing here?"

He wiggled his toes on the marble floor. "Just in case my parents got wind of anything from last night, had to throw them off the trail."

"Think one mandir appearance will appease them and out-weigh the hedonism of a Western lifestyle?" I smirked.

"Seems to be working so far. They're ecstatic. My mom almost cried when I told her I wanted to come."

"Aw. That's sweet, but don't get her hopes up."

"Of course not. She asked if this was going to be a regular thing now, and I told her no."

"How's it being back so far? I see all the guys are talking to you."

"Eh." He glanced over his shoulder where the men had divided into age groups to do whatever they did. "More like recruiting. They want me to do this and that. Like I'm going to perform in a play or lead Sunday school for the kids. Those brats get on my nerves."

I snickered. "Don't call them brats."

"But they're so hyper, man."

"The kids are just excited to see you. And I'm sure the older ones are extending invitations so you feel that you can jump in wherever you'd like. They're welcoming you."

He shook his head. "Nah. They're trying to suck me in. I'm not falling for it."

He was probably right. I said, "Aside from that, looks like you're doing well here. Thought you would've called it a day halfway through and sat out in the parking lot or grabbed some fries at the McDonald's down the street."

He puckered his lips. "I almost did. At least three guys asked me when I was going back to college, and two uncles offered for me to work for them."

"I take it they were being passive-aggressive?" I asked, knowing how a single wrong word or the slightest tilt in tone could change a humble offering into an emotional weapon.

"Yep. Telling me that I was still young and needed to finish college so I could be respected and find a nice wife and make the community proud. Blah, blah, blah."

Most would respond that they meant well and wanted to see him succeed, but we knew better. They wanted to keep our community elevated, to say we all did these high and mighty things, come join us and be successful, too. But even if they meant well, it didn't come off that way. It just felt as if our entire worth was based on subjectivity.

"At least no one's telling you that your ovaries are drying up."

He guffawed. "TMI."

"Not more than a hello, never a call or text, never a moment to ask how I'm doing or get to know me, but somehow always jumping straight into my business and what I'm doing wrong. I thought this would stop as we got older."

He raised a brow. "You know we're Indian, right? The prying and judgment never stop."

"Ah, yes. Lots of generational toxicity to unravel and deconstruct, but not a battle I'm up for at the moment."

"How are you holding up?"

I shrugged.

He flicked the edge of the dupatta hanging from my shoulder like he often had when he was a kid and thought it was fun trying to provoke me. "I don't like seeing you like this."

"Like what?"

"Sad. Depressed," he replied solemnly.

His words took me by surprise. "I'm smiling and talking and getting out."

"I know you better than that."

"It hasn't even been twenty-four hours. It'll get better," I confessed softly. "Hey, I went by your house before going home and dropped off a cupcake. Your mom said you were in the shower. Didn't know she meant you were showering to come here."

"Oh yeah. She told me you dropped by. Thanks. It was really good."

"I know you usually don't do desserts. Was it too sweet? The lady behind the counter said it was semisweet."

"Not as sweet as most cupcakes. I appreciate it. I sent you a text."

"Haven't had time to check, with my mom being on me so hard right now." I dropped my head with a groan and added, "They won't treat me like an adult until I'm on my own again. I should move back out. It would be less stressful for everyone, and a grown woman needs space."

"You read my mind. I was thinking the same."

"That a grown woman needs her own place? My parents weren't really one hundred percent okay with it before, but I had roommates to help with rent and address their safety concerns."

"Rogue will protect you," he replied confidently.

I grinned. "She's fury incarnate. You just want me to have my own place so you can come over and crash whenever you want."

"You caught me. But seriously? It might be a necessary move."

"You're right. Guess I need a *real* job now, huh? Maybe I can get more freelance work or start applying vigorously for production jobs again. Maybe I'll have better luck this time."

I brainstormed over other ideas.

Rohan shoved his hands into his pockets. "You're going to sell that script by the end of the month. *That* is your real job."

"I appreciate the confidence. But I don't think so. Seriously and honestly."

He regarded me for a moment before nodding at someone in passing. "Did you get a cupcake for yourself?"

"Yep. And one for the bartender . . ."

"His name's—"

But I interjected, "Oh no. Suppose I have to keep calling him Thirst-Trap." I shrugged dramatically and heaved out a sigh.

"I can't with you . . ."

"He liked his cupcake. Doesn't feel like enough. Yours, either. I should take you to dinner or buy you a car."

"That's not jumping an entire lane at all, is it? Was he . . . cool?"

"Surprisingly, yes. He either doesn't remember seeing me at my worst or is excellent at covering up his true emotions."

"Or maybe he's forgiving. It does happen, whether you believe it or not. There are wackier people and wilder situations going on out there. Even people who don't judge so easily. Did he by chance say anything about the script? Maybe that guy who took it realized it wasn't his and called the pub to send it to, I dunno . . . lost and found?"

"No. Not like me being a scriptwriter came up."

"Really? What did you guys talk about, then?"

I sighed and glanced at Mummie. Her rigid gaze fell over

us. "My mom called and cut the visit short to make sure I'd be home in time to attend mandir."

"You coming again?"

"Not if I can help it . . . but I don't think that I'll be able to win this fight as long as I live at home."

"I think you're right. Don't stress, though, okay? Things will always work out. Hey, what are you doing the rest of the evening?"

"Evening?" I glanced at the clock on the wall. It was seven already. The program had been so long and my family always got here so early, dragging me with them. "Take Rogue out and sleep. I still have a throbbing headache. I might sleep all day tomorrow, too, and then look for more work. Guess my parents will finally be happy with me."

"Do *not* give up."

From across the room of dispersed groups, my mom called me over with a jerk of her chin. I told Rohan, "I better go. Talk to you later."

"Yep."

We parted ways as I walked toward my parents. Three aunts and two uncles from my mom's side, a handful of older cousins, a few aunties and uncles from mandir-led classes, and oh yes, the most respected of our elders, the ones who took care of the mandir and delegated duties and approved whatever happened here.

I . . . was not expecting this to happen here and now.

My steps faltered as the covert conversation came back to memory in full. My parents last night, discussing an intervention. In a matter of minutes, everyone would know about my "wild" ways and become a united front in dealing with me.

My stomach tied into knots and my cupcake was about to come up.

What in the world? Was I a teenager again, needing reprimanding like a child? Did my parents think so little of me that they were willing to open up the floodgates like this? To let everyone in, all in an effort to put up a wall of unified voices and arguments and pressure to subdue me into submission?

My breathing turned ragged and hot as anxiety bubbled over my thoughts.

This wasn't loving or helping, but did they see so little in me that they thought this was?

My skin turned chilly and Mummie's impassive expression turned into concern. She met me partway when my legs went numb. I couldn't move. I was a frozen disaster.

"Beta, are you okay?" Mummie asked, her brows creasing with worry.

My lips moved, but not a single word emerged. I wanted to ask what all this was about, if she truly deemed it necessary to put me through something that was easily going to traumatize and isolate me. Because if a few upturned chins and gossiping folks could make me leave this place and never want to return, then how would a group of my elders telling me to get my sorry excuse of a life together make me feel? If the former made me doubt my self-worth and curl into myself every time I came across someone from this community, then how much would this intervention crush me?

I blinked for several seconds, unable to speak, unable to respond to my mother, who gently touched my arm, asking me, "What's wrong?"

Maybe I didn't want to cause a scene. Maybe I didn't have it in me to stand up for myself when over a dozen people waited to descend upon me like vultures preying on my faults. Maybe I didn't have the guts to speak up to my elders, to even reason my way through confrontation. Maybe I was simply at a loss for words and actions. Whatever the reason, it didn't matter.

Because I stepped backward, away from her, away from them, away from confrontation.

"Are you sick?" she asked, touching her hand to my forehead.

"Yeah, I am . . ." I was severely sick to my stomach.

"Oh, beta, you're burning up."

I finally looked at her, at the motherly concern in her eyes. She really just wanted me to be my best, didn't she? But what was my best if it wasn't what made me happy?

"I'm . . . going to go home," I said, my voice drifting away.

Before she could say something, or maybe she had—I didn't register anything—I turned from her and left.

Chapter 18

My headache, and my hangover, had eased by Monday, helped by liver-pounding amounts of ibuprofen and depression-style hours of heavy sleep. It was all very much needed, and I vowed to never drink that much ever again. There was no reason to. I didn't have a particularly excellent time drunk, and the consequences weren't something I'd want to go through again. Days of feeling exhausted and sick, my skin crawling, my insides spasming, my bones aching, my head rioting . . . no thank you.

I awoke to Rogue's butt on my shoulder, her feet in my face, when she unleashed a sulfuric fart and woke herself up. She immediately startled and went to the other side of the bed, looking at me from over her shoulder with the biggest, saddest eyes, like she'd done something wrong.

"It's okay. Come here," I told her, even as I swatted away the smell.

She gingerly returned and I petted her before sitting up.

I vaguely recalled Mummie checking in on me as I slept. But she must've, because there was a full bottle of water on my bedside next to a temporal thermometer. It was difficult to be upset with my parents when they still took care of me. She'd even left a text mentioning that there was soup in the fridge. Because she knew soup always made me feel better when I was sick.

My parents, much like myself, weren't perfect, but they were good.

At least my parents were at work and I didn't have to talk to them just yet. I had some time to gather myself and figure out what to do. Not just with them, but with my future in general.

Blinking away tears and shoving past lingering anxiety about the state of my life, I whipped my hair into a high bun and glanced around my room. It had yet to be cleaned. Was it time to finish my drunken, ragey train of thought from Saturday night and finish throwing away the rest of the sticky notes, pack up all these books, and wipe down the dry-erase board for a final farewell?

With the dry eraser in my hand lifted to clear off the remnants of the storyboards of my heart, of this latest project and ideas for the next and a niggling of yet another, I couldn't quite commit. Or otherwise, what? Redraw all of this?

The velvety side of the dry eraser hovered centimeters over the colorful drawings and scribblings. It hurt my heart to be this close to ending things. It wasn't that I hadn't tried, because years of college and a decade of writing and years of submitting and rejections . . . dug a hollow, rotting core in the pit of my creativity. The darkness swelled and touched the last figments of patience and faith and endurance.

I let out a sigh. The board was half-gone anyway. I swallowed and commenced to finishing off the job, wincing as my dreams faded into white. Front and back of the two-sided board. I hadn't seen it this clean since I first bought it, which felt like a lifetime ago.

I moved on to clean up the ripped-apart Post-its, torn notebooks, and shredded textbooks, salvaging only what I could. Which, aside from the textbooks, wasn't a whole lot. Sheesh. Ragey me sure had gone at it in the worst possible way.

Behind me, on the bed, my phone pinged. I leaned over and read the screen.

Rohan: How's it going?

I bit my cheek. If he knew what I was doing, he'd lecture me. How was my younger cousin always lecturing me? Did he get tired of supporting me with nothing to show for it, nothing produced to conclude it was all worth the time and energy? Did he ever think of calling it a day and agreeing that it was time to move on?

Maybe. All I knew was that I'd been frustrated now and then trying to get him on his feet when he was going through his worst times, when he'd been depressed and stuck in eerily dark days for nearly a year. Getting him to get out of bed and shower was an entire ordeal. But after my selfish moments breaking with impatience, I always returned to him and continued to be whatever sort of crutch he needed for support. And eventually he walked again. He was motivated, joyful, himself again. I'd never considered one of those seconds wasted. So maybe he didn't consider any of these times with me wasted.

I responded that I was okay, which was the truth. Not great, not wretched, but okay. And since he was at work, there wasn't a lot of back and forth and probing.

I set the phone down as another text came through.

Thirst-Trap: Did you lose a folder and thumb drive?

My heart skipped a beat. Had the messenger bag guy seen the error of his ways and returned my proposal to the pub? My information was on the front page, and maybe the messenger bag guy had chickened out in texting me himself, as if I didn't know my own folder.

Thirst-Trap: Let me know what you'd like to do.

Tarik didn't text after that, and it was for the best.

I gingerly picked up the phone, as if touching it would activate a video call that I wasn't ready for. Since the text came up on screen and I hadn't actually tapped on my messages, it wouldn't have shown a "read" message. At least, I was pretty sure that was how it worked.

I then noticed a notification on LinkedIn. Everyone had good news, it seemed. Lots of jobs out there, I supposed, just none that were working out for me. Sheesh, this mass migration of Californians into Austin had really saturated the job market, and I just wasn't competitive enough. Maybe I *should* return to school.

I stared at the profiles of my former classmates, the ones who had been with me on numerous projects and who had gone on to exciting internships and successful careers across various media formats.

Veronica's post was front and center on my news feed. She'd just announced her huge promotion from production assistant to assistant writer! A huge leap indeed! The post had already garnered three hundred twenty likes.

Maybe when she was out with our former classmates on Friday night, she had been celebrating her newest accomplishment.

I took a deep breath and congratulated Veronica on her promotion. The woman was killing it, and I was glad for her. I added, in a private DM, that we should get together soon.

She immediately responded with a "thanks."

I smiled, sliding the app off my screen, and tucked my phone into my purse. Not quite the response I was hoping for . . .

Ping!

Hmm? I retrieved my phone. A message. From Veronica! I grinned. Just hearing from her made me so happy. I wanted every detail.

Veronica: Hey, girl! Thanks for the congrats! Thought texting would be faster, lol! How's it going? And yeah, let's meet up. I'm free the Sat after next if you want to get coffee and catch up? I was actually just thinking about you. It's been a couple of months since we chatted.

Isha: I love hearing from you! And YES to coffee that day. Things are . . . okay . . . on my end. Still trying to sell, ya know? Still loving your company?

Veronica: More than ever! Promotion helps, ha! Working as an assistant doing grunt work all that time really paid off thanks to the mentorship program I got into at work.

Isha: I'm so happy for you!! <3

Veronica: Thank you! Sorry to hear about your script. Hey. Are you still doing the freelance editing?

Isha: Yep!

Veronica: Getting a lot of work?

Isha: No. Trying to expand.

I added an arbitrary laughing emoji even as I frowned.

Veronica: The reason I was just thinking about you is because we have an opening for a copyeditor at my company. So . . . if you want, you can send me your resume or apply directly, and I'll tell my hiring manager to keep an eye out for your material.

Isha: Seriously? Would they even consider me?

Veronica: Yes! I already mentioned you to my boss, and he thought your background of copyediting and scriptwriting could be a good fit. And ya knooowwww . . . we are a film production company. So you could play the long haul like I did, and get your foot in the door. Let me know! Here's the link!

I blinked a few dozen times. Was this really happening? Veronica had been the elite student in our 400-level classes. She was perceptive and skilled. She'd already worked the bottom of the ladder at a film company and moved up to assistant after she graduated. When she said working the long haul to get to the position she now had, she *meant* it.

Veronica was Filipina, so we commiserated over some common points. Her parents had also seen her creative endeavors as a waste when both of her parents and all of her siblings were nurses with high-paying jobs. They'd given her a hard time, but now she had the income and official title to prove them wrong. Not that those things were the only things that mattered. She never gave up, and for her, that meant living on her own as a poor college graduate with her boyfriend in a tiny apartment, scrimping and saving.

She was, in the bluntest words, an inspiration.

I immediately clicked on the link, reviewed the job posting, and applied. Then texted Veronica. Aside from a thumbs-up, she didn't reply.

Eh. This was probably just another shot in the dark, according to my luck, but an internal referral could help.

With a yawn and a sudden wave of exhaustion, I eventually lay down with Rogue. She cuddled up to my side. It didn't matter if I'd slept three hours last night or ten, nap time was the best time.

My phone, muffled between blanket folds, rang in my ear. Ugh. What time was it?

My eyelids were heavy, and dragging myself out of sleep seemed like a battle to the death. It felt as if I'd slept for hours, but the blinds were open and daylight snaked in.

I lifted my phone to mute the caller, except I accidentally answered.

Maybe if I stayed still and quiet, they'd hang up.

"Hello?" a familiar, throaty voice spoke.

Rogue had her chin buried in the blankets, but her eyes were visible enough for me to see that she was curiously watching me. Her ears perked up at the sound of Tarik's deep voice. She even lifted her head. Yeah? Liked his voice? Apparently, so did my lady parts and the sudden drop in my gut. How did he sound so damn sexy on the phone? His voice was hoarse and gritty, what I imagined his voice sounded like when he first woke up.

"Isha? You there?"

Oh, right. He knew my name.

"Hi," I said, breathy . . . for some reason.

There was a brief pause before he went on. "This is Thirst-Trap."

"Oh my lord," I muttered, shoving my face into the pillow.

He chuckled. "You know, I overheard you call me that so many times, I can't even count."

I smiled into the phone and adjusted myself so that I lay on my stomach on the edge of the bed because of course my little six-pound dog took up three-quarters of the bed.

"Did you get my texts earlier?" he asked.

"Oh yeah. How *did* you get my proposal?"

"One of the waitresses found it underneath the bench seating when she was cleaning up after closing the other day. She left it in my office with a sticky note that said 'lost and found' and I didn't get a chance to look at it until this afternoon."

Huh. So that guy really *hadn't* taken my proposal? "No worries. You can just toss it out."

"Are you sure? Looks important. The flash drive, too?"

"Nothing terribly important," I replied, deflated.

"Are you all right?" he asked, concerned.

"Suppose that's relative."

"What's on your mind?"

"Are you . . . bartending me over the phone?"

"I guess so. What's up? What happened? And does it have anything to do with you two ending up at the security office?"

Well, at least he didn't mention the vomiting. "Don't really feel like talking about it, to be honest."

"Are you sure? I'm an excellent listener."

"Apparently! With your superhuman hearing."

He laughed. "You were actually pretty loud."

"Oh . . ." Heat rose to my face.

"If you don't want to talk about why you sound so down, do you want to talk about something else?"

"Like what?" I rolled onto my side and petted Rogue.

"This folder. I'd rather give it to you and let you dispose of it if you really don't want it, rather than trash it myself. I wouldn't feel right."

"Oh, now, see? I think you're just trying to get me to go to the pub again. I'm done with drinks for a while. Saturday was much too rough."

"I make nonalcoholic drinks, too."

"So . . . you *are* confessing to trying to get me to go there again."

"You caught me. I could meet you somewhere else, if you want."

Was he asking me out on a date, or was I reading too much into this? "Are you at work right now?"

"I'm in my office. Taking a break," he replied.

"I owe you a shirt, don't I?"

"Ah, yes. I only gave you a pub shirt to ensure that you'd

have to come back to return it. They're very pricey and rare, you know?"

I smiled. "I'm sure they are."

"How about you come down to return the shirt? If you're not going to come just to pick up your folder, that is."

"Seriously?"

"Yeah," he answered.

"You want that shirt back?" I asked, arching a brow.

"Did you toss it out?" he asked, sounding as offended as if I'd thrown out a kitten.

"No. Actually, it's washed and neatly folded."

"So . . . see you at four?"

I sighed. How had we gotten into this situation? "Persuasive, aren't you?"

"Yes. That was a nice shirt!"

"Won't you get into trouble?"

"With who?"

"Your boss? Interrupting your work. Again."

"Nah. I work for a real cool guy, thought you knew."

I smiled. "You sure do."

"So, you coming down?"

"Okay," I said after a moment of deliberating.

"Great! See you then."

I hung up the phone with a giant smile on my face and squealed. Oh! I grabbed the phone. I did hang up, didn't I? All right, cool. Cool. No big deal. He hadn't heard me squeal like a schoolgirl. I was just going to stop by for a few minutes, return the shirt, pick up and then promptly trash the proposal, and maybe take a drive around town. Maybe he could make me a to-go drink. I was in the mood for an Italian cream soda.

And then . . . we might never see one another again? That

was a sobering thought. I kind of, sort of, really liked him. And I had a feeling that he liked me, too. I just didn't know how much, if it was enough to keep talking.

It was ten past three. I had enough time to let Rogue out to potty and get ready before anyone came home and before traffic clogged up during rush hour. By now, the smell of vomit and dumpster had been washed out of my hair and skin like nobody's business. If I didn't smell like plumeria and waterfalls by now, then there was no hope.

My hair stayed in a messy top bun while I patted on light makeup to look more awake and less dazed. But yeah, also to look nicer. I opted for a tan faux suede miniskirt with matching boots and a black sweater that hugged my curves just right.

"Well, damn," I commented aloud when I checked out my reflection in the dresser mirror. I wasn't exactly aiming for sexy AF right now, but if this guy didn't drop his jaw at how put-together I could look when not a hot mess, then he needed glasses.

And yes, I opted for glasses. No contacts for me again. Ever.

On the way to the pub, I stopped by a bakery to get Tarik a better apology/thank-you gift. But it was also a habit I'd picked up from my mom. We never visited someone empty-handed. We always showed up with food.

Instead of a single, large cupcake, which had been delicious but consumed in a few man bites right before my eyes, I went to a local fave. This bakery made incredibly delectable tiny pies, both sweet and savory. He might finish these off in a few man bites, as well, but at least they were a bit more filling and a whole lot more thoughtful.

Tarik had me all figured out with drinks and now I tried to

figure out his tastes with tiny pies. He might appreciate something filling, and something to repay him for the salad: a spinach, mushroom, and ricotta pie. A Tex-Mex veggie pot pie that smelled divine and had cheese oozing out the top with tiny specks of peppers. On the sweet side, I bought cherry, key lime, apple bourbon caramel, and of course Texas two-step with decadent local pecans. These pies were gourmet and expensive as hell, but worth every dollar.

I would definitely need to find a job after this, though.

Chapter 19

With a box of tiny pies in my arms, the shirt folded neatly on top, and my purse hanging from one shoulder, I struggled to open the door to the pub and grill. I didn't want to put the box down on the dirty ground, but I also didn't want to tip it over and ruin the perfect pies.

Tarik saw me through the glass pane to the right of the entrance and jogged across the room to open the door.

"Thanks," I said, squeezing between him and the doorframe. He smelled as delicious as the pies.

He released the door behind me as I spun partway toward him. His gaze fell down the length of my body and dragged back up. His cheeks were tinged with a cute flush. He cleared his throat and took the box. "Let me get that. What's this?"

"Well, it's a shirt."

He smirked. "I mean the box underneath the shirt."

"Pies. To properly thank you for Saturday night and for calling me about the folder. I honestly thought this guy stole it on Saturday, or had mixed it with his folders and he thought I was lying about it being mine. So at least that mystery is solved. I won't go to my grave hating him and wondering what he did with my work."

"How's your ankle?"

"Better. Only hurts once in a while now," I answered, although it was a little swollen.

"That's good to hear. It's nothing serious?"

"No."

He walked ahead of me and cocked his chin toward the hallway. "Let's go to my office."

While the pub wasn't packed, it was busy enough with several customers eating or having drinks in their post-workday outfits. Bars always seemed like a nighttime or weekend thing, but it made sense that lots of people would need to unwind after hectic days in the office, particularly downtown.

We walked down the empty hallway and into his office. He closed the door behind me and set the box on his desk, next to a covered platter. In front of his desk were four different barstools.

"What are these? Trying out new styles?" I asked, drawn to the dark-cushioned stool with a footrest bar and a small back.

"Yeah. Thinking about some minor renovations. These are the top contenders," he replied.

I sat down. My butt felt incredibly welcomed on this one as I pushed against the footrest bar and gently spun around. I let out a giggle. "I like the spinny ones."

"I see that." He walked around the line of stools to stand in front of me, gripping the small, circular seat of the stool as it slowly stopped.

His thumb inadvertently grazed my thigh. A definite look

of shock lit his face at the same time I felt the same sort of shock ripple down my body and ignite at the minuscule spots where our flesh made contact.

Here was Tarik, standing over me, gripping the edge of this seat like he was about to break it in half, smelling like a man who'd just stepped out of a sudsy shower, and giving off enough heat to bake a cake.

"I . . . like this stool," I said.

"Oh yeah?"

"Ones with the back are hard to find but make all the difference," I rambled. "I could sit here forever with that little bit of support. The cushion is good. Not too soft, like it's old and worn, but not so firm that it hurts. The spin aspect is great. The footrest bars are helpful for shorter people. The colors are nice. And the height . . . is perfect."

Oh, why had I glanced down to see just how perfect the height was? I could've wrapped my legs around his waist and just . . . *mmm*!

I wanted to fan myself but kept my hands clasped in a tight ball on my lap. What was happening? Was he attracted to me? Was this a fleeting moment that could be easily ruined if I kissed him?

My skin was much too hot. I could feel my armpits pumping out sweat on manufacture overload.

Tarik smirked and released the seat. "I was thinking this one." He touched the seat beside me.

"It's ugly," I replied. "And has no back. Backs are important. Have you tested these?"

"Yes. These are my favorites."

"I mean have you had others test these? Specifically, women?"

"I've had the staff test. But now that you mention it, the

women did prefer your seat for the most part." He rubbed his jaw as if this decision would make or break his establishment. And he was utterly adorable for it.

"It's cute how seriously you're taking this."

He glanced at me midrub. "I'm cute, huh?"

"Thirst-Trap cute."

He laughed, revealing gorgeous teeth and the deep dimples that I'd missed so much.

"Here," I said, and jumped down to sit on his top-choice stool. "I'll be an extra tester. This is firmer and my butt isn't as welcomed as it was with the green one. But it does have the footrest bar, and that's extremely important for shorter people to hoist ourselves up on, but also to readjust while sitting and just have a place to rest our feet without them dangling in the wild. It spins halfway, which is okay. But let's say I wanted to turn from the bar and check out the band or the karaoke singers while I enjoyed my drink. Or do you prefer to have customers facing the bar the entire time to keep them drinking?"

"I do prefer to have them facing the bar."

"Tricky." I tested the others, but they didn't come close to the green one.

He then lifted a hand for me to sit on the nice leather swivel chair at his desk. I sank right in and practically disappeared.

"Like my chair?" he asked, pulling up a folding chair and sitting down kitty-corner to my right so that the covered platter took up more desk space for him than it did for me.

I laughed. "It's like it swallowed me whole. How are you this big?"

"We can trade chairs. My butt barely fits on this," he said with a chuckle, but he didn't make a move. Instead, he opened the box and swallowed with hunger.

"Yeah. Hard not to salivate when you see those," I commented, pleased.

"These are expensive," he said, noting the very specific and singular bakery that specialized in tiny pies. "You really shouldn't have."

"No. I really needed to. You did a lot for me. A cupcake wasn't going to cut it after all."

"Thank you. Did you want to split?" He held up one of the plastic forks from inside the box.

I gnawed on my lower lip, something that didn't go unnoticed by him. "They're for you, you know?"

"I can see it on your face how badly you want some."

"That clear, huh?"

"Yep." He handed me a fork. "You're drooling."

"No, I'm not." But I was! I mean, tiny pies were the best.

"Not sure if my drinks go with any of these, but we'll find out." He uncovered the platter, sliding a white napkin off two glasses on a serving tray. "It's mango with cardamom and lime and garnished with mint. Nonalcoholic."

I greedily took a sip and closed my eyes as the tropical delight sprouted across my tongue. "You can keep the pies. I'll just drink this."

He laughed, plowing a fork through the ricotta pie. "I love these pies. I don't typically get them except for special occasions because they're pricey. And of course, on Pi Day."

"Ah! So I guessed well enough. Did I get any of the flavors right?"

"Definitely. Can't go wrong with pecan pie or any variation thereof. This ricotta one is good, too."

I wrapped my hands around the tall glass and tapped the side, watching him and taking small sips to savor the drink.

"You actually brought the shirt back?" he asked in between bites.

"You told me to."

"I was joking to get you to return. I told you Saturday that you could keep it."

"Oh . . . well . . . I'll just take it back with me, then."

"Mmm. Before I forget, here's your folder." He pulled out the drawer between us and landed the folder on the desk.

I eyed it and asked, "Did you read it?"

"Just the first page to figure out who it belonged to and if there was any return information."

"Oh, sure. Makes sense."

"It's a script?" he asked, his eyebrows arching high with unabashed interest.

"Yes."

"That's cool! Are you a writer?"

"Mmm-hmm," I mumbled with trepidation, noting with great pain how I used to respond with enthusiasm before this past weekend. Excitement and pride had kept me going but had also dwindled over the past year.

"What's with the lack of enthusiasm? You writing porn or something?" he asked around a bite.

I guffawed. "No!"

"Nazi love?"

"What?" I spat.

"Then what? You seem indifferent."

I shrugged. "Most people don't get it. I get a superficial 'cool' or a nod of acknowledgment, but most don't care."

"I apologize if my 'cool' came out sounding superficial. Let me try that again." He cleared his throat, dropped his hands to his lap, and said effusively, "I think it's actually *incompre-*

hensibly amazing that you're a writer. I've never been creative, so to see someone who thinks that way and can create entire worlds from nothing is pretty damn inspiring."

"Oh. Thanks," I replied softly, not expecting such a genuine and uplifting comment, and now kicking myself for sounding like I'd called him out.

"Why would you want to trash your script?"

"It's not that I don't love my work, it's that it's getting painful."

"What do you mean?" he asked, and moved on to the next pie. If he could consume a large cupcake in a few bites, there was no reason why he wouldn't eat tiny pies just as quickly.

He lifted his chin as he waited for my answer. There was something about being this close to those mesmerizing green eyes that slowly unraveled me. "Does it have anything to do with Saturday night?"

I groaned, rubbing the back of my neck and pressing my fingers in when I discovered a sore spot. "Are you ever going to let that go?"

"No."

"Well, it's not nice to probe."

"Even if I came through for you several times?" He grinned as if he'd claimed checkmate.

"Even then . . ."

"Not that I'm trying to pry, and in no way feel that you owe me an explanation. Just . . . you sound so down at the mention of this script. You can unload on me, you know? If you want to. Um. Anyway." He leaned back. "I did save some for you."

I craned my neck and peered over the lip of the box at the half-eaten pies. "You just share your germs with people?"

"Oh! I'm so sorry! I should've cut them in half first. No. I don't expect you to eat after me."

I laughed. "It's okay. You don't have anything contagious, do you?"

"Nah. I even have my health history on my phone medical app if you need to see."

"Thought you didn't know me well enough to get into your medical history," I teased.

"Maybe we're getting closer?"

"I trust you. Besides." I jammed my fork into a pie. "I need something to settle my stomach if I'm going to tell you this sorrowful ride of mine to anywhere except scriptwriting success."

He pushed the box toward me, then leaned in, his forearms on the desk, and suddenly that much closer to my face. Why was it so hard to think straight with him being so close, with that charming lopsided smile of his and those perfectly sharp canines?

Well, I was real enough to admit that there was an undeniable attraction to him. No one could blame me. But once he heard my story, ya know, on top of him having seen me at my worst, then there was no way he'd ever be in the slightest bit attracted to me.

So here it went. I busied myself with pie and drinks while I relayed the severity of my lack of a career and what had transpired Saturday from pitch session to losing my agent to the brawl to the clown and the dumpster to the ill-advised trespassing and ending with the security office.

When I finally looked at him, expecting pity or amusement or plain ole disinterest, I found none of those things.

He was sitting back against the small folding chair, watch-

ing me with serious intent as if every word enraptured him like
the greatest story ever told. His brows knitted in concentra-
tion, his eyes alive with fascination, his lips parted as if he had
comments.

I swallowed, bracing for his words. "What?"

"You're giving up?"

I shrugged. "For a while, maybe. It's exhausting and dis-
couraging and just . . . heartbreaking and soul-rendering. It's
as if validation hinges on someone buying my work, and if no
one does, then I feel that the work is worthless, and by exten-
sion *I'm* worthless."

He sat quietly for a minute, to the point where the whirl of
the A/C haunted the room and the sound of my swallowing
echoed right alongside the gushing, frigid air.

"Oh. Shouldn't you get back to work?"

He waved off my comment. "It's fine. I have enough staff
for the moment."

I looked around at the large office made small by the desk,
chairs, barstools, shelves, and boxes. "I was here Saturday
night because Seth said Matthew McConaughey was going to
be here. He's my former professor from UT and I thought he
could help me. Does your family really know him?"

"My grandparents are friends with him. It's a long but
funny story. My grandma tells it better."

I smiled at his smile.

"You know? I'd wanted to own a restaurant forever. I kept
getting denied by banks or outbid by other buyers. My parents
didn't think it was a good idea and wouldn't support me in it,
especially with a bar attached. There's too much competition
in Austin, particularly on Sixth Street. The banks wouldn't
give me good enough loans. When I was ready to give up, at

least for a long while, my grandparents told me to try one more time."

He smiled as he spoke fondly of them. "They always say, well, you never know what might've happened if you'd tried one more time. No surprise that the banks wouldn't give me the right loan, but my grandparents surprised me by giving me a large sum. I'd never asked them for money. I'd never asked anyone outside of the banks. They just did it. It took me about six years to finally get this place, and another two before it returned revenue. They say that typically new businesses fail within the first two years, so if I was making a profit by then, I was doing well. Even if I wasn't making money hand-over-fist, which I wasn't."

He leaned forward, passion bouncing through him. "When I bought this place, it ended up having a lot more issues than what we'd thought. Black mold. Broken pipes. Rowdy neighbors. I had to renovate, and that cost a lot of money. My grandparents gave me more. Never asked them to. But they always believed in me. I kept them up to date on everything, since I felt I at least owed them that much. They never judged me or made rules or took over decisions regarding this business, only offered advice. They gave space but made sure I knew they were always there for me. I went through three bad chefs and at least two entire staff turnovers before I got it right. Now it's a good return investment, and suddenly my parents are proud."

I scoffed. "Wait, are you Indian? Because that sounds like some genuine Asian parenting."

"No," he said with a laugh and went on to explain, "I'm part Egyptian, part French Canadian."

"Ah."

"But the point I was making is that it can take a long time. The fact that I had a successful business before thirty is a miracle. It took years of trying, of failing, and then years of fixing. It took years of taking breaks but not giving up. I always think, if I'd never tried one more time, then I wouldn't be where I am today. If I didn't have the unfailing support from my grandparents, I wouldn't be here today. I ended up paying them back, finally, a few months ago. They didn't expect it, didn't want to accept. But I gave it back to them with interest. Not because I owed them, but because I wanted to show my appreciation and do what I can to ensure their golden years are good."

My heart warmed at his story, at his endurance. It was true what they said, that success was an iceberg. People on the outside only saw the tip of success, when beneath the waters was a mountain of obstacles they'd overcome.

"Wow. What an amazing story. And amazing grandparents. They must be very proud. Have they seen what you've done with this place?"

He grinned extra hard, which had me grinning. "Yes. They come by all the time. They call ahead to let me know, and I always make sure they have prime seating. Every staff member knows them, so they get seated and served immediately. It's an incredible thing to see their pride. But you know what? They've always let me know that I make them proud, regardless of this place."

"That's so sweet!"

"They're wonderful. Sometimes failure is hard, especially when we keep getting hit by it. Sometimes all we need is a break to get ourselves back in the game. Maybe you could take a temporary break instead of a permanent one? You just never know what'll happen the next time you try."

I gnawed on my lip for a few seconds before asking, "Can I confide in you about something else?"

"Of course."

I took a deep breath and pushed around crumbs as I acknowledged one of the hardest things to say aloud, even more so than admitting my career struggles. I wasn't sure why I was telling him about my parents' abysmal disappointment in me and their plot to involve others for an intervention. I just . . . I don't know . . . had to tell someone.

But I found myself relaying everything with ease. Tarik was a great listener and alleviated any tension or awkwardness. He had seen the worst of me but didn't make me feel that he had. Plus, he wasn't connected to my family or community, and I had the choice of never seeing him again. Which always made things easier.

At the end of my confession, when he didn't say anything, I blew out a breath, dragging my eyes to meet his. He was watching me with intensity. If he didn't think badly of me before, he surely had to now.

"I know," I whispered. "I'm acting like a child, therefore my parents are treating me like one."

He slowly shook his head. "That's not what I think."

I scoffed. "Coming from you? You're mature and have your life together. This whole adulting thing? You're doing it well."

He rubbed his chin and then took a sip of his drink. "No one's perfect. Every adult has something to work on. We all have our vices. You get carried away with drinking once in a while. Does that make you worthless? A catastrophe? No. Maybe it's something that you have to work on, but we all have something to work on. You took a risk and went after your dreams instead of a quote-unquote proven path and it hasn't paid off yet. Does that make you a failure? No. Every step forward, no matter how big or small, is a step toward your future self."

I chewed on the inside of my cheek.

"It's in the eye of the beholder, right? Success? What we want to be and what we should be? I wasn't successful to my parents until this place made a return, but that doesn't mean I was worthless until that point. It took a million steps to get here. Maybe your million steps are almost done, and you just need a few more to get there."

"That's incredibly inspiring."

He cracked a smile. "I know."

I laughed as we both relaxed.

He went on, "I think your parents mean well, but they obviously don't have any idea what this is doing to you. It sounds like they love you and support you, even if it's not all for writing. So maybe you need to have a talk and be open and frank." He swallowed. "Something I wish I would've done with my parents. They'd created a toxic, suffocating environment because they're the parents and always right? I suppose. Probably would've saved me a lot of heartache and self-doubt and anxiety if I knew how to stand up to my parents."

I couldn't imagine someone with the confidence and stability of Tarik being unable to stand up to someone, much less his parents.

He ran a hand over his hair, laughing. "Not to get too intense. Wow. Sorry."

"No. No, don't be. I really appreciate this conversation and you being so honest," I replied, mulling over the word *toxic*. No one wanted to think critically of their dear loved ones, yet that word stuck out and jammed itself into my thoughts. It had such a volatile meaning. Was my family being toxic?

"You don't have others to talk to?"

"My cousin, but he's heard it already. I don't want him to get tired of it."

"I'm sure he wouldn't."

I sighed. "I've taken up enough of your time. Thanks so much, really, for everything. I don't even know how you're this kind."

I reached for the folder when he asked, "Are you really just going to throw that away?"

"I mean, that was the plan, but maybe I'll hold on to it. Don't worry, I do have backup copies."

"Do you mind, if you're comfortable with it, if I read it?"

I paused and looked into a pair of imploring and, perhaps, the most genuine eyes I'd ever seen when it came to someone wanting to read my work. I nodded and slid the folder across the table to him.

"I'll have it back to you," he said. "Thanks for trusting me with your words."

I grinned.

"Sappy?" he asked.

"A little," I teased. But endearing was more like it.

I reached down, placing the shirt into my purse, before taking a final sip of my drink. I wasn't letting any of it go to waste.

Tarik placed his forearms on the desk again and leaned toward me. How could he be so casually this close to me? My heart rammed against my ribs, and I fought the desire to glance at his mouth. But there I went, my gaze dropping to his lips when he asked, "Are you dating anyone?"

Good thing I'd already swallowed my swig of this near-perfect drink. I scoffed, sliding my finger down the cold, slippery surface of the glass. "Yeah, right."

"What does that mean?"

I shook my head. "Nothing."

"'Nothing' kind of sounds like definitely something."

"You probably wouldn't get it."

"Try me."

His closeness had my head reeling, despite there being an entire desk corner between us, despite there being a vast, open space around us. The heat of his body prowled across the expanse of space and wrapped around me in pulsating waves, making my skin flare up like a furnace on overdrive.

I blinked a few times and pushed myself back into the reality of what he was truly asking me. I tapped the glass, now filled only with pebbles of melting ice, and joked, "I mean, I barely know you to tell you my dating history."

"Then maybe we should start combining some things on our to-do list. Food, histories."

"Are . . . you asking me out?"

"I guess I am."

"Why would you, a man who has his life together, ever be interested in me, someone who clearly has a lot of work to do?"

"I mean, the fraction of you that you think is imperfect isn't the sum of you. I'd just . . . really like to get to know more of you. No pressure whatsoever. If you're not interested, I understand," he said nervously and swallowed. The movement of his throat had my gaze locked.

My lips quirked into a one-sided smile. He was beyond sweet. "As in a date?"

He nodded. "As in a date."

I almost, *almost* asked if he was certain he wanted a date with someone like me—given that I'd vomited all over his back alley—but then his gaze fell to my mouth, and I swallowed down those words. Why ruin the moment? Why sabotage what could be? He flashed that grin again, and my entire body tingled. Like wanna-get-caught-in-this-trap kind of tingling. Either I was extremely attracted to Tarik or I'd hit the fertile section of my cycle. Both made reasonable sense in that my chemical rage was tilting toward overdrive.

Or maybe, just maybe, the sexy-as-hell look he was giving me had my ovaries exploding like cellular fireworks. I swear, if we kept staring at each other like this, we might never leave this office.

Chapter 20

I stood in my room the following morning, hands on my hips, my stare intently focused on the blaring whiteboard. I deliberated over options. I'd had lots of time to think as the events of the weekend clarified and settled. Yes, I'd made some *stupid* decisions driven by depression and desperation and drinking, but talking it out with Tarik (who was I kidding . . . Thirst-Trap forever) helped compartmentalize things. I couldn't give up, but I had to make extraordinary changes.

First up, applying to every new position that popped up within my industry, even if the position didn't have to do with writing or creating. I might've been too vain to apply for an IRS desk job, but I wasn't too proud to start from the bottom at a production company of any kind.

Second, I had to start looking for places to live that were actually affordable. Thanks to skyrocketing rent, my search pushed me farther and farther out of town, even past bordering areas that had also exploded with an influx of population, and into the bowels of the country.

I tapped my chin and wondered why I restricted myself to Austin. It might not go over well with my parents to know that I was moving out again, but it would be easier to explain if I found work outside Austin. There was nothing really keeping me here aside from Rohan and maybe Tarik. But Tarik was new and there was no safe betting on a guy. I couldn't stay because of him.

Additionally, I applied for several positions at various film production companies in L.A. and New York as an assistant and many others as remote work. A sense of accomplishment and moving forward had me feeling all sorts of giddy. But I knew better. This was the hopeful high before rejections and ghosting hit, deflating optimism like Pennywise popping that red balloon.

I would, when I was up to it, begin applying to pitchfests and contests and look for a new agent. Who knows? I might even get inspired again to write the next script. Until then, and as always, I had to keep hustling. I had just enough in my bank account to rent a place on my own for a short while, to get out of this mental pit. If things worked out, my little apartment could come with a nook in front of a window, an optimal place to be creative.

Let's see, let's see. Who did I know who needed a roommate? Was there anyone outside Austin? Think, think, think.

I texted Veronica to ask if she knew anyone. She immediately replied.

Veronica: Yes! I might. I know a lot of people in Austin and NY, but have to think who might be looking. Hey, sorry that it

took so long to respond the other day; have to get ready for
three weeks of meetings just to catch up with the new job.
Didn't think I'd ever have homework again, but here I am. Not
that I'm complaining. I'm excited and want to show my best.
Anyway! I was about to text you before your message came.
Good thing you applied, because my boss was sort of waiting
for you to. Haha!

Her text was accompanied by an email ping from her production company wanting to set up an interview. My heart
pitter-pattered and I had to tell myself to calm down. This
wasn't the first time someone was nice enough to go to bat for
me for a position. Every time I got excited, confident, things
never worked out.

I carefully read and reread the email before clicking on the
link to set up a virtual appointment. Jobs like these oftentimes
required a few rounds of interviews and dreaded tests. While
I didn't mind behavior and cognitive tests, I would never understand why applicants were given a math portion for positions that had nothing to do with math. And contrary to
popular belief, not all Asians excelled in it. I certainly didn't.

After responding to Veronica to let her know about the
interview happening tomorrow afternoon, I ate a snack and
relaxed before diving into yep . . . ya guessed it . . . applicant
testing. Just behavioral this time with a questionnaire gauging
creativity.

In order to fully avoid my parents until my plan could become more concrete, and also because I knew they hadn't forgotten about that intervention, I made sure to leave the house
by six, before they returned from work.

Since Rohan tended to be busy during the week with over-time, I decided to get some fresh air, taking Rogue with me. I packed my tote with water, snacks, and Rogue essentials, and headed out. As much as I loathed going downtown, I always enjoyed visiting campus. Maybe the days of unfiltered dreams might spark my soul back to life.

So here I was, holding my arthritic miniature Yorkie, star-ing at Littlefield Fountain with its iconic horses and the UT Tower looming just beyond.

"It's too hot for you to be on the ground," I muttered to Rogue, and kissed her head as she tried to scramble out of my arms. She probably wanted to mark this entire fountain as hers. So territorial.

Even this late in the day, there were a lot of people around, but I, for once, didn't mind. I didn't mind the crowds and en-ergy of my beloved UT. Clusters of three and four students and staff and business folks chatted or strolled by, their shoulders slack at the end of a work/class day.

Not far from here, a good walk and a half for younger me, had been my classes with Matthew McConaughey. If only he still taught here, if only I had a way to access him through the school like a normal person. It had been easy back then, and now I was kicking myself for not staying connected with him. Assuming he'd wanted to stay connected to his stu-dents.

Hmm. What if . . . there was a way to get his contact infor-mation through the system? Surely the university database kept records.

Agh! No! Stop it! That was madness, and I wasn't even drunk!

Although . . . how difficult would it be to get into the school system and find his email address or phone number? Was it just sitting there, gathering electronic dust, waiting to be found and used?

No, no, no! That was a criminal offense. Even if I knew someone who had access to the faculty information, that was a line that couldn't be crossed.

I wiped beaded sweat from the back of my neck when my phone pinged.

Thirst-Trap: Afternoon.

I smiled up at the monumental bronze statues of galloping horses and adjusted Rogue in the crook of my arm so I could reply.

Isha: Hi.

Thirst-Trap: Whatcha up to?

Isha: Staring at bronze balls.

Thirst-Trap: Sure. Sounds like an interesting hobby.

Isha: Haha! I'm at UT looking at the fountain statue.

Thirst-Trap: Are you by yourself?

Isha: Why? You want to join me?

Thirst-Trap: Possibly. Definitely.

Here I stood, at the base of airy fountain mist, grinning like a fool as waves of people moved past me.

Isha: Well, I AM on a date.

Thirst-Trap: Oh yeah? Who did I lose out to?

Isha: My child. Her name's Rogue.

Thirst-Trap: That's an interesting name for a child.

Isha: Child/dog.

Rogue started to twist and turn in my arms, most likely having seen another dog nearby. I gently readjusted her and frowned that Tarik hadn't responded. I wouldn't mind if he wanted to join us.

A low growl sounded from Rogue as she squirmed to turn her head, jostling me in the process, even head-butting me trying to check out something behind us.

"Calm down," I told her.

"She's probably trying to warn you of approaching danger," a deep, gritty voice said in my ear.

I yelped at the same time Rogue launched herself off my chest and went for the man behind me. She'd almost made it into attack position, but I snatched her just in time and hugged her to me, turning from him so she wouldn't see him.

I willed my racing heart to slow down and glanced over my shoulder at a sweaty Tarik standing with his hands up in surrender. He was wearing the hell out of a damp green T-shirt and black basketball shorts.

"I didn't mean to scare y'all," he promised.

I kept Rogue secure to my chest as I turned and gently slapped his arm. "Yes, you did!"

He laughed. "I'm sorry."

"What! My dog almost killed you!"

He cracked up even harder, his face turning all sorts of red, all while Rogue snarled and kept her eyes trained on him. She had the look of death and total annihilation in her eyes.

"Were you stalking us? Pretending like you weren't anywhere near while you watched and waited for the perfect moment?"

"Yes," he said matter-of-factly. "I saw you but wanted to make sure it was you."

I let my shoulders slacken. "Congrats on succeeding in surprising us."

"Rogue saw me coming a mile away," he commented, but Rogue wasn't falling for his charming looks or sensual voice.

I patted her against me like burping a baby and ignored the ache in my right breast from where she'd launched off. A paw-kick bruise wasn't the sort of action my breasts ever anticipated.

"Not at all happy to see me?" he asked, taking a step toward us.

My frowning façade broke. "You're sweaty."

"I thought women liked man sweat," he teased, acting like he was coming in for a hug as I turned from him.

"Ew! No!" Although, secretly, hell yes. There was a hefty dose of sexy pheromones wafting off him and if we weren't in public with campus police rolling by, we'd be in trouble.

His sweaty chest ever so lightly touched my back as he

lowered his head to my ear, the one farthest from a growling Rogue, who was about to lose her crap.

I scrunched up my shoulder and backed away from his teasing. Not because I wanted to, because the good lord knew better, and definitely not because I didn't want his sexy sweat all over me, but for the sake of Rogue, who was now shaking with frenzied attack energy.

I cradled her and cooed to her and snuggled with her to get her to calm down.

"She really hates me?" Tarik asked, hurt dripping from his tone, as if Rogue had been the love of his life and had slashed ties. "Dogs usually love me."

"Not when you try to scare their mama," I replied, my back still to him.

From the corner of my eye, his arm appeared, as if he might hug me this time. Instead, he offered his hand to Rogue. She didn't sniff or bite. She simply glared at him.

Mm! It was her formidable *I'll cut a bitch* stare. She had enough practice with her toys and was looking to draw blood.

"I'm sorry, Rogue," he told her.

"She'll be fine," I promised with a hefty sigh as she began to calm against my chest. "I should get her out of the sun. She's always happier with food and water. Do you want to sit with us?"

"I'd love to."

We walked around the large fountain and up the steps onto the South Mall, a sprawling courtyard between the fountain and the tower. I limped on the last step, an abbreviated bolt of pain surging up my ankle.

Tarik lifted a hand as if to catch me by the waist before I

steadied in a nanosecond. He didn't touch me and retracted his arm, asking, "Your ankle?"

"Yeah."

"Did you RICE it?"

"Hmm?"

"Ya know: rest, ice, compress, elevate?"

"Oh, nah. I took some ibuprofen. It'll be fine." Although, dumb me. I really should've applied ice and kept it elevated. Hungover Isha wasn't thinking about it, to be honest. And as much as I'd slept, I safely presumed that counted as enough elevation.

Aside from the steps, the level ground dismissed any up and down that could aggravate my ankle, which thoroughly helped.

There weren't a lot of students sitting around between classes or meeting people at this time of day, which gave us first pickings of shaded areas. First, I checked for birds in branches before choosing a tree. We were *not* getting pooped on today! When I'd ascertained the perfect location, I dropped my purse and sat down, securing Rogue in my lap.

We sprawled out on the grass on the South Mall, flanked by the Six-Pack, as clouds rolled overhead to provide extra relief from the sun. Tarik stretched his long legs in front of him, feet spread apart, and leaned back on his hands.

"Nice legs," I teased.

"My eyes are up here, you know?"

He glanced at Rogue, who gave him serious side-eye shade, and quirked a smile. "She's protective, huh?"

"Extremely. Don't let her small size and adorable bark mislead you. She'll go straight for the throat."

She let a low growl rumble through her chest when he leaned toward her, the sound sending vibrations through my hands.

"Aw, be nice," I said, cuddling against her. "This is Thirst-Trap. Don't you recognize his voice from the phone? You liked his voice before."

"Did she?"

"She was absolutely mesmerized."

He cautiously, slowly lifted his hand to her again. This time, she sniffed. When she finished a full deconstruction of his scent, she dropped her lower jaw and panted so that her tongue stuck out. And suddenly, she'd transformed from attack dog to utter adorableness.

"I'm dead," he said, as mesmerized by her as she was by him. "She just killed me with cuteness."

I smiled and watched their intrigued interaction. Rogue was a sweet girl, but she'd never let down her guard for strangers as quickly as she had for Tarik. And Tarik? Dare I think that he might be in love with her?

"Were you out jogging when you spotted me?"

"Yeah. I live nearby but can't jog in the morning when it's much cooler because I'm asleep. I have to get in some exercise before work and try to catch the shadiest parts. Which is on campus." He wiped glistening sweat from his brow and neck.

"Oh! Would you like some water?" I asked, loosening my hold on Rogue to sift through my tote. She went limp on my lap, resting her chin on my thigh to watch Tarik. The girl was practically in love with him, too.

"That'd be great," he said, and took the extra water from me. He drank half the bottle on the first swig.

I set out Rogue's travel dish, pouring water into one side and a few kibble into the other, then sanitized my hands when she crawled off my lap to sit on the grass at my feet. She lapped water and ate and then lay down on her stomach to watch a butterfly in the near distance, her plump behind facing us.

"I also have snacks!" I said with a grin.

Tarik seemed pleased when I presented him with a container of cheese cubes and roasted almonds. He sanitized his hands before sharing, which earned him extra points.

"Food, drinks, and a view? Can I consider this a date?" he asked, popping an almond into his mouth.

I pushed down rising nervousness and nodded. "You can buy next time."

He chuckled. "Sounds like a plan."

He turned to me and said, "You know you just agreed to go on a date with me. I mean, for a second time."

Oh! I had, hadn't I? Well, there was no backing out of it now. "I don't know if you can top this date, to be honest."

"It is pretty amazing."

He dared to pet Rogue and she let him. She even rolled onto her side for a belly rub. Shameless!

"See? Dogs love me," he declared. "Is her name where I think it's from? Marvel?"

"Are you one of those guys into comics?"

"Quite possibly one of the biggest Marvel fans out there."

Be still my heart. "Rogue is named after Rogue from X-Men. But to be clear, I'm the biggest Marvel fan out there and I have an autographed drawing to prove it."

He held his hands up. "Can't dispute that."

I glanced around as a breeze swept through and sighed. Nostalgia tackled me in the gut as the excitement and energy from college days swam through my memories. I was momentarily thrust back to a time when I was carefree and happy and beheld an entire future chasing my passion as obtainable and without blemish. I'd never thought I would end up being this fraught with pessimism and failure.

"I really miss campus days," I muttered.

"Me, too. They were good times."

"Did you attend UT?"

He poked a thumb at himself and declared, "Proud Longhorn alum. Majored in business. Thought about going for my MBA, but the master's students I knew were all pretentious assholes."

I coughed on my water. "I mean, well . . . it's a prestigious program."

He tilted his head to the side. "But no one has to be a jerk about it."

"Do you regret not going?"

"No. I got out of corporate America and bought the bar. It was the better decision for me."

"My parents would beg to disagree."

He shrugged. "So would mine. But it's not their blood pressure going through the roof trying to work in an office."

"I'm glad you found, pursued, and thrived with your calling."

"Thanks. Me, too. You'll be thriving soon, too," he added, nudging my shoulder with his. "It all started here, right? One of the best universities in the country with classes taught by one of the best actors in the country."

I almost, *almost* opened my mouth to spew a ludicrous plan of getting into UT's database to track down Matthew McConaughey but stopped myself just in time. Wouldn't want to scare him off because he thought I was off my axis.

Tarik and I both leaned back, our hands in the grass, and watched the stretch of land ahead of us. A funnel of buildings to the end of campus, disrupted only by the fountain and a line of trees. This was, hands down, one of the most iconic and scenic spots on campus.

I didn't have to look down to notice how close our hands were to each other on the lawn when his finger caressed mine. Such a soft, fleeting, innocent brush that sent raging butterflies through me. I hadn't felt this giddy since high school, or this turned on since we were last in Tarik's office. Maybe, just maybe, even if my career didn't take off the way I wanted or if I had to eventually change gears from my bigger-than-life dreams, maybe I had . . .

I sucked in a breath. Could I dare think it? Could I even mutter the thought in the recesses of my mind? Had I found someone who liked me in this vast, messy life of mine?

"I have to get ready for work soon," Tarik said, solemnly breaking our perfect serenity.

My phone pinged with an email notification right as he moved away to sit up. "What a shame," I told him as my gaze flitted to my screen.

"What's the smile for?"

"Oh!" Was I smiling? I guess I was! Relief and excitement stormed through my words when I replied, "My college friend, who works at a production company, recommended me for a position with her boss. I have a virtual interview with them tomorrow."

"Congrats!" He nudged my shoulder again with his. "I told you. Thriving soon."

"Thanks!" I replied as I clicked on the scheduling link and confirmed the interview. There was no way to ignore how badly I needed this, and there was no way to escape the hope bubbling in the pit of my soul, despite knowing how devastating the blow would be if this job didn't land.

As if Tarik sensed my anxiety like heat fumes rising from scorched Texas summer sidewalks, he said, "Since your schedule is about to get booked, should I try to slide into a time slot now?"

"Depends," I said.

"Oh yeah? On what?" The corner of his mouth tilted upward.

Why was it impossible to not stare at his mouth? How obvious could I be? "Do you like pizza?"

His lips curled up higher into that lopsided smile, showing those perfect, pointed canines. "There's an exceptional pizzeria not far from here. Slices bigger than your face. Tomorrow is a slow night for us. I can meet you there?"

"Sounds like you're going in for the official date."

"Or maybe I just really, really want to know how your interview goes."

My skin warmed. It was going to go great because put-together Isha was confident, especially virtually. And put-together Isha knew how everything was riding on this.

Chapter 21

I hadn't been on a date in a grievously long time—did people even meet in person anymore?—but leaving an interview where I didn't embarrass myself left me in a good place. This time, I remembered not to stand up for any reason and give my breasts or crotch any screen time. The last time I had a virtual interview, I stood up to get something and had forgotten that I was wearing short shorts. I made sure to wear slacks this time just in case.

Plus, it helped that I was on my merry way out the door to both avoid my parents and see Tarik. Yes, the man had me feeling all sorts of ways. If only Mummie could see me now . . . not wearing sweatpants and making an effort!

I tugged down on my miniskirt over tights on the sidewalk and took a moment to breathe, letting my muscles relax before putting myself in front of Tarik again. When I was ready, when the shaking had subsided, I pulled back my shoulders and moved ahead.

The only parking spot to be found was a few blocks from the famous pizzeria, which was fine. It was nice to get a little walk and a little movement for my ankle as it slowly healed.

It was rush hour with migraine-inducing loads of traffic, both cars and pedestrians. I was glad to have found a parking spot where I did and enjoyed discovering new places on my trek. Like this boba tea and snow dessert shop and a place that served only baked potatoes. Carbs had never smelled so good.

Up ahead, the pizzeria appeared with a neon green-and-red sign. I'd looked up the restaurant on my phone and found that it had high ratings, a ton of positive reviews and awards, and had even been featured on local TV and in magazines. I expected the prices to match the praise.

Inside, the place smelled divine. Open fire pits cooked pizzas and breads and desserts to perfection. Fresh salads and sides filled up bowls. Entire pizzas sat on metal pedestals in the centers of tables. And was that a tiny individual s'mores grill set someone was eating over? Why yes. I knew what *I* was having for dessert.

The wait was another fifteen minutes, so I put us down for two and walked back outside to get some air and catch Tarik on the way in, if nothing else than to make sure this was indeed the right place.

Rohan: Whatcha doing? Feeling better?

Isha: Definitely, thanks! Slept on it. Talked it out. About to get pizza.

Rohan: You didn't invite me?

Isha: Thought you'd had enough of me after last weekend.

Rohan: No such thing as too much Isha. Cuz you the ish.

I laughed. Oh my lord. This boy . . .

Isha: LOL. I haven't ordered yet. There's a wait. Thirst-Trap invited me to try it.

Rohan: I seeeeee. He's making his move.

Isha: You're more than welcome to join. You can impress your soon-to-be boss?

Rohan: Third wheel to you and Thirst-Trap? Nah.

Isha: LOL! Want me to bring you a slice, then?

Rohan: Sure. You know what I like. No biggie, though, I'm making dabeli. But . . . uh . . . I understand if you get too BIZZAY . . .

Isha: Eh. In that case, can you stop by my house and take Rogue out?

Rohan: And be an enabler?

Isha: Of what? Getting . . . BIZZAY?

Rohan: LMAO! I mean drinking.

Isha: No drinks! He made me nonalcoholic drinks, and they were even better than alcoholic ones. It's my way now.

Rohan: OK. Get your thirst quenched. Just don't tell me about it.

Isha: Omg. Bye!

Rohan had me cracking up in the middle of bustling crowds. While we were adults and he was my bro, it was just a little weird to joke about intimate things with my guy cousin. But still amusing.

I slipped my phone into my purse and glanced up. Tarik strolled toward me looking gorgeous, glowing in the early evening. I bit my lip, loving how my body reacted to just seeing him. My heart fluttered in my chest, butterflies danced in my belly, and my skin flushed a full degree warmer. And then my entire body roared to furnace levels when his gaze skimmed the length of my body.

He seemed to instinctively mumble "Damn" under his breath. "You look very beautiful," he said instead.

"I know," I replied. "So do you."

"I try. What was so funny?" he asked, stopping in front of me, his hands in his jacket pockets. Oh, such a delectable height. Something about a handsome guy towering over me, smiling down like the sun, and making my goodies tingle had my knees ready to buckle. Good lord, was I living in a rom-com?

But nothing like the thought of my family to void all sultry images. "My cousin. The one I was here with on Saturday. Rohan. He loves pizza."

"I know Rohan," Tarik said with a laugh. "He has a good sense of flavor."

"How would you know?" I prodded.

"I believe my brother picked Rohan as a final runner-up for taking over my menu. I haven't tried anything from him yet, but Seth raves about his dishes."

I slowly smiled. At this very moment, Rohan was making his famous dabeli from scratch. He was baking tiny slider buns after meticulous proofing, boiling and mashing potatoes, roasting and adding aromatic spices, buttering and grilling those buns, smothering them in both spicy and sweet chutney, and topping them with peanuts and pomegranate seeds with a sprinkling of diced onions and cilantro. My mouth was watering.

"What's that look?" Tarik inquired.

"You won't regret hiring Rohan."

He held his hands up. "I didn't say anything about hiring. I don't want to disappoint you if things don't work out."

"I know. It's business, and no favoritism."

"Glad you understand."

"But let's just say, your taste buds aren't ready for what Rohan can cook."

He cocked an eyebrow, his chin leveled so that he had to lower his gaze to meet mine. "Is that so?"

"Seth knows what he's doing. Expanding the menu the right way will have your returns exploding."

"I look forward to trying his food."

"Cuisine," I corrected. "It's a level beyond mere food."

He leaned toward me. "Well, now you've raised my expectations sky high."

I flinched. I hoped I hadn't ruined Rohan's chances by being honest. I sighed and tapped his chest. "You're not ready."

He laughed and asked, "Shall we go in?"

He opened the door for me, sending a whiff of cinnamon-laced cologne. We'd sat at a cozy table for two next to the window when he asked, "How was the interview?"

"It went well. The fact that I managed not to make a fool of myself for once says a lot."

"When will you hear back?"

"They said soon. They're looking to fill the position ASAP, and my friend had already talked me up to them. I'm trying not to get my hopes up in case it doesn't work out, and I'm sure there will be another interview or test."

"Test?" He arched a brow.

"I did pre-interview cognitive tests. The position is for copy-editing, so I assume they want me to prove my skills and will have me copyedit a sample."

"Feeling confident?"

I nodded. For the first time in a long time, I felt assured. At least for a job that had little to do with screenwriting. Tarik would never know about my spreadsheet detailing two-hundred-plus failed job interviews.

We ordered from our pretty and voluptuous waitress, who couldn't seem to pry her gaze off my handsome date. *Date* sounded surreal and otherworldly, and for a moment it made me forget how spectacular a man Tarik was. What was he doing with a girl like me?

Tarik was right about this place. Pizza slices bigger than my face. We shared a cheese pizza. It seemed like a simple thing: dough, sauce, cheese. But together, the flavors were a complex symphony on my tongue.

We watched others walk by outside and laughed at the awkwardness in which I tried to manage such a cheesy slice. How far could cheese stretch!

"You've got it all over your chin," Tarik said, reaching over the table to gently wipe dribbles of cheese or marinara from my face.

"Oh my lord," I muttered, grabbing a napkin to blot my chin. "This is so good. Rohan *would* love this. I should get him a slice to go."

He smiled. "It's sweet that you get along so well with your family."

"Yeah. He's essentially my brother from another mother."

He laughed.

I sat back and patted my belly. I couldn't possibly take another bite, yet I found myself longingly looking at a neighboring table with their cute little iron grill surrounded by big marshmallows, chocolate squares, and graham crackers.

"You want dessert?" Tarik asked.

"How can you tell?"

He smacked his lips. "Got it."

"How are you even hungry?"

He nodded at the waitress when she turned from another customer and caught her eye. "I'm not starving, but we've been here for an hour. Plenty of time to work up an appetite for dessert."

Gosh, an hour already? How time flew when one was in his presence.

"You want another pizza?" Tarik asked.

"No!"

"I can order another one. At least one for you to take to Rohan."

"No. He can have this one slice."

He pointedly glared at the partially eaten slice on my plate. "That's doing him so wrong."

The waitress stopped at our table and asked, "Can I get you anything else?"

Tarik nodded at me, and I leaned in on my arms against the table and watched the waitress watching Tarik. She just couldn't take her eyes off him, and he knew. His lips twitched as I smiled. Was he uncomfortable with that sort of attention?

"I just want s'mores. Do you want to split them?" I asked him.

He leaned toward me, his hands beneath the table as he touched the very edge of my knee in the briefest of seconds. "I love s'mores."

He ordered s'mores for us to share and a small cheese pizza to go for Rohan.

"Got it," the waitress said, and sauntered off.

Tarik said, "I'll have to make you my famous s'mores martini one day. Nonalcoholic, if you'd prefer."

"That doesn't even sound good."

He grimaced as if I'd stabbed him in the back. "Ouch. Have I ever made you a drink that you didn't fall madly in love with?"

"That sounds like infatuation. Love doesn't behave that way."

"Know so much about love, huh?"

I shrugged. "Eh."

He crossed his arms. "All right. We've had food, and dessert is on the way. Back to my original question that you've not answered: are you dating anyone?"

"I thought this was a date?" I countered, unable to maintain eye contact.

"You know what I mean."

"Are *you* dating anyone?" I looked at him, which felt like a mistake. Now I was sitting here in the full breadth and glory of those intense green eyes.

"No. Are you asking me if I want to?"

I laughed. "Do you even have time to date? Seems like you work a lot."

"You've known me for five days. As far as you know, I've only worked for five days my entire life."

"Hmm . . ."

"Tell me about you."

I sucked in a breath and admitted, "I'm not dating anyone. I am a hot mess, as you know. You want to date that?"

He cracked up. As the waitress set down the miniature fire pit with literal flames between us, we instinctively sat back and quieted. The awe of s'mores.

"Enjoy!" she said, and walked off.

We both stared at the beautiful setup of a cast-iron cup filled with flames kept in control by the slotted top. It sat on a platter beautifully plated with large marshmallows, chocolate squares, graham cracker stacks, short metal rods, and a small pot of caramel drizzle.

We dragged our gazes up until we each met the other's eyes. Tarik replied, "I'd love to."

"Love to what?" I asked, confused, as I stabbed a marshmallow with a poker.

"I'd love to date that," he clarified in a steady tone.

My breath hitched. "Oh. *Oh*."

He smiled shyly and lifted a hand for me to go to town on the s'mores. "Tell me you'll think about it?"

"Yeah," I said with a shallow gulp, and pushed up my glasses. "I'll think about it."

Tarik quickly moved the conversation to other things. We gradually finished the s'mores as if he didn't want the evening to end any more than I did, nibbling on the corner of a cracker.

We finally, perhaps reluctantly, called it a night. I kept waiting for the waitress to bring our check so that I could pay for my half, plus Rohan's pizza. When she returned with only Rohan's order to go, Tarik began to scoot out of his chair.

"We haven't paid yet," I said.

"I handed her my card when I went to wash my hands," he replied.

"Hey."

"Hey what?" he said, offering his hand to pull me up.

Suddenly, we were practically chest-to-chest and neither of us budged. "You didn't have to pay."

"You brought me pies."

"That was a gift."

"You lavishly showered me with snacks yesterday."

"Oh my lord."

"How about . . . you pay next time?"

I tucked a few wayward strands of hair behind my ear. "A next time, huh? Think you're clever?"

"Yes."

I cracked a smile. "Okay."

"Just so you know, you agreed to another date with me."

I playfully elbowed him.

He carried Rohan's pizza as we walked out.

The temperature had dropped since we started dinner and I shivered in the chill, remembering just how short my skirt was and how thin these tights were.

"Where are you parked? I'll walk you to your car," Tarik offered.

"Just a few blocks down."

It was hard to keep a conversation going while walking side-by-side against pedestrian flow, not to mention the cold had me walking faster than normal. I flinched every now and then when my ankle screamed, but I hoped he didn't notice when he walked slightly behind me to allow space for others to stroll past us.

When we reached my car, I took the pizza from Tarik to place on the passenger seat. I closed the door and faced him to bid farewell when he said, "I had a good time."

"Me, too. Always a good time when there's good food."

"And you." He smiled.

I tugged on his sleeve. "That was really cheesy, my friend."

"Yeah, yeah," he muttered.

"I mean so cheesy it put the cheese pizza to shame."

"Are you done?"

I laughed. "For now."

"Well, I guess this is good night?" he said.

I nodded, stifling my giggles. He stretched out his arm and promptly retracted it to scratch the back of his neck, as if maybe he wanted to hug me or shake my hand or anything else remotely awkward. He turned to leave.

My heart was beating furiously against my introverted nature, urging me to make a move despite my brain having decided this was enough social interaction for the week. But there was something about Tarik that made me want more. The way he had my body thrumming, the way he put my thrashing thoughts at ease, the way he didn't make me feel drained but completely comfortable and renewed. Those types of people were too few and far between.

"Hey!" I called out. We weren't about to end like this.

He turned back. "Yeah?"

"Just walking away like that?"

"I was planning on calling you later. You know, when you can hear me above your cackling."

I crossed my arms. "No one is worried about you calling them."

"So you don't want me to call you?" he teased, taking the few steps back to me.

"I suppose that would be all right."

"It's okay to admit that you want me to call you. I mean, have you seen me?" He swiped a hand across the air to indicate his body.

"So full of it already."

"You're the one who calls me Thirst-Trap." He stepped even closer, our chests once again nearly touching.

Tarik's warmth and smell and everything delicious about him invaded my space in the best possible way. I wanted to close in those last inches of distance between us, to press myself against him and see if his body responded to me in the way I reacted to him. To see if maybe he'd glide his arms around my waist. I bet it felt good to be in those arms.

I stole a breath and said, "You're never going to let me forget that, huh?"

"I mean . . . you did get caught. In this trap. So . . . nah."

"Oh my lord . . ." I laughed.

"Or am I only Thirst-Trap when you've been drinking?"

"Um . . ." I swallowed. No, definitely not. He was Thirst-Trap twenty-four-seven.

His smile devastated. His closeness elevated. His scent, the sound of his voice, everything about him being this close had my head spinning harder than any drink I'd ever had.

I was certain he was about to kiss me. I knew he wanted to. I knew that he knew that I wanted him to. Yet he didn't.

He took a step back and blew out a breath with a heave of his chest. "I'll call you later?"

I nodded, once reeling from his closeness and now reeling from disappointment.

Tarik turned to walk away again. And again, I said, "Hey!"

"Yeah?" He pivoted partway.

Ah, screw it. I walked toward him, clutched his jacket, pulled him into me so that our chests met, and kissed him.

This wasn't a peck on the lips.

This wasn't even a first-kiss-in-public sort of delicate, classy graze.

This was . . . explosions, earthquakes, a rumbling in my gut and every other good part. My head soared from the mere touch of our lips. But when his hands landed on my waist and pulled me into him, our bodies crushed against each other, our tongues meeting in an intoxicating dance, it turned into a maniacal yearning. And when his mouth parted from mine, it was a devastating need.

This was unlike any kiss I'd ever had. Gentle yet bold. Considerate yet passionate.

I gasped. As I regained my senses, because for the love of god, we were in public next to rush-hour traffic, I pulled away even as he tried to keep me close.

He didn't let me go just like that. He nipped my lower lip, turning it into a fleeting suckle that had me moaning against his mouth as we somehow managed to pull away. Had we not parted, had we been *anywhere* except on a sidewalk, I might've even orgasmed from this kiss alone. Yes. It was *that* good.

"Well, *damn*," he muttered against my mouth, his chocolate-infused breath crashing against my lips.

"Yeah," I conceded, breathless, weak.

Damn, indeed.

Chapter 22

I stood at the front door to my parents' house, one hand around the handle, the other holding Rohan's pizza as I deliberated over options. He'd texted to bring the pizza to my place because he was here and it looked like this might be the intervention I'd been dreading.

As soon as I walked in, my breathing finally under control and ready to have that long-awaited sit-down with my parents, every coherent thought and justification and valid point flew out the window.

Because I hadn't opened the door to my parents sitting in the front room. I opened the door to . . . the intervention.

My heart rammed itself up against my chest as my brain cells registered all the worried faces. Well, until a second ago, they'd been chatting and laughing and drinking cha. Now, all eyes were on me, even as I settled the pizza on the small table beside the banister.

My knees buckled, then locked. I felt the strain in my knee-caps, the taut tension up my legs, the fire on my skin, and a slight dizziness evolving.

Here was the thing: I'd been taught my entire life never to speak out against my elders and to do what I was told. I'd seen my entire life how my parents were concerned about what others thought of us, to keep up best appearances, whether real or pretenses, in order to evade gossip and hurt. Now I stood at the cusp of standing up for my decisions, decisions that were deemed so horrific that my parents were willing to let others through our perfect façade.

Needless to say, but this was a bit . . . extreme.

There weren't nearly as many people as I'd expected for the intervention, or perhaps this was the pre-intervention. A test of the waters, if you will, to see if my parents had to actually pull in all the big guns.

I could do whatever I wanted. I could only say so much to my parents. Even less to the extended family present. And even less if they were to bring in aunties, uncles, and community elders.

Because one, I didn't want to hurt my parents or make them appear to be horrible people who'd raised a rude child in front of others. Two, I had no leg to stand on to justify my decisions.

I wondered if things had been this intense for Veronica.

"Feeling better?" Mummie asked.

"Yes," I said carefully, and simply stood there. I didn't even want to take my shoes off in case I needed to make a run for it.

Lord. Grow up. Be a woman!

"Good. We need to have a chat," Mummie said.

"Yes," Papa added. "What we're going to say, what we're all here for, is to help you. So don't get upset or take this the wrong way."

I brushed clammy hands against my sides.

But then, as I looked at each concerned face, I knew they all meant well. They all loved me and wanted to see me thrive. And I could understand how they saw my situation as circling the drain when they'd all worked two jobs or double shifts regularly, when they owned houses and cars outright, had sent children to college, and had traveled the world.

My phone pinged, cutting off my thoughts and drawing me back to the here and now.

Veronica: Yay! My boss raved about you!!

Her text was accompanied by an email notification. The production company wanted to set up another interview.

"Isha?" Mummie said.

"Hah," I replied, glancing up at her.

Because I respected and loved my parents, I let them begin with the same old "You have such potential."

But because I respected and loved myself and had to barricade my mentality when no one else could, I said, "Thank you for everything you've done, but this isn't necessary. And I need you to understand why."

My parents shook their heads. Mummie turned toward her sisters to say, "So the reason we asked you to come today—"

"Hey," Rohan said, startling me. I almost jumped out of my skin. He popped his head from around the hallway, from the kitchen, as he was always snacking. And true to character, he had a dabeli in one hand and Rogue in the other.

Rohan took one look at me, his brows furrowed, before he nodded. "What's up?"

"Um, hi," I said, confused.

He held up the mini bun filled with a curried mashed-potato patty and pomegranate seeds. "I'd made you dabeli to eat later to cheer you up."

Everyone in the room melted at his kindness. Plus, everyone in existence devoured his dabeli. The boy had talent.

He casually walked into the room and announced, "I'm taking a new job."

"Huh?" his mom asked, as perplexed as the rest of us.

"Yeah. My friend is helping his brother run a restaurant and he wants me to be in charge of the menu so they can expand their food items."

His dad arched a brow. "So . . . you want to leave a perfectly fine government job at the IRS to . . . cook?"

Rohan didn't seem fazed at all when he replied, "Well, I would be more than a cook. Head of the kitchen and menu. I'd oversee cooks in how to make my creations, and we may partner into doing a food truck. And I'd keep my IRS job until tax season is over. And if things don't work out, then I'll return to the IRS if they call me back next season."

"Oh!" his mother said excitedly. "Two jobs! Such a hard worker my boy is," she said while elbowing my mother, who hadn't taken her eyes off me.

"For now, but this isn't a permanent thing. Tax season is over in two months. This isn't the ongoing Indian side hustle you keep wanting me to get into," he added with a roll of his eyes.

"Following your passion?" I finally asked when his parents merrily discussed this turn of events.

Rohan smirked, like he wanted to smile but also might be

joking. Ugh. This boy and his not-straight face. "Inspired by Motiben. Here, try this. It's a fusion dabeli, but no one else has tried it yet."

He held the dabeli to my lips like an honorary offer. I'd never felt so esteemed. "I'm so proud of you."

"Yeah, yeah . . ."

In that one bite, a firework of spices and hints of sweetness went off in my mouth. A fusion of Indian and Tex-Mex.

"Oh my word, is that hot sauce?" I asked, taking the slider-sized burger from him and inhaling the rest.

"Yep. Careful. There's habanero in it."

I coughed as the tail end of the pepper hit the back of my mouth.

Rohan patted my back with Rogue's paw. "Calm down, weakling. Original recipe has ghost pepper, but for you, it's toned down."

"Thanks." *Cough.*

I blinked away tears and finished the last bite, mumbling, "Very good, though."

He walked away and returned with water, which I greedily gulped. "I was inspired by Motiben to go after what makes me excited to get up in the morning, to have an actual career in cuisine, to run my own kitchen and maybe one day a food truck, and make a name for myself. I want people to see my name in the paper and local magazines and have a line out the door before the place opens."

His parents pretty much fawned over him, but I couldn't blame them. I was happy for my little cousin, going after what made him feel alive.

While my aunt and uncle coddled him, my parents tried to lure them back into the reason they were here.

"As I was saying . . ." I turned to my parents, preempting *that* conversation. "I know what this is about. I appreciate your love and concern, and I'm sorry that I worry you. I'm sorry that I didn't live up to your standards." I swallowed hard on those words.

Rohan pressed his lips together and nodded reassuringly, then glanced at his feet. He didn't watch me as others were, but he didn't leave me to stand alone.

I petted Rogue, who nodded off with her little chin on his shoulder. "Well, let me start from the beginning. I should've told you that I changed majors. I should've talked to you when I was having difficulties with classes and needed a break."

My parents nodded. Mummie said, "Hah. You should've."

I sighed, my muscles relaxing as the support from Rohan beamed beside me like a beacon, as the hope of a potential job that happened to be a foot into the door waited in my inbox, and as a new friend/possible love interest offered newfound support and hope helped me to stand up. After all, I knew that in the very end, no matter how enraged my parents might become with me, they would never truly stop loving me.

So why was this difficult to say?

A few gazes flitted to the stairs behind me. Oh, *great*. Mohit cautiously walked down a few steps and paused.

I went on, nonetheless. "You worked hard for us and obviously have a strong work ethic. Even though I don't have the degree you wanted me to get, or work forty-plus hours with that Indian side-hustle mentality, I still worked hard. I worked above and beyond for my classes, and I worked endlessly on my craft. But the thing is, you want me to be in a box that you understand and approve of.

"While I get it, you want me to thrive, this isn't how one

encourages a child to thrive. It might've worked with Mohit, but it doesn't work on me. I never came to you during college because I was scared of letting you down and disappointing you. We didn't have the open environment for me to be able to safely discuss."

"What are you talking about?" Mummie asked. "How do you think you can't be frank with us, huh?"

"Well, that attitude right there," I said softly. "Whatever you say and believe is always right. It might be for you, but not for me. If I pursued anything other than what you wanted, it was a waste, and you'd try to, and still do, push me into the box."

"What's wrong with being a nurse or doctor or engineer?" she spat. "You'd have a good-paying job by now. Just look at Mohit—"

"Please. Don't compare us. It's like me comparing you to another mom who doesn't make her kids feel like crap."

She paused, and suddenly the room turned eerily quiet.

"See?" I said, my heart pounding and my head dizzy. "I would never do that, but see how it hurt you? I don't ever want to hurt you, which is why I never stood up to you. You think you're helping me when you're making me feel like I'm worthless."

I blinked back tears, my chest numb, my limbs nothing, as if they didn't exist. "Of course, I want you to be proud of me, but you're not and that's okay. I'm not perfect to you, but you're . . . not perfect ! . . . to me . . ."

Mummie swallowed and her eyes glistened. Oh my word, why was I doing this? I was a horrible daughter!

Yet I went on. "I wouldn't ask you to change. I would never tell you that you're not meeting your full potential. I don't bring up all the things that you missed in my life. Because it's toxic. And I want us to be healthy.

"I moved back home because I was struggling financially. But being home, as much as I love you all and appreciate your kindness, my mentality can't take it anymore. There's a difference between encouraging me to do more and berating me with passive-aggressiveness. But you're right. I need to mature and move forward. It's not for a lack of trying, but I can't mature and move forward living at home where, yes, you help me more than most would help their kids, but also where you treat me and see me as a child."

I chuckled. "Believe me. I've tried very hard. I'm not giving up on my creative ambitions, but I'm going to take a different route that will support me. Um . . . so, in essence, I'll be moving back out."

There was a collective gasp and tears started streaming down Mummie's face as she mumbled, "Why would you move back out?"

"*What?* You're the one who keeps telling me I need to get my life together, the one who put this whole intervention together."

"I just want you to get a full-time job."

"I'll find a job that I like, where I'll thrive and make strides toward the career I want. Not the IRS." I turned to Rohan and said, "No offense."

"None taken," he said.

"We sort of need space, don't we?" I asked my parents. "So you can see that I can take care of myself and not feel that you're providing everything for an adult. But don't worry!"

I pulled out my phone and showed them the email. "I'm going to take on more freelance work and have an interview this week for a major company. I just think it's best. And for me, too, to help me feel and act like an adult again."

Papa sighed and finally spoke. "You don't have the monetary means to support yourself."

"No, she does," Rohan said suddenly. "We're going to rent an apartment together."

My jaw dropped. As had everyone else's.

He cocked his chin at me, his gaze falling on mine. "We talked about this. It'll help me to finally get out and be more responsible. I'm ready for the big move. And then get set in my business ventures, and I guess, one day, very, *very* far into the future, the next step is . . . finding the right woman?"

And that was all it took for his parents to clap and cry with joy. This guy, whom they couldn't drag out of his room during his depression, was ready to get into the world and move forward. And talk of entertaining the idea of considering a woman for a future marriage was always the deal-maker.

I leaned toward him and muttered, "Thanks for taking one for the team, but you don't have to do this."

He shrugged. "I think it's a great idea," he said to everyone. "New jobs for us, and Motiben can help me learn how to do finances and responsibilities. She's my safety net. And at the same time, ya know, we can protect each other. You won't have to worry about us."

"It's unconventional for a male and female cousin to live together," Papa started.

Rohan scrunched his face, like he couldn't understand. "Fua, we're brother and sister. There's nothing strange about it. I found a few two-bedroom apartments not too far from here and closer to work. Definitely affordable, and they have availability on the first of next month."

"What will people say?" Papa asked.

I rolled my eyes. "Don't take this the wrong way, but who cares? We need to be concerned about how *we* feel, how we make each other feel, not what random people say. They're no one and have nothing to do with us. They can say or think whatever they want, and they will no matter what we do, but they're never going to help us the way we help each other. They don't care about us, so you really should stop caring so much about them. Everyone *I* care about, anyone *we* should care about, is right here in this house."

"Isha . . ." Papa warned.

My shoulders slumped. "This is hard to say because I don't want you to ever think that I don't love, appreciate, or respect you. But the fact is . . . you treat me like the worst failure sometimes, and pushing me into jobs that won't help me advance toward my dreams tells me that you think my dreams are worthless, or at least dead or unworthy of pursuing, and that you care more about what others think than how I feel."

There was a mixture of anger and pain brewing in their expressions, and a horribly deep sense of sympathy from my aunt and uncle.

"And what?" Mummie asked. "We just let you continue down this path because us wanting better for you makes you feel bad? You just embarrassed us in front of our family."

I scoffed. "Weren't you about to gang up on me? Spill out all your worries of my underachievement in front of the family? How embarrassed am I?"

Papa snapped, "Our opinion of you doesn't matter? The pain we feel knowing you're in this situation? The awkwardness we feel when others inquire about you?"

"See?" I said with shaky words, my eyes blurry from tears.

"This is why I never talked to you about college majors and careers. This is why I could never tell you how you make me feel. This is why, even as an adult, I can't openly talk to you. But it's the truth, and my truth should mean something."

A crushing silence fell around us. My parents glared at me while everyone else stared at the floor.

I sniffled and wiped a few falling tears. "I never want to hurt you. And it's hurting us both for me to keep living here. So I'll be moving out soon, and . . . yeah . . ." My voice trailed off.

I took Rogue into my arms, focusing on her so I wouldn't cry, attempting to smile at her, but felt my lips quiver.

Mummie said, "Isha. There is more to life than living paycheck to paycheck. Stay here and go back to college for a real degree. Make something of yourself. Think about a future. Depend on yourself and not us. Look at Rohan. He's thinking ahead to what he needs to do to find a good wife and have his own family, his own home in the future. And you? You're not thinking of what you need to be to attract a good husband for later. What sort of man will want to be with a girl who can't take care of herself, who can't be serious in life?"

Tarik crossed my mind, despite trying not to think of him. Of course, no one ever said he was interested in a future with me.

I knew I wasn't the best catch, or even the best version of myself at this moment, but Mummie's words cut deeper.

"You will want an established, secure man one day, but stable men want stable women. No decent, serious man will want you this way. Everything is tied up for a future that you're not seeing. This conversation isn't over," Mummie said.

Anxiety clawed across my ribs. Perhaps she was right. Her reasoning was logical.

"But it is," I replied softly, still focused on Rogue's sleepy face as she yawned and pawed around her eyes to scratch. "You're never going to be happy with who I am. But I at least need to be happy with myself. Thank you, again, for everything. I better set up this interview and start packing."

Without looking at Rohan or glancing at anyone else, I walked upstairs with Rogue. My legs had never felt heavier. My body burned, my skin tingled, and my heart was going wild. If I could just make it to my room, then I could collapse in bed.

Mohit backtracked up the stairs and waited at the top. "Are you okay?" he asked, concern etched across his furrowing brows.

I nodded.

"For what it's worth, Motiben, I never thought anything less of you."

I cleared my throat. *Don't cry. Don't cry.* "Thank you."

I walked numbly around the corner into my room and glanced at my phone when it pinged with a text from Tarik. He'd had a great time tonight and hoped we could see each other again. How could a meaningful text like this hurt so much? He didn't want to date a loser like me. He'd soon realize what my parents saw as clear as day. I was a walking disaster who couldn't figure out how to move forward in life.

The text went unanswered.

Just as I closed the door, someone knocked.

"Can I come in?" Rohan asked.

"Me, too?" Mohit asked.

I let them in and Mohit closed the door.

Rohan stuffed his hands into his pockets as I tidied up books.

"Rohan. Why didn't you tell me that you took the menu job earlier?" I asked, trying to focus on the good instead of my racing heart.

"I haven't yet. But I'm going to as soon as I leave. I'd been seriously considering it, and when I saw them talking to you like that, and how hard you've worked trying to get this far, and how I had a chance fall into my lap . . . I dunno. I just remembered you saying to go for every opportunity. Plus, if I take the job, I could really help you more with rent. I was telling the truth about how you inspired me to get after my goals."

My chest warmed as I faced him. "I'm glad you took the chance."

"All right . . . don't go all crybaby on me."

"I'm not!"

He pouted.

I cleared my throat because I was going to cry. "It shouldn't take too long to pack," I said. "Better start looking at apartments. Where were the ones you found? You don't have to move out with me and waste your money—"

A breeze hit me, quickly followed by the anise-scented body wash Rohan used, and then Rohan himself, his arms wrapping around my shoulders.

"You never hug anyone," I muttered into his shoulder once the shock wore off.

"It's okay, Motiben," he said, simply. No witty comeback. No dry humor. No sarcasm. No comment that made me wonder what he truly meant. Just a hug and validation.

Then Mohit rammed into us, hugging us both. "You know you're the best, don't you, Motiben?"

That was all it took. I started bawling, trying my best to keep my sobs contained as these two guys crushed me.

"Let it all out, crybaby," Rohan cooed.

I half laughed, half cried.

"Can I move in with you, too?" Mohit asked.

"What?" I mumbled against . . . I wasn't quite sure who was where at this point.

"Oh my lord," I said, pulling away and wiping my face. "I can't take care of you both."

He laughed and Rohan smiled, and my worries and pain subsided.

It hadn't been too bad after all. So what if my parents were embarrassed and pissed at me? What was new?

They'd get over it. And I, hopefully someday soon, would be in a better place financially, mentally, emotionally, career-wise, independence-wise, and well . . . just in a better place with *myself.*

Chapter 23

I f one could turn their life around as deftly and efficaciously
as an elder Indian daughter who'd isolated herself from her
parents solely because of failed familial expectations, then the
world had hope for me. In a matter of a few days, my parents
estranged themselves, for which my guilt hadn't yet subsided.
To add to the mental and emotional seclusion, I'd skillfully
evaded Tarik. We were fun and good feelings, but my mother
was right. Stable men did *not* want unstable women.

Thankfully, to alleviate the tension at home, my parents
were all tied to something at the Houston mandir, which
meant they were gone and would be helping their sister location for the next four days. This was the only source of solace
and relief I'd get from them, but that didn't prevent my parents
from texting and calling to hammer the fear of God, and quite
possibly demons, into me.

All calls and texts remained unanswered, unless they came
from Rohan or Mohit. Food and mental health were the pin-

nacle things they asked about. Not work or college. And once in a while, kitten videos.

I'd nailed the second interview, sweaty armpits and all, and left the downtown-based company with a prayer to the universe to help me out for once. I was prepared to sacrifice to any and all deities at this point.

I then applied for an apartment with Rohan. Bless his soul, he'd found one that we could both afford but was also decent and allowed pets. There was, of course, a wait, but thank goodness the boy had impeccable credit history. While his parents were still a bit unsettled about him moving out, not to mention getting it from my parents for allowing Rohan to aid me, or so I assumed, they seemed happy having him move forward. Which meant they still trusted me with their precious boy.

I'd also expanded my reach for more freelance work, anything really, before packing up the rest of my boxes with things I wouldn't need for a while. Like these textbooks on scripts.

Until that steady job or career boost came along, I was determined to work all day, write all night, and hustle like it was going out of style. Besides, who needed sleep?

Of course, clothes and shoes and makeup stayed in place in case another interview popped up. It was easy to move clothes on hangers from one closet to another, and keep clothes neatly folded in drawers for the move. I really didn't have much, seeing that almost everything I owned was in this bedroom or in the bathroom. Whatever else I had from my previous apartment was already packed and sitting in my parents' garage, ready for its next destination.

I sat down at my disturbingly empty desk and swiveled in the chair, deciding to take a mental break from scriptwriting.

Just for a short while. I needed to recharge creatively before diving into the next project.

Once Rohan and I were settled into our new place, I could get back into the right headspace to query agents again and get back into pitchfests and conferences and networking. Maybe, just maybe, I'd get this position with Veronica's boss and meet someone who was willing to mentor me and give me a chance to prove my skills the way they had with her.

Biting my lip, the queasiness of the confrontation and embarking into the unknown turned less heavy, less extreme, less dramatic. I was an adult, and this was what adults did. I found myself enjoying a slight wave of giddiness tingling through my insides. Yeah. Everything was going to be fine. No one said success only came in one's twenties, or that success only had meaning if it was reached by thirty.

It was okay. Things would be okay.

I nervously laughed into the void.

It had to be. There were plenty of people who found their stride, their career, their passion, their love, their everything well into their forties, fifties, and beyond. I recalled a LinkedIn post about a man getting his PhD in his fifties. An article about a woman who found the love of her life in her sixties. There was an Olympic athlete who competed in his seventies. A woman I read about a few months back who accomplished yet another life goal in her eighties. There wasn't a set age limit, a moment when it was too late for everything.

My parents were wrong if they thought I should have everything together by now. It was okay if I didn't. It was okay if I was still striving and working toward my dreams. And it was okay to evolve.

I glanced at my phone, expecting Rohan to change his

mind about living with me, expecting him to say it was all a setup to get me out and on my own again. Thankfully, no such text came.

I pondered Rohan's menu opportunity and wondered how it would all unfurl for him and where he would be in a year. Probably managing the entire kitchen or having one of his own. Maybe he would even take the big step of starting a food truck. His adventure awaited, and I was so excited to see where life would take him.

My phone screen lit up.

Thirst-Trap: Just checking in on ya. I haven't heard from you in a while. Hope everything is okay.

By a while, he meant a couple of days and a handful of texts. Was I awful for ignoring him? After all he'd done?

Thirst-Trap: Going to catch my ego in check here and just ask if you want me to stop texting you? If I don't hear from ya, I'll take that as a yes. ☹

Oh, hell. Not the sad emoji. I dragged in a deep breath and sputtered. Ah, too deep. My chest burned. No matter what I thought of myself, I couldn't take that out on a man who'd done so much for me. He deserved to know the truth, no matter how pathetic. Then we could have a clean break. It shouldn't be so bad, really. It wasn't as if we were a couple or had been dating for more than a day.

More than that, more than anything else on this planet, I couldn't screw up Rohan's chances of working with him. I might've made a complete mess of my life, but Rohan had a great opportunity to break into the food world.

"Ah, woman up," I muttered.

Rogue caught my attention from her spot on the bed. She made aggressive eye contact and I blinked first.

"You're right, Rogue. I have to be mature."

I tapped my screen to unleash an unabashed explanation, my fingers ready to text away, when I accidentally hit CALL.

Of *course* I'd done that!

Before I could hit that glaring red END CALL icon, Tarik answered.

I froze when he didn't speak for seconds on end. Perhaps he'd butt-answered? And he would keep doing whatever it was that he was doing and the call would disconnect without any awkward interaction?

"Hello?" He finally spoke.

I closed my eyes, my hands trembling, and said, "Oh, that was quick." Why did I say that!

"I was texting my brother and accidentally answered on first ring," he explained, his voice gravelly.

"Oh, funny. I was about to text you and accidentally called."

"Accidents aren't always bad," he replied.

"Did you just wake up?"

"Yeah. Just lying here, catching up on messages," he answered. His throaty, hoarse voice made my insides churn.

Hearing his voice when he first woke up was the sexiest thing in the world. He managed the pub. Understandably he went to bed late, which meant waking up early afternoons. I loved to hear it. He sure took the edge off.

"Oh! Sorry."

"No, don't be. You?"

"It's almost noon. I've been up since six."

"Such an early riser," he groaned.

"Wait. So you're still in bed?" I bit my lip, and it was all I could do not to imagine being in bed beside him.

"Yes. The curtains are closed and it's still dark in my bedroom."

I vanquished the images of him in bed but couldn't help it, imagining sheets gathered at his waist, one arm above his head, his hair messy. Did he sleep without a shirt on? Or in the nude? "So what are you wearing?"

Even his morning laugh was throaty. "Calm down, woman."

I shifted in my desk chair, grinning. "No. Tell me."

He cleared his throat. "All right. I'm wearing gray sweatpants and a red T-shirt."

I pouted. "Aw. You didn't even pretend to be topless?"

"Are you topless?" he asked, suddenly sounding a little more awake.

"Eh. You'll never know, I guess. This should've been a video call for that."

"Thanks for the idea. Next time. Nothing like a surprise video call."

"No! I at least need a text warning. How dare you?"

He chuckled. Then we both went dead quiet. I had watched Rogue nibble on her chew toy for what felt like a good minute when he asked, "Are you okay?"

"Yes. No. Sort of. I don't really know."

"Did something happen? Did I do something?"

"No!" I was quick to reply. "God, no. You're perfect."

"Is this one of those things where a girl thinks a guy is too perfect and therefore boring?"

I pushed my fingers through my hair and tugged at the ends. "Far from that. I apologize for avoiding your texts and not responding."

"Being left on read hurt a little bit, to be honest. I don't mean to come on strong. I absolutely understand if you want space or if this was a temporary thing."

I took a breath, my body quivering.

"Isha?" he said softly. "You can be honest with me."

I gathered up all my courage to tell him how I was not, and never would be, good enough for him when instead, I said, "I really like you."

A pause.

All right. Not the reaction I'd expected, but also not the confession I'd anticipated. This was fine, totally fine. This was good, in fact, because it would make it easier to leave things between us.

I swallowed and went on. "Um. I spoke with my parents. They actually had the intervention for me. Walked into it after our date. I decided to pursue what I need, and nothing went over well. They're beyond disappointed in me. In fact, we're not even really talking right now except for them telling me how I'm in danger of destroying any type of sufficient future. But they said something that stuck, and I think it's true. And that's why I didn't respond to your messages."

More silence. Was he still there?

I continued, "I'm a total mess and need so much to happen for me to be in any way composed and reliable and put together."

Dead silence.

"Tarik?" I said, nervous.

"What exactly did your parents say?"

"Aside from getting my crap together, getting a *real* degree and a *real* job, they said I should be thinking ahead because no stable man wants an unstable woman. I mean, I know. Dependable people want other dependable people. They're right, but I'll get there. And I know it sounds dumb, to feel so damaged, so impacted by a few words."

"It's what parents do, even when they don't mean to."

I scratched my arm, preparing for the already growing spasm in my chest in having to say goodbye. "So anyway. That's the reason and you should know. It has nothing to do with you, and I hope this doesn't affect you taking a serious, honest consideration of Rohan for your menu. He'll be amazing."

"So I won't see you again?"

"Did you hear any of that? Why would you ever be interested in a disaster like me?"

He cleared his throat. "I feel like we had this conversation before."

"Takes a new meaning when someone you love and trust tells you to your face, all truth, no holds barred."

"Do you trust me?"

"Yes," I replied. To a great extent, I *did* trust Tarik.

"Then why don't you trust me when I say that I do *not* see a walking disaster or a failure or someone who I don't want to be around? If you don't want another date, or to ever see me again, I'd be profoundly disappointed, but I would respect your decision. But if you think I don't want to be around you because . . ."

I'm not good enough for you.

"Then at least let me voice my side. I've seen your wild side."

My skin burned and I cringed. He meant the gross AF side.

"And you've told me the parts about you that hurt the most. I just don't see you the way your parents do, and I hope you don't either."

My pulse raged behind my ears, so loudly that I was sure he could hear through the phone.

When I didn't respond, and honestly, I couldn't even think of anything, he said, "By the way, I really like you, too."

"Oh . . . you do?"

He laughed. "Do you hear yourself?"

I smiled.

"I thought it was obvious, shamelessly showing off my sultry legs and all."

I cackled.

"But let me just be clear with ya so there isn't any room for misinterpretation: Isha . . ."

My eyelids fluttered. Lord, I loved how he said my name, like a late-night moan from his kissable lips.

"I would love to see you again. Even if it's not a date."

I was grinning so hard that my cheeks started to cramp.

"Would that be all right?" he asked.

"Yes. More than all right."

He went on, a smile to his voice. "I do have a question for you. Non-date-related: are you busy this Sunday evening?"

"My only plans were packing."

The sound of sheets rustled on his end. "Packing? Where you going?"

"Moving back out on my own."

"That's great news, right? You sound sad."

"It is. It's just not under the best circumstances with my parents."

"I thought they wanted you to move forward in life and get back on your feet."

"Oh, they do. But apparently in the way they want."

He groaned. "I'm sorry to hear that. Are you all right?"

"Hmm. I will be. They need time to cool down, and the distance will help."

There was a pause, and I could practically hear him frowning. When he spoke, he had a nervous yet excited edge to his voice. "My grandparents are having a small party at their house. It's some family, some friends. Very casual. It'll be outside on their lawn . . . and . . . anyway . . ."

I smiled into the phone, my heart galloping at this very *non-date.*

"Do you want to come? I understand if—"

"Are you asking me to meet your family?" I interjected, jumping up from my chair.

Rogue startled and glared at me as if to say *Calm the eff down, I was just falling asleep.*

"Just the grandparents. Listen, I know you're still down from everything that happened last weekend, and now with you moving out and what your parents said. I want you to feel supported. My grandparents are great that way. I told them about you—well, not all the details or personal things, and no mention of us having gone on a date, so no pressure there, but they want to meet you."

"Really?" I touched my chest from sheer, undiluted happiness. "Just to support me?"

"Like I said, they're great that way. I read the script and . . ."

I held my breath for his thoughts, unsure of why I needed his truthful accolades.

"It's amazing. You're amazing," he added softly.

I clamped down on a squeal. "I know."

He laughed. "I'm serious!"

"So am I!"

"Well, it really was an engaging script. I hope I can read the rest one day?"

"I think that can be arranged."

"I told my grandparents you're a writer, and they were immediately invested. They love helping others out, and they love nourishing talent. So they want to meet you and see what they can do."

My breath caught. "Oh . . . that's so sweet."

"You don't have to answer right now—"

"Yes!" I blurted. "I mean . . . I'd love to meet your grandparents and spend some time with, um, them."

He chuckled. "You meant me. It's okay to admit it. You like spending time with me."

"Ha!" I said, even as my skin tingled with all the feel-goods.

"You can come with Rohan, if that makes you more comfortable. My brother is inviting him. Haven't heard if he's replied or not."

"He's at work. He probably won't get the message until his lunch break. Some people work a nine-to-five, you know?"

"Ah. How could I forget? But you'll want to join us."

"Oh yeah? Why's that?"

"I'll be making drinks, nonalcoholic ones as well, so make sure you come . . ." He let the last word linger.

I groaned. "Don't say it."

". . . *thirsty*."

I dropped my head, grinning like a fool. "Oh my lord. You said it."

Chapter 24

Sunday evening couldn't come fast enough. After doing my hair, which required straightening and then curling because of the heinous amount of frizz (screw you, Austin humidity!), my sore arms painstakingly went through every outfit. I wanted to be comfortable, but also cute. I wanted Tarik's jaw to drop when he saw me, much like it had on our date, but I wanted to be respectful of his grandparents.

Since the party was outdoors and in the early evening, that meant no skirts. I was not going to embarrass myself constantly fighting the wind trying to blow up my skirt, or flash anyone. I hadn't tucked my skirt into my panties in a long time, and it wasn't going to happen tonight. Also, it might get chilly once the sun set.

Skinny jeans seemed too casual. So I opted for burnt-orange wide-leg slacks and flats, since I didn't want to ruin their lawn or break my ankles with heels. And a shimmering bronze blouse that buttoned across the chest from top left shoulder to lower right waist. A silver bracelet. A light layer of makeup and of course bronze lipstick to match the top.

There! Presentable, elegant, comfortable, windproof, lawnproof, and still figure-flattering. It hit all the marks.

I pushed up my glasses, gave Rogue a kiss, and headed out as soon as Rohan texted that he was outside. Rohan was always going to go. He never said no to a party.

"Still laying low?" he asked when I shimmied into his car.

"Maybe indefinitely," I muttered, adjusting my small purse. "Have to move out when they're not home. Sunday, mandir time work for you?"

Rohan eased onto the street, giving me a side glance, and said, "Best time, bro. We know we have exactly three hours. Just need to find some help."

"Sounds like a plan." I bit my nail anxiously. "Ugh. I really, really hope I get this production job. It sounds so perfect, and it helped my college classmate land her dream role."

"Don't stress. All you can do is try, and if it doesn't work out, try again. You're going at things from different angles, so that opens up more opps, ya know?"

I clucked my tongue. "So wise, little one."

"I know."

"Your parents still happy?"

"Oh yeah. But I think your parents are giving them a hard time about enabling you."

I groaned. "I'm sorry. Don't listen to them, and hopefully your parents won't get roped into anything."

He shrugged. "We all know family members get all up in each other's business."

"Truth if I ever heard it."

"Can you give me directions?"

"Yep." I plugged the address into GPS and navigated through traffic toward Lake Travis.

The lake was huge and elongated and split into smaller lakes and diverted into rivers, so it didn't necessarily mean Tarik's grandparents were wealthy or notable. And it didn't mean they lived on waterfront property or even had a water view. I wasn't expecting anything extravagant.

So when we pulled up to the same neighborhood that we'd been kicked out of last weekend, I grimaced as Rohan slowed way down to turn onto the primary street.

"Are you sure this is the address?" he asked, noting how we were so close to that looming security office. "Not a joke?"

"Mmm-hmm . . ." I checked my phone to verify this was indeed the right place when it rang. "Hello?" I asked on the first ring, having accidentally hit ACCEPT.

"Hi." Tarik's smooth-as-honey voice came through. "Are you close?"

I glanced around. "Um . . . we might have the wrong address."

"No. It's the right one. Don't worry about security. Is that you driving slowly up the street in a black sedan like you're casing the place?"

"Yes . . ."

"See you soon," he said, and we hung up.

At the top of the hill, where the sidewalk met an entryway to the property, Tarik appeared and waved us down, looking absolutely adorable in a pair of khakis and a blue button-down shirt.

"Aren't you glad you didn't wear basketball shorts for once?" I asked Rohan, noting his black slacks.

He grumbled and pulled into a wide roundabout driveway

where we parked next to some pretty fancy cars in front of a very opulent house.

"Dude . . ." he said, looking all around before getting out. "We're in Matthew McConaughey's neighborhood!"

I slowly emerged from the car, my breath hitching. Such bouncy grass and perfect hedges and well-kept everything.

"I'm glad you could make it," Tarik said, giving Rohan one of those guy slap-handshakes when I walked around the car to meet them. "Heard great things about your mock menu from Seth."

"Thanks. I've got lots of ideas and recipes I've been working on," Rohan replied, his face lighting up, which had me melting with joy.

"Awesome! I can't wait to try it. Seth is a die-hard fan," Tarik replied. Then he turned to me.

We awkwardly stood in place. We'd never greeted one another physically. But seeing that we'd locked lips and had been chatting since, it seemed like maybe a handshake . . . or a side hug . . . was in order? In the end, we did neither.

"You look very nice," he finally said.

From the corner of my eye, I saw Rohan walk off. Where did he think he was going? But he was the type who'd rather walk by himself than be a third wheel. Soon enough, he greeted Seth in the near distance.

"Thank you," I replied. "You look adorable."

"Adorable? That's exactly what I was going for."

"Well, it's working."

"How's your ankle?"

"Back to normal. I'll try not to trip over curbs, but that might be a lot to ask of me."

He laughed. "Good to hear. Any news on the job hunt?"

"No. Still waiting. And waiting to hear back on the apartment. Which, by the way, how would you like to help us move when the time arrives?"

"Oh, I'd love to. I'm a master at Tetris-loading moving trucks. I swear, one trip is all you'll need."

I laughed. "We don't have too much. I just don't like lifting things."

He smiled. "Do you want to meet my grandparents?"

"Oh . . . wait. Do they actually live here, as in the same neighborhood with Matthew McConaughey? Um, I'm not allowed back here. You know that, right?" I whispered.

"It's fine. You're invited this time."

"So you do know those guys! The ones at the security office?"

"Yeah."

"Oh my lord. Was that whole thing an act then, you bribing them into letting us go?"

He walked me toward a blue-linen-covered table filled with lovely drinks topped with purple and pink petals. "Oh no. That was real. It's an actual crime, you know? They can't let it slide by a second time, so don't get caught."

He handed me a flute with light pink, bubbly liquid. "Only nonalcoholic drinks for you while you're here."

I gasped, taking the glass from him with one hand, and with the other I slapped his chest. He feigned pain, clutching the spot, but laughed.

"Har har," I mimicked. "But yes, absolutely correct."

"Oh, this must be Isha," an older woman in beige dress pants and a pink blouse and loaded with pearls said as she walked toward us.

"Yes! Grandma, this is Isha. Isha, this is my grandmother," Tarik said, standing beside the two of us.

She gave a slight bow of the head and smiled warmly. She had the same dazzling smile as her grandson. "So nice to meet you. Tarik's told us so much about you. Said that you're a scriptwriter. Oh, you must meet our friend. He's into that, too. Come. Come."

I glanced at Tarik as he nodded. A giant grin swept across his face. What was he so giddy about? There was nothing new about grandmas loving me, and it wasn't as if we were seriously dating for this to mean something momentous. There was no impending engagement on its way.

"Oh, that's him over there," she said, and pointed at a small circle of people holding either drinks or small plates and chatting, enjoying the setting sun on their faces.

I had to do a double take, quite possibly a triple take.

The way she said "our *friend*" made it sound like some person who dabbled in writing on the side as a hobby. Not. Freaking. *Matthew McConaughey.*

I was in no way honestly expecting to see him because things like this never happened to me. That was called kismet, and kismet seemed too poetic and fantastical for the likes of my inferior soul. Or was kismet about to turn dark? Dangling this in front of me only to trample my dreams in some sordid, cruel way?

"Oh!" she said, turning to greet Rohan and Seth.

I needed to thank Seth for trying to set up my encounter with my former professor at the pub, and for sending Tarik to bail us out. But I was a bit distracted.

I turned back to the small circle and stared. Ten seconds ago, they were just strangers, and I was composed. Now that crowd ballooned into intimidating proportions. My eyes just about plopped out of my skull.

But then I, *eventually*, regained my composure. I was a professional . . . and this was a gathering that we were both invited to. We were . . . dare I think it . . . equals here?

In my head, I went over how to approach him as the proceeding scene bloomed in my thoughts.

I'd slide up beside him and politely interrupt, saying, "Oh, Matthew McConaughey, right? I'm Isha."

Then he'd say in that slight Southern drawl, "Yeah, nice to meet ya."

And I'd continue with, "You were my professor at UT a couple of years back. I've been meaning to connect with you again. You really praised my project outlining the Indian diaspora in Austin."

And he'd say, "Oh yeah? I remember! That was one of my best student assignments. I use it as an example for others as a gold standard, but of course, no one has been able to compare. How's it going? Have you broken into the field yet?"

Then I'd answer with, "I landed an agent but no bites from producers. We've since parted ways. I had this awful pitch session last weekend where I spilled coffee on their laps, I was so nervous!"

And he'd laugh and comment, "That's one way of making an impression."

Then I'd say, "I was hoping to connect again because I could really benefit from your feedback on my latest script. I think it's something you'd really enjoy. It was inspired by some key points in your lectures. Specifically, about world-building and character development. Just like you mentioned, I took to the whiteboard and created backgrounds and details in storyboard that never make it into the script, but really round out world and character and plot. I see the difference. You've changed my entire approach to writing, and it's better for it."

And he'd grin down at me with that dimpled smile from that marvelous, transcendent height and say, "All right, all right, all right."

"Are you okay?" Tarik asked, cutting through my thoughts like a machete.

"Huh?" I blinked back into the moment, the perfection of my daydream wilting away. "Yeah."

"You don't have to talk to him, if you're not ready."

I turned to Tarik and asked, "Did you know he'd be here?"

A sheepish expression fluttered across his face. "I had a feeling. Sometimes he comes to these things. He's friends and neighbors with my grandparents, even though my grandparents don't quite understand how big of a deal he is."

"You didn't tell me? I could've prepared a presentation, or brought the flash drive, or—"

"Or . . ." He gently interrupted and snaked an arm around my waist, sedating my rising anxiety. "You would've been nervous and needed a drink and end up running around this neighborhood again and eternally being banned."

"Oh yeah . . . That."

"Or worse: you might not have come." He frowned, as if the thought of me skipping out severely wounded him.

"Wait." I whipped my head back toward Rohan, who lifted his glass to me while chatting with Seth and his grandmother. "Was Rohan in on this?"

"Yep. Like you said, the ultimate bro."

"You mean the *Brohan*."

He chuckled. "This is a safe space, a relaxed party. You

don't have to meet him if you don't want to. And if you want to meet him, you don't have to talk work."

A relaxing wave washed over me as I replied, "He was my professor at UT. I should say hello."

"Are you nervous? Do you want me to go with you? Or wait for Grandma to initiate an introduction?"

I scoffed, closing my eyes for a brief second and banishing all the jitters. The amassed anxiety and worries and self-loathing and mishaps and tears and depression of trying to find my way in this business melted away faster than makeup on a Texan's face in midsummer's 110-degree heat. All the thrills and excitement and ambition and confidence that I'd ever felt for my work came rushing into my bones and shimmied into my soul. This was probably what Tony Stark felt when he summoned the powers of the universe through the Infinity Gauntlet. Powerful. Confident. Necessary. Inevitable.

I happened to glance down at the delicious nonalcoholic drink in my hand, then looked up at Tarik and laughed. I handed him the glass and said, "Hold my drink. I got this."

And with all the swagger of a woman who knew her work was big-league material, I marched toward my former professor, politely inserted myself into the circle, and reintroduced myself.

Isha Patel.

Former student.

Current badass writer.

Future award-winning producer.

ACKNOWLEDGMENTS

I don't really know what to say about this book. I just wanted to write something silly and funny, inspired by my cousin (the actual Brohan) and all our wacky adventures! I didn't know if publishers would want this kind of book, but I had a blast writing it!

I want to thank Brohan for being so amazing and wonderful and just the best bro/cousin. I hope you understand how wonderful you are and what sort of impact you have on the lives of others. I'm blessed to have you in my life.

Special shout-out to Meet, who inspired some of Rohan (the character); Rogue, who is my actual 6.6 pounds of ferocious Yorkie; Mena Massoud and Henry Cavill for inspiring Thirst-Trap; and *Tribeza* magazine for the real-life layout of my book beside Matthew McConaughey's book, which acted as the catalyst for this entire story.

Thank you to my agent, Katelyn, who entertained this wild idea and told me to run with it! I wouldn't be where I am with this book without your insight and endless patience. OMG, you're a saint! Thank you for helping me reach my decades-long goal of being able to work with Berkley and the fantastic Cindy Hwang.

My incredible editor, Cindy, saw something in *Isha, Unscripted* and took the story up a notch, helping to mold it into what readers are holding today. Thank you for making some of my dreams come true! I still can't believe I get to work with you.

I want to thank all the readers who keep coming back for my worlds, and welcome new readers who took a chance on Isha. I hope you enjoyed and will join me on the next adventure!

Isha,
Unscripted

Sajni Patel

DISCUSSION QUESTIONS

1. Isha is twenty-eight years old and finds herself without sufficient income in an inflated city, which forces her to move back home. While it isn't unusual for unmarried children to live at home in the Indian culture, this opens up issues around boundaries. Isha finds herself succumbing to her parents' pressure to find a "real job" and is unable to stand up to them. Why do you think this is?

2. Are Isha's parents justified in pushing her to find a job, any job, despite what she wants in a career? Are they justified in *how* they push her? Do you think this comes from a place of love?

3. We often hear about close sibling bonds, particularly with sisters, but what about cousin bonds? Are you close with your cousin(s)?

4. Isha is an adult, but her parents often view her as a child, and even more so given her situation and what is expected of her. Do you feel this worry over one's child is normal for parents? If so, to what extent?

5. Isha is driven by desperation early on. Have you found yourself in similar situations where you were willing to take a leap of faith, no matter how wild? What were the results?

6. Have you ever had dreams you wanted so badly that not reaching them hurt? If so, did you continue pursuing those dreams?

7. Tarik witnesses some of Isha's worst moments. What do you think makes him want to know more about her instead of turning his back on her?

8. Tarik has found success in his pursuits and appreciates the support he's received along the way, as well as acknowledging those who didn't support him. Do you think this is why he encourages and supports Isha with her dreams?

9. Do you think Isha and her parents will ever come to terms with her final decisions in the book?

10. Have you ever met a celebrity? Which celebrity would you want to meet?

Keep reading for an excerpt from the next romantic comedy by Sajni Patel!

Bhanu

I worked in UX. Don't know what that is? Don't worry. Ninety-nine percent of people I've come across had no idea what in the world UX stood for, much less what it was (user experience, btw). It was simple, really. To put it humbly, I was the all-powerful bridge connecting creativity to technology, functionality to experience. If you've ever used an app or website and didn't find yourself frustrated with navigation or have any negative experience, then you, my friend, experienced good UX design and had an entire dauntless team to thank for the smallest clicks and details that made your browsing exploits so flawless that you didn't even realize you were having them.

That, of course, was oversimplifying. A great deal went into the tiniest things down to color specs. Tons of meetings and research and late nights went into every thought. But I supposed, like every other career out there, no one really knew all the behind-the-scenes madness unless they were in that field.

It was six in the morning, and even the sun hadn't decided to peek through rain clouds on the horizon on this early Pacific Northwestern day. I'd buzzed around getting coffee and waffles in my elegant, flowing cardigan, feeling very much like a princess. One who'd been isolated in a tower but not-so-secretly enjoyed it. I spoke of . . . *remote work*. When else could a girl feel like a princess in baggy pajamas and no bra?

Fret not, I *had* donned a bra and shimmied into one of a dozen meeting blouses to look the part, brushing my hair into a low ponytail as coffee cooled, and patted on light makeup while munching on waffles. I wasn't typically a breakfast person, but there was something about waffles that I couldn't shake off. So bad was my waffle addiction that I'd splurged on one of those heavy-duty waffle makers that made four perfect squares at a time. And yes, I was eating all four this morning. A few blueberries in the mix, smothered in butter, a dollop of whipped cream, and I was the happiest person in the world.

Odd-hour meetings were part of UX work. Although my company was based in Seattle, we worked with clients from around the globe. Those clients paid pretty pennies for us to collaborate with them on their next big tech designs. Usually websites and once in a while apps. When I say websites, I don't mean WordPress. I mean industry giants with complex coding and hundreds of call-to-action buttons leading to a million user interfaces to push product and make sure their company rose above intense competition.

UX was cutthroat.

I prepped my slides for my segment, making sure the presentation was ready to go, and went over the hurdles our clients were sure to toss out. They had a lot to say and seemed particular for no valid reason. Mainly because they didn't know what they wanted or what worked best. So, we let them talk nonsense and then our teams adeptly explained why they were wrong. But kindly. Of course.

Like, sir, why would you insist on *that* ugly shade when color theory clearly explained why it wouldn't work? It didn't fit the mood, the atmosphere, the purpose of the app, and created horrendous legibility issues. And testing showed that eighty-five percent of users were either disturbed or distracted by said ugly color.

These were typical annoyances a UX team almost always had to deal with.

I sat down at my sprawling desk, made too small by all the stuff on it, with an *oomph*, careful not to spill coffee, and shoved another bite of waffle into my mouth. I'd love to say that I was extra careful with my desktop and laptop out, plus a tablet and phone because we were techy-techy, but nah. I enjoyed waffles with butter and sans syrup, so there was at least that. Less sugary, sticky mess to attract ants.

A hefty sigh left my lips. All screens up. Slide deck prepared and now locked. Virtual platform on. A few large squares showed the bright-eyed faces of coworkers blinking back at me as we prepared to go live. Those squares quickly multiplied as others joined.

The entire team wasn't required to join, seeing that the leads would present, but was always encouraged to sit back and listen and learn.

The overall dynamics of a UX team included a PM (project manager) to oversee everything and be the main source of contact between the team, our clients, and bosses. The rest of the team was broken down into research, design, UI (user interface), content, and coding, with each team managed by a lead.

I was a senior lead UX researcher. I was the one who over-saw mind maps, extensive user studies, field tests, and more to make sure every aspect, every click and tap, every color, typography, size, responsive design, et cetera, was at its quality best.

As lead, I worked with the leads of other subteams, which made me Mama Duck who pushed and protected her vast army of researcher ducklings while often butting heads with extremely particular designers and particularly overworked devs (coding developers).

But that was because we were passionate. And we made beautiful, thrilling designs.

I glanced up to see our lead dev hop onto the screen, but I was too busy enjoying this fine cup of cinnamon coffee to care. His eyes skimmed across his screen, a little wrinkle in between his brows as he focused, and then a smile cracked his uptight-ness. Probably looking at cat videos. He looked like a cat guy. An annoying cat guy.

Snapping out of it, I messaged my team in the private chat and then opened up a chat with the PM. Gabrielle declared all was a go.

My heart did a shimmy in my chest. No matter how many times I presented, which was at least once a week, it was a little unnerving when it came to presenting directly to overtly opin-ionated clients. Would they slash our research down to the nub, or would they let us do what they were paying us to do? Hmm, it was always a shot in the dark as to what their mood would be. The guys never seemed this stressed, which had me wonder-ing if guys had it easier. What a dumb question. Of course they did. Our clients probably respected male leads and took their word as gold. After all, what did I, a woman who'd worked in the field for over five years with a masters in UX theory, possibly know about some damn buttons?

Carol, the big boss overseeing multiple teams on various projects, started the show and handed it off to Gabrielle. She smiled, flashing dimples, and essentially looked like a doppelgänger of Gabrielle Union. She also had a slightly deeper voice and made these wild facial expressions that promised nobody wanted to argue with her. She was, hands down, the best PM ever. A shield against the higher-ups for us and a moderator between leads at times. She was a well-oiled organizing machine, and ever so eloquent.

Carol dinged me. I was up next.

"Thanks so much, Gabrielle," Carol said with an accent, for some reason, rolling the *R*. It was funny until she announced, "And now let's hand the floor over to Bhanu."

Damn it, Carol.

My name is Bhanu. Pronounced *Bon-ooh*. It was almost always expected to have to correct someone on the pronunciation, to the point where it had become standard. But Carol—granted she wasn't my direct boss nor did she have a lot to do with me personally—and I had been working together at this company for years, and half the time she still said my name wrong.

She reminded me of an old classmate, Cathryn, who had once complained, "Ugh. I'm so sick of people misspelling my name."

"Try having people mispronounce your name," I countered.

She'd looked at me with big gray eyes and said, "Well, your name *is* a little hard."

"Bitch, it's two syllables."

Just kidding. I hadn't said that, but I *was* thinking it. I thought a lot of things that didn't actually come out of my mouth for fear of being labeled hostile, unlikable, et cetera. It came with the territory of being a woman, and even more so as a woman of color.

These days, with people being a little more considerate and "woke," many were prompted to ask for pronunciation, so they didn't butcher my name. Carol had asked more than once.

My name wasn't *Ban-ooh* or *Bane-ooh*. Yet, here we were.

Behind some of those many squares were a few coworkers snickering at my immediate roll of the eyes.

Oh, Carol. This shouldn't still be a thing, ya know, the lack of respect to say a name correctly.

"Thanks, Cairo," I muttered.

She gave a confused look but there was no time. I dove right into my presentation. In between segments, I checked my image in the little box at the corner of my screen to make sure my blouse hadn't wandered down the front to expose this sexy sports bra. The fact that I even had on a bra was about the best anyone could expect from me, if we were going to be honest.

I adjusted my pajamas at the waist, tapping my feet in fuzzy, pink pirate socks underneath a throw blanket.

I offered a few visuals as I spoke. A couple of graphs, but not too many, otherwise I'd lose the clients' attention. They could try to argue against data science, but look, numbers didn't lie. They couldn't keep saying they needed, for some unknown reason, a big-ass header on the landing page. God, we get it, you love your logo.

During our last meeting, we'd presented low-fidelity wire-frames, which were basics. Boxes and lorem ipsum fillers for later text. This time, we had a prototype, which the UX design and UI leads would go into next.

One of the hardest things for clients to grasp was how agile UX was. We worked in a constantly rotating circle. They couldn't just say they wanted this app and bam! We'd have a working high-fi prototype fully designed within weeks. No. We had to start with research, conduct testing, create storyboards and site maps, create and adhere to UI design patterns for consistency, among a hundred other items, and then actually code the thing. And then we did it all over again, testing each element until we nailed the best version.

Data science was hard to argue against, but then I turned the presentation over to Juanita, the UX design lead, and that was when the clients essentially forgot everything I'd just said.

"What about offering more options in purchasing?" one asked.

I bit my lip, wishing Juanita could tag me back in so I could pull up the journey maps and storyboard slide showing how users moved through their app. I'd spent forever drawing these! These weren't little stick figures with thought bubbles wondering how does one even open an app.

I retrieved my calm.

Gabrielle messaged me and aha! Back in the ring to reiterate, once again, after the clients nearly dismantled Juanita. She was an amazing lead and held on. It wasn't her fault they were being hardheaded and dismissive.

I delved deeper into algorithms and pinpointed a few design suggestions that had particularly strong feedback. I then answered a few questions and, without thinking to hand it back to Carol, handed the presentation over to the lead dev, Sunny.

"Thanks, Bane," he said, and jumped right into his overarching structural gameplay for the code team, going through an actual functioning prototype.

I glared at the screen and blinked. Damn it, Sunny. Could we go one day without this?

My name was definitely not Bane. As in the bane of his existence . . . or even Bane from Batman. As hot as a Tom Hardy Bane had been, I just didn't think that was a compliment in any way.

Anyway, he wasn't worth my calm this morning. I was too chill to respond, which probably disappointed whoever had bet on today's pool of Bhanu versus Sunny. He went through his segment, talking way more than he needed to. Sheesh, most devs in this business were known introverts, but here he was, loving the sound of his own voice. It was deep and gritty, more like Denzel Washington than a nerdy coder—ahem—but yeah, whatever, not my thing.

I lowered the volume and muted myself, wrapping my fingers around my warm cup.

The rain was a constant drizzle outside my Tacoma apartment, per usual for this time of year. The fireplace was going and added a nice, cozy warmth to the one-bedroom place. I sat in the converted office corner of the living room, where the watery streams running down a frostbitten window had me feeling all sorts of ways.

Working remotely worked for me. A single woman, no kids, somewhat introverted, and approximately one year away from being a cranky old hag yelling at kids to get off her lawn. There was no traffic, no rushing in and out of the rain, no wearing uncomfortable clothes because they were "presentable" (what did sweatpants ever do to anyone except love them?), no starting fights when someone touched my lunch in the fridge, no being forced to sign cards for people I barely knew or being coerced to chip in for coffee when they never bought the kind I liked, and best of all? I could mute anyone I wanted. It was essentially a superpower.

My thoughts drifted during Sunny-and-his-Denzel-voice's segment. Then our client-facing portion ended once Carol thanked everyone. She disappeared with them, leaving Gabrielle in a breakout room with one lead at a time.

"Bane. Bane? BAAAANNNNEEEE," Sunny said dramatically, reminiscent of how movie heroes cried out in vengeful declaration against their archnemesis.

Ugh. Unmute.

"Yes?" I asked.

"Can we get the results of the CTA buttons ASAP? It may only take a day for you to get research done and about ten seconds to design, but adjusting any detail in code can cost us a week."

"I'm aware of that," I replied, swirling my coffee. He wasn't going to get to me today, no sir.

"Are you, though?" he asked, chin on his knuckles, elbow on a chair arm as he swiveled back and forth. Oh, that familiar, dry look, like he loathed talking to me.

The number of black squares onscreen had diminished, leaving a handful of people still on camera, all team, all muted. Except Sunny. Because he loved his Denzel voice.

His hair was disheveled, like he'd just popped out of bed to make it to this meeting. I'd like to say that was a side effect of remote work, but he always looked like that. Devs were like little workaholics stuck to their many, many windows glowing with a billion lines of basic.

Back when we were in-office, I'd often walk into his section of the floor, a large area with cubicles and glass-walled meeting rooms covered in Post-its and scribblings, to find Sunny typing away while studying three gigantic computer screens filled with a dozen windows in alternating coding languages for various pages of any given project. My soul sort of died a little every time I saw it. While I understood basic HTML, CSS, and JavaScript, and could yes, in fact, create working, responsive prototypes from thin air, that stuff wasn't easy or quick.

Too many lines. Too many numbers and phrases and a hundred generational variants for one simple thing. Lord, I'd rather be working in a cubicle again. Spare me a slow death.

I wondered if he had as many computers set up at home. Probably. And right now, he was glaring right at the virtual box my head was in. I smirked, imagining his bottled-up load of loathing and no Bhanu in person to unleash it upon.

Sarah, one of my researchers, unmuted herself to chime in, "Sorry about that! It's my fault. I'm uploading to the system now. Results are pretty solid, and I think the design team will lean toward keeping CTA buttons as is. Good news, right?" she added nervously.

I scowled. No team member of mine should be groveling at the feet of anyone. That was what I was here for. No. Not to grovel! But to erect barriers around my team so they could work without feeling the weight of others' demands.

"Thank you, Sarah," Sunny said at the same time I said, "You don't have to apologize."

Sarah opened her mouth but didn't respond.

Without missing a beat, Sunny added, "She's right. You don't need to apologize. It's the lead's job to make sure these things are on time."

"Thanks, Sunny," I replied bluntly, and then said in one breath, "And it's the lead's job to discuss this in private with fellow leads, which is the very job description of a lead, and not try to inflate an already gigantic ego that's about ready to burst and splatter brain matter on our screens in some severely traumatic yet I-warned-you sort of way." I blinked. "Or did you bet in today's pool?"

His face dropped. His swiveling came to a dead stop.

"Oh. Didn't think I knew about the office pool of Bhanu versus Sunny? You guys shouldn't be betting during work and on coworkers. But lucky for you, I'm a chill pill today." I toasted him with the coffee mug my sister had given me, making sure the decorative side faced the screen so he knew without a doubt that, just as the writing said: I TOOK A DNA TEST, AND I'M 100% THAT BAD BITCH.

Besides, I also placed a bet on today's pool. I believed I'd just won thirty bucks.

"The research is live on real-time for the design team to look at and make their final decision." I glanced at the time on the upper right corner of my screen, adding, "And with an hour to spare on its deadline, nonetheless. I'll be moving that Trello card to complete. Mmkay? Thanks. Hit me up if anyone has questions. Have a great day, teams!"

I went dark mode and muted myself but watched Sunny's look of exasperation.

After Gabrielle spoke privately with each lead in a breakout room, she spoke with all of us together.

"Are you still going on vacation?" she asked.

"Yes," Sunny and I said simultaneously.

She, and the other leads, eyed us like there was some naughty gossip to be had. Ugh. There wasn't. Trust me, never would I in a million years hook up with the Denzel-voice grump.

I immediately piped up, "I'm still going to visit my sister, but will be working."

Gabrielle frowned. "That's not what a vacation is. Or proper work-life balance."

"I'm sure I'll get bored. My sister's working and it's not like we have a super-fun agenda planned. Literally going to be sitting at a resort all week."

She sighed dreamily. "Must be nice."

"I guess." I didn't really feel like putting on "real clothes," much less leaving the apartment. In fact, with grocery delivery and food delivery and even alcohol delivery, I could go a month without stepping foot outside. "I didn't know you approved two leads to leave at the same time."

"We're in a good place with the project. Junior researchers and devs can handle it for a few days."

"Well, I'll be—"

"Enjoying the beach," Gabrielle said pointedly. "I better not see you logged on or working." Then she said to Sunny, "You, either."

"Ah . . ." he started, looking both perplexed and anxious. "Sure," he conceded.

"Wow. For people going on vacation, you two sure seem to be dragging your feet."

I shrugged. I couldn't speak for Sunny—what with a name that surely indicated his cheery disposition—but I knew that I just wasn't in the mood for a vacation. Was there such a thing? Apparently so.

As soon as we finished our meeting, I logged off the chat, double-checked that my camera and mic were off, slid the cover over my camera, and went to the bedroom to change. Ah. Sweet T-shirt of mine. Even though I'd worn a blouse for an entire two hours, there was nothing better than getting back into pajamas.

I packed in between small meetings with my team and checking off work items. Hmm. What to pack? Tech was always a given. I needed my laptop, phone, tablet, and chargers. Undies and socks, sure. Toiletries, purse, wallet. Um . . . clothes? I wondered how many pajama bottoms I'd have to pack for a week away, seeing that my sister didn't think a weekend getaway was enough.

Speaking of that little sneak, my phone lit up with a text from her.

Diya: You better get your frumpy ass to the airport on time. Don't try to ditch me. And for the love of all that is holy, please get out of sweatpants. Better trim up down there, because I expect to see you in a bikini by the pool. See you tomorrow! Love you!

Ah. To be blessed by such sweetness.

Sajni Patel is an award-winning author of women's fiction and young adult books drawing on her experiences growing up in Texas, an inexplicable knack for romance and comedy, and the recently resurfaced dark side of fantastical things. Her works have appeared on numerous Best of the Year and Must Read lists, including in *Cosmopolitan*, *O, The Oprah Magazine*, *Teen Vogue*, Apple Books, AudioFile, *Tribeza*, *Austin Woman*, NBC, Insider Reviews, PopSugar, BuzzFeed, and many others.